THE
CHAOS
OF
TIME

BRIDGET SHEPPARD

THE CHAOS OF TIME

ISBN: 979-8-218-05643-8

Editing: MP Smith
Cover Design: Lindsay Heider Diamond
Interior Formatting: Colleen Sheehan

THE

CHAOS

OF

TIME

PROLOGUE

Berlin

*H*e never trusted the apparent age of someone's face. He knew flesh could be too easily altered. This man looked young—somewhere in his late twenties perhaps. What Christopher knew is that he didn't recognize the person standing in front of him, and he hadn't initiated any kind of meeting. He'd been eating outside at his favorite restaurant, watching with interest as a young couple several feet to his right argued, when the stranger stopped in front of him, his body language making it obvious how uncomfortable he was.

"You're Christopher?" The man's voice came off as confident, despite the truth his body told.

Fascinating. An American accent. Related to the organization? *Christopher thought to himself, his interest stoked.*

For many years, Christopher had been a project manager for the California chapter of a United States-based criminal organization providing a variety of services to high-end clients. Intricate terminations (the organization's word for murder) made up a large part of the business. Christopher and his fellow project manager, Mary, had worked out of Sacramento before Christopher was transferred to the New York chapter's Manhattan office. Shortly after his transfer, the California chapter was demolished with the aid of a journalist named Kassidy Turner, the ex-girlfriend of Kurt Leonard.

Leonard was a Bay Area tech giant and one of the chapter's top clients. For years he had sexually harassed, assaulted, and raped a number of his tech company's employees. He'd used the organization to terminate most of the women, as increasing paranoia left him thinking the MeToo movement, in which women around the world spoke up against their assaulters, would give his victims the bravery they needed to report him to the police.

When Kassidy Turner discovered Leonard was behind the murders, local police and the FBI began an investigation, finding more information along the way. Leonard was arrested and shared the information he knew about the organization with federal authorities. One of the California chapter's last acts was to have Leonard terminated before he could go to trial. Since the organization blamed Leonard for its downfall on the west coast, and because it wanted nothing more to do with Leonard's women, Kassidy Turner kept her life. The leader of the California chapter, a man most of his employees knew only as John, fled the country as the FBI searched for him. As far as Christopher knew, there were no current leads on John's whereabouts.

Although Christopher was working in Manhattan by the time the FBI was taking the California chapter apart, he could see the writing on the wall. The FBI wouldn't stop at California. The bureau had been gaining bits of information about the nationwide organization over the years, and it would eventually take it all down. He had no interest in going to prison. Christopher took a red-eye flight from JFK International Airport and had been in Berlin for almost a year. He'd become involved in his own exploits, most of them for entertainment purposes. No one related to the organization had contacted Christopher—or rather, been able to track him down. He had wanted it that way, but he had to admit his routine was growing a little dull. If the man looking down at him was connected to the organization, it could provide an interesting change of pace.

"Have a seat, Mr.?" Christopher responded, motioning toward the chair across the table from him.

The man hesitated, but sat down, not offering his name.

"I have a client who needs your assistance," he said.

Christopher sat back in his chair, making himself comfortable. "I'm typically approached via referrals from people I've already worked with."

"You and I, in a way, have related business from the past," the man responded.

Christopher eyed him for several moments, interested, but needing more information. "Yet, I don't believe we've met."

"We haven't. But I was somewhat connected to Kurt Leonard's—hobby," the man responded, looking around him, although the street was loud and Christopher found it hard to believe anyone could hear them. The man was showing himself to be quite the novice.

Christopher tried to make himself sound surprised as he said, "Ah, Mr. Leonard. So, his ghost is alive and well, then?"

The man sighed, looking far too tired for someone his apparent age. "And sometimes I feel like it will never stop haunting me. But in this case his actions could result in a large profit for me. And you, if you're interested."

Christopher leaned forward without a word, not bothering to answer.

"I was, what I guess you could call, a contractor for Mr. Leonard," the man continued. "I filmed many of his encounters. I still have much of the original footage. Although, as you know, he had many of the women—," He didn't seem to want to say a word referencing the murders, "but a few are still alive. One of the survivors caught the attention of one of my higher-paying clients. I already know where she lives, but don't know how to become involved in her life—how to involve my client in her life—without raising suspicion. That's where you would come in."

Christopher chuckled. "So, your business is what? A high-end dating service?"

The young man didn't so much as crack a smile. "A little more than that. My clients request specific women. I make sure to find and supply those women. The women aren't exactly—given a choice."

Christopher nodded, assuming the women were killed once their services were no longer needed.

"Why request my help? If this is your business, you must have done this many times before."

The man sighed and looked away from Christopher for a moment, as if needing to really contemplate his answer before giving it. "It is a relatively new business. As I said, I used to be a contracted videographer, filming whatever situations my clients wanted me to. Then I discovered the money I could make in selling the people in my videos. I often film streets, parks, stores—finding people of interest for clients. When a client sees someone he wants, I begin following her, learning her routines: when she is at work, when she is home, when she is alone. Then I secure the woman in question for my client." He looked Christopher in the eyes, as if to gauge his reaction, but Christopher had none. The man continued, "This case could be a little more complicated. The women are not usually well known. Taking them is just a matter of breaking into their homes at night while they're sleeping or coming up behind them as they jog alone. This woman was in the news at the time Mr. Leonard was arrested and killed. She's smart. She kept herself safe from him for years, but then she came forward. I'm assuming you know which woman I'm talking about."

Christopher nodded. Alexis Miller was one of Leonard's victims. She had changed her identity and hidden herself away after Leonard raped her, her intuition apparently telling her Leonard would not let her live. Although the FBI had discovered the whereabouts of the other few survivors, who were alive due to sheer luck, none of their names were shared in the media. Alexis Miller had contacted Kassidy Turner and was finally willing to reveal herself to law enforcement to help bring Leonard to justice. She had been interviewed by several news outlets around that time and was set to be a witness at Leonard's trial before he was killed.

"So, I'm sure you can understand this project will take a more elaborate plan than I'm used to. I'm told you have worked hundreds of such projects. It also doesn't hurt that you're familiar with the woman's past." The man's words were rushed, but then he paused a moment, studying Christopher. Perhaps it seemed he wasn't convincing him, so he continued, "My client is willing to pay me whatever it takes. I can guarantee you a large sum for your participation."

"It would be a difficult thing to plan from Berlin. I will not be returning to California any time in the near future," Christopher stated without allowing so much as a blink of his eyes.

The man watched him, and Christopher stared back. He didn't need the work or the money. This person knew he was valuable, so it seemed appropriate to drag his decision out. He enjoyed seeing discomfort spread across the man's face.

"A very large payment. More than you could dream of making on any of the low-level jobs you're working here. My client and I would be assisting you on the ground in California," the man added.

And as if he needed to convince Christopher of their ability to help, he pulled up a picture on his phone. It was taken from a distance and showed Alexis Miller walking down a street, holding her phone to her ear with one hand, pushing long red hair away from her face with the other.

"I've already found her in Sacramento."

Christopher smirked. He didn't know why, but he wanted to take the job. It was sure to be challenging, not for his skills but for his tolerance regarding the young man and his client. It could also be quite entertaining. "Half of the money up front, and I will agree to help you. However, I don't work with people without names," he threw in the last words, just to push a little further.

The young man attempted to stare him down again.

This only made Christopher's smirk grow. He's so delightful! So predictable!

"My name is David," the man grumbled back. "I think I can make half up front work, but we need to get started. My client isn't used to waiting."

"He'll get used to it." Christopher shrugged and took a sip of coffee.

CHAPTER 1

Early June
Sacramento, California

In his nightmare, Luke found her again. She was on the kitchen floor of their apartment, the life had bled from her. He screamed, but there was no sound. He reached for her and was instantly covered in blood. He hadn't killed her, so why did he feel like he had? He screamed again for help, but no one came. But there was an incessant ringing. That wasn't familiar. What was that? It kept ringing; he didn't know how to stop it. *Wake up! Wake up! Wake up!* he yelled at himself.

He knew what would happen next. He wanted to wake up before that, but he couldn't. The ringing had disappeared, but now it started again. He looked around the kitchen. Where was it coming from? *No, wake up!*

Luke always knew he was dreaming when he had this nightmare, but that didn't help, because he could never force himself out of it. He had to see it through to the end. He turned to look at her again. Her eyes were open now. She was staring at him, her face filled with disappointment. *Emma.*

He shot up in bed with a strangled cry. His heart slammed in his chest, his breathing fast. *Get a grip. Just the same dream. You're fine.*

He always had this nightmare around this time of year—next week was the fifth anniversary of her death. Sometimes he'd have it every night for weeks, sometimes just for a few days. But it was always similar: finding her in their apartment kitchen, where she'd been killed—having to look at her eyes to be ripped back to reality. But what was the ringing in this one?

The noise started again, and he cringed. His phone. He checked his bedside clock. It was five in the morning. He could guess who it was. He'd been expecting the call. He never knew exactly when it was going to come, but it came every year since he'd moved to Sacramento about four and a half years ago.

Five o'clock meant eight o'clock in North Carolina where the call originated. He was still slowing his heart. The ringing stopped. Luke checked his phone and saw four missed calls, but no voicemails. The phone number was the one he'd expected. *Susan.*

He needed to get up. He was six-foot-five, and as he got older and continued carrying the weight of his job and his past on his shoulders, he found his tall frame felt more and more like a burden. He swung his legs out of bed and put his face in his hands. He needed to shave today. He'd been so wrapped up in work, trying to distract himself from this anniversary, that he'd let some things go. He couldn't keep doing that. His knew his attitude had been shitty. The members of his team were starting to notice. But there was never any impact to his work. If anything, he worked harder when he was angry and depressed.

The ringing started again. He couldn't keep ignoring her. Susan never stopped until he spoke to her. He had so many emotions connected to these calls. His guilt was still strong after all these years. Of course, she was still grieving too. Her daughter was dead. The woman he'd loved was dead. The grief hit him at the most random times, but especially during this time of year. Talking to Susan made him feel the sadness and anger even more.

He took one more breath and answered the phone, trying to keep his voice even. "Hello?"

"Luke, you have to do something!" Her voice was as desperate as it was every year, always making him feel horrible for the response he had to give.

"Susan, good morning. I know this time of year is very difficult. I'm sorry for the pain you deal with every day, but nothing has changed. It's no longer in my jurisdiction, and even if I still worked there, they wouldn't let me have anything to do with her case. Believe me, I wish," his voice faltered, "I wish there was something I could do. I would give anything."

"How can you say that when you ran away? Across the country!" she accused in anger, but then she started to cry.

Luke was used to this. Susan always threw his cross-country move into the conversation. She wasn't a bad person, but in her grief, she often said things to hurt him. "I didn't run away. I took a job I'd interviewed for before she died—a job they delayed so I could have some time after she was killed. You know she was going to start a job out here too. That was the plan before. We were moving out here," he answered in a calm voice, explaining the same thing he did every year.

"You didn't have to leave so soon. You didn't even wait a year. You could have stayed here, tried to make them do more. I don't think they're even investigating anymore. They never knew for sure that those serial killers murdered her. They never found them, and now they've stopped looking!" Susan was almost yelling by the time she said the last few words.

She was referencing the Sunset Killers, a serial killer duo that murdered a number of women over several years in Mecklenburg County in his home-state of North Carolina. They were so named because they'd always murdered their victims around sunset, even as seasons and the time of sunset changed. Many of the victims were killed in their homes with no trace of identifying information left behind. They murdered two other women in the city of Charlotte just months before Emma was killed. They'd gotten sloppy and left bodily fluids behind them at the scene of one of those murders, which was how they were finally identified. But although law enforcement knew *who* they were, no one had been able to figure out *where* they were. They seemed to have fallen off the face of the earth.

"They're still looking for them," Luke responded. "You're right, they never found any concrete evidence, but they believe it was the Sunset Killers. Her murder mostly matches the others. I know they're still looking into Emma's death, because a lot of law enforcement in that area knew her, and they want to know for sure. But you have to understand that after five years of finding nothing—"

"How dare you! How dare you act like it's okay to give up because of the passage of time. Most days, I feel like she was just here. I can still see her face, hear her laugh. I still have that picture of you two at your coworker's wedding. It's sitting on my mantle. She loved you. She would have done anything for you. And you've given up on her! You're a coward, Luke! She would be so disappointed!" And with that, she ended the call.

He stared at his phone for a moment before putting it back on his nightstand. He laid back down, but there was no chance of any more sleep. He knew Susan didn't mean any of it, but the words still hurt. *God, I'm sorry, Em. I'm sorry.*

Emmaline was her given name, but she always thought it sounded too much like a southern belle, so most people called her Emma. To Luke, she was Em. And to know her was to know she was anything but the belle stereotype. She was smart, stubborn, and strong. She'd never needed protecting, except for that night. He should have been there.

He could still see her face too, but most of the time it was in his nightmares. He sighed and wondered when to expect Susan's next call. Probably in a couple hours. She always called to apologize.

He sat up and decided to get the day over with. When it was almost eight o'clock and she hadn't called back, he found himself getting annoyed. *Shit, Luke, you're a selfish ass. Let the woman hate you if she wants to.*

Luke knew Susan's anger and bitterness were also the result of her husband, Nicholas, divorcing her two years after Emma died. Luke knew the man had been dealing with his own grief at the loss of the couple's only child, but Susan said his leaving was the ultimate betrayal.

Luke told himself not to dwell on when Susan would call again, but somehow the second call always made him feel a little better about himself.

Maybe it would just take her longer this year. As the minutes ticked by, his annoyance increased.

When he stormed into a Midtown coffee shop, his mood hadn't improved. Too many things were flying through his brain. He couldn't wait to bury himself in work, to pretend like his personal life didn't exist.

He waited in line longer than he should have, because one of the baristas at the register was being chatty. By the time he got to her, his face felt like it was in a permanent scowl. He looked up from his wallet, ready to give his order, when he noticed she looked familiar. Familiar, but not. She was petite with red hair and blue eyes. He cast a quick look at her name tag. Alexis. Where did he know her from? He rarely forgot a name or face. He rarely forgot anything; it served him well in his career. But her identity did not come to mind.

"Oh!" An immediate look of recognition settled on her face. "Hi, Detective—Kruger!" She remembered his last name with a smile.

"Good morning," he responded in a professional tone. So, someone he knew from work. But he wasn't in the mood to try to figure out who she was. He just wanted to get his coffee and get the hell out.

Amusement filled her eyes. She knew he didn't remember her. "I'm Alexis Miller." She lowered her voice. "The case involving Kurt Leonard. I—I was one of his—" She stopped herself, clearly uncomfortable saying the words. "I reached out to Kassidy Turner."

Kassidy Turner was his colleague Brett Green's fiancée, but Luke had first met Kassidy when she came forward with suspicions against Kurt Leonard.

Luke had only spoken to Alexis Miller in person once before, during an interview regarding what Leonard had done to her, although he swore she looked different back then. After that, the FBI took over the case.

"Right. Hi, Ms. Miller," he said, but his attention was on the menu board behind her, trying to give her the hint that he'd like to order. He didn't want to focus on the past. He needed to stay in the present and try to speed time forward past Emma's anniversary.

"I can't believe it's been more than a year since all that. And now Brett and Kassie are getting married in a couple months." Alexis smiled to herself, and Luke remembered Brett saying Alexis and Kassidy had become friends.

"Yeah, time flies," he said, offering a weak smile. He took his debit card out of his wallet, trying to envision his coffee.

"Are you okay?" Her eyes met his, and he saw true concern there. "You seem unhappy. Maybe sad?"

That put him over the edge. Most days, Luke didn't mind chatting for a few minutes. Because of his job, he understood that people dealt with scary, frustrating, messed-up things in their daily lives, usually when they least expected it, so he liked to be kind, to give the people he met time to talk. But he didn't care to talk about himself. He couldn't give people the same openness they chose to give him. He didn't like people knowing his true emotions. The fact that she'd so easily seen his, annoyed him, although he knew he must look like a mile of bad road.

"I'd really like to order my coffee. I've been standing in this line for at least fifteen minutes, I'm late for work, and I don't have time to talk right now. Can I order?" He tried to use a calm tone, but it came out curt.

She looked stunned. He felt like a jerk. But he wanted to get out of there. "Yes. Sorry," Alexis said.

He saw her face go red as she looked back down at her register. He gave his order and checked his phone as he paid, hoping to see a missed call from Susan. There wasn't one. He moved his attention to the machine that should be processing his payment, but a note came up on the screen advising him to wait for the cashier. He turned his eyes back to her. She was looking over his shoulder at something, confusion written across her face. The look in her eyes and his natural sense of curiosity made him want to turn around to see what she was seeing. But his coffee was so close he could almost taste it, so he cleared his throat with a volume she couldn't miss.

"Oh, sorry!" She jumped, punching something on her screen to allow the payment to go through.

"Thanks," he mumbled, distracted by the ringing of his phone as he stepped away to wait for his drink, but instead of Susan's number on the screen, he saw his mother's. He'd have to call her back. Without meaning to, he flashed a look back at Alexis. She'd been watching him as well, but looked away when his eyes met hers.

CHAPTER 2

"What an ass. Sometimes customer service sucks," a voice murmured in Alexis's ear, making her jump. She hated people sneaking up on her, especially men. On top of that, this man's voice was the familiar one she'd heard floating around the shop. She knew it, but couldn't place it.

Alexis whirled to find him standing next to her. He was around her age with dusty-blond hair and brown eyes. He had probably a good eight inches on her five-foot-two height. He gave her a sheepish smile when he realized he'd startled her. He was wearing an apron and a name badge. He must move fast, because just a few minutes ago he'd been at the front of the store with her manager.

The confusion she'd felt upon hearing a familiar voice but seeing this man, a complete stranger, had thrown her. She'd been staring at him while Detective Kruger was trying to pay, further pissing off Detective Kruger, who seemed to have come into the shop already angry.

"Um, yes, sometimes," she managed to respond to the blond.

"Sorry! I'm Zeke. I just started. They asked me to shadow you for today." He stuck out his hand.

It's fine. You're fine. It's just a handshake, she gave herself a quick pep talk and made herself shake it. Alexis still struggled with any form of physical contact with men, but she'd come a long way from the woman who couldn't be in the same room with a man without standing by a door in order to have the opportunity for a quick exit.

"Oh, okay. Nice to meet you. I'm Alexis."

Another coworker came over to relieve Alexis at the register so she could make some of the drinks. Zeke followed her.

"Have you worked in a coffee shop before?" Alexis forced herself to ask Zeke as she made the drink she knew was Detective Kruger's. They were slammed that morning. Two of her coworkers had called in sick, so orders were dragging.

"Yeah, at a couple big chains, so management here wanted me to see how things work in a smaller-scale shop." Zeke gave her a smile that was perfect in its lopsided way, and she found herself blushing.

She wasn't interested in getting involved with a coworker, or anyone for that matter. She hadn't been interested in a relationship since her rape. But she couldn't deny Zeke was attractive. His brown eyes sparkled back at her as he smiled. Although his hair looked a little mussed, Alexis could tell it was by design, making her think he was going for some kind of surfer vibe.

His appearance fit really well with the laid-back, beachy feel of Valle Coffee Co. The shop was named for its founder, who'd moved to Sacramento from Southern California with the dream of starting his own coffee house. Alexis loved it here. She'd never been a barista before moving to Sacramento, but something had told her to take a chance on this place.

She carefully placed the detective's coffee on the pickup counter. Heaven forbid she spilled it. He'd have yet another reason to find her annoying. Kruger took the drink, but was engrossed in his phone. She frowned at him as he left the shop. She didn't want to agree with Zeke, because the detective had been very kind when she spoke to him a year ago, but it was hard to reconcile that version of him with the one she'd gotten today.

"Sometimes technology ruins real human interaction," Zeke said from just behind her. She gave a little nod, but moved to put some space between them.

Alexis could see the vast benefits of technology as someone who'd worked in the field, but she'd left a lot of it behind after she'd come forward about Kurt—when she'd come out of isolation. It was challenging enough for her to live in the real world most of the time.

It wasn't as easy to keep in touch with friends without being on social media, but she still used email and texts. Since she'd disappeared from the face of the earth for almost three years, she didn't have more than a handful of friends anyway.

She reflected on those years of seclusion. She'd worked from her apartment as a database administrator, and only left to go to stores when she had to. Even then, she drove well out of her way so no one could be sure of where she lived. She'd never visited her mom, but called her on the phone every day. At the time, her mom was the only one who knew about her identity change and why she had become a recluse. She kept telling Alexis to go to the police, but Alexis was too scared. She would never allow herself to be that scared again. She liked being back in the world, being able to interact with people, not looking over her shoulder every other minute.

Zeke's shift was the same as hers, so he followed her around most of the day. She didn't mind after she got used to having him there. He was funny and nice to everyone in the shop. He made the day speed by.

At the end of their shift, he gave her a wave, got on his bicycle and rode off. He'd told her he lived downtown. She walked the several blocks to her little apartment. She had just enough time to eat before heading to her other job.

Her phone rang as she stepped through the door.

She threw her keys and purse on the couch, answering the call as she headed for the kitchen. Eileen Kelly still felt like Alexis's safe place. She found herself letting stress go as she said, "Hey, Mom!"

"Hey, baby," her mother replied. "I'm just on a break and wanted to see how your day's going."

"Good so far! Just left my barista shift, and I have painting tonight. A new guy started at the shop today. I swear his voice sounds familiar, but his face isn't. But I was pretty proud of myself. Shaking his hand wasn't easy, but he was shadowing me for most of the day, and I felt okay about it."

"That's great! See how much progress you've made! I'm proud of you," Eileen gushed.

"Thanks, Mom. It's just hard to see it at times." Alexis shoved some leftovers into her microwave.

They chatted for a bit longer before Eileen had to go back to work. As it always was after she talked to her mom, Alexis felt much more at peace.

As she was scarfing her food, her phone rang again. She smiled at the name on the screen.

"Hey, Kassie," she greeted her friend. The two had become close over the last year, and they got together a few times a month. Kassidy and her fiancé had bought a house in Sacramento just a couple months before.

"Hey, Lex! How're you doing?"

"Good. Just inhaling some food before my painting class. I've gotta be doing better than Brett's coworker." She wanted to run Kruger's behavior by Kassie to verify whether the man's personality was really like that. Although Zeke's company had improved her day, she couldn't get the detective's scowl out of her mind.

"Wait, who?" Kassie sounded interested.

"Detective Kruger. He came into Valle Coffee this morning. I remembered him, but I think it took him a bit to remember me since I've changed my hair and my contacts. He looked like there was a storm over his head. I mentioned that he seemed upset or sad, which I know I shouldn't have done. I think I go overboard sometimes, compensating for all the time I wasn't around people. He lectured me about how long he'd been waiting and how he was late for work. I don't remember him being like that, but I guess it's been a while since I've talked to him."

"Hmm, doesn't sound like him, but Brett did mention something about him seeming off the past couple days," Kassie said. "I'm sure it didn't have anything to do with you."

Alexis didn't respond. Maybe she'd taken it too personally. That was an easy thing for her to do these days. Maybe the guy was just having a bad day. She'd never seen Kruger in the coffee shop before, so she hoped she'd never run into him again.

"Anyway," Kassidy must have sensed Alexis was ready to move on, "I called to ask you something. We weren't going to do any kind of housewarming party with the wedding coming up, but we decided to throw something small last minute. It's this Saturday at six. Are you free? I know sometimes you have painting on weekend nights."

Alexis glanced at her schedule, which she'd stuck on her fridge. "I do have a class Saturday night, but I'll find someone to cover for me. I think Aaron still owes me from a couple weeks ago."

She'd been painting from the time she was two according to her mother, but after college she'd never had much time for it. During her isolation, there'd been nothing but time, so on something of a whim, she'd gained her master's degree in art education, just in case she was ever able to get her life back. Now she taught adult painting classes in several locations throughout the city. She also worked part time as an instructor for a studio offering wine and paint events.

"Are you sure? I don't want you to lose—"

"I'm sure! I'll be there!" Alexis interrupted before her friend could finish her sentence. She knew Kassie was going to say she didn't want Alexis to lose money and that Kassie meant it in a supportive way, but Alexis didn't want anyone worrying about how much money she had. She still had some savings from her days in technology. And with what she made in her current jobs, she was doing fine.

"Great! Can't wait to see you, Lex!" Kassie knew to let the subject go.

"You too! Say hi to Brett for me."

She smiled at her phone as they hung up. She was glad to have Kassie in her life. Although she'd made a few other friends in Sacramento, none of them were as close to her, or understood what she'd been through the way Kassie did.

Checking her watch, she jumped. She tossed her dishes in the sink, grabbed her purse, and ran for the door. She'd have to remember to call Aaron later.

Alexis let herself sleep in on Saturday. She usually got up early to paint, but she was beat. It felt strange to have a whole day in front of her with no work. She wanted to try to embrace the laziness she must have somewhere inside her.

When she climbed out of bed, she pulled open the bedroom curtain of her second-story apartment. She loved her view of the Sacramento streets below, because the city always seemed so alive. But instead of the usual sights of people walking their dogs, running, or pushing baby strollers, she spied a man across the street taking pictures with his phone. Her heart began to race, and she ducked away from the window. She stood there, forcing herself to take deep breaths. *There has to be a logical reason he's out there.*

It took her several minutes to calm down and make her legs move. She'd woken up craving a bagel, but that meant she had to get out of her apartment first. After a quick shower, she braided her hair, threw on shorts and a T-shirt, stepped into flip flops, and was out the door. She jiggled her front door handle several times after she'd locked it. Better to be safe than sorry.

Her car was parked across the street, not far from the man who was still snapping photos. It looked like he was aiming at the apartment building next to hers. Her interest now outweighed her nerves.

"Good morning," Alexis managed, giving a curious tilt of her chin toward his phone.

"Good morning! Geoff Morgan," he answered, holding out his hand for her to shake. She did so reluctantly. "My real estate firm is handling the sale of this building. Gotta get some good shots." He flashed her a smile and handed her his card. It looked legit. She tucked it in her pocket. She'd be checking his real estate license later. "If you're looking to rent, the new owner is sure to overhaul all of the units. They'll be the jewels of the neighborhood."

"I already have a place, but good to know. Have a nice day." She moved to her car and as she got in, she watched him from the corner of her eye. He appeared to be making some notes on a pad of paper. He was tan with bronze-colored hair and at least six feet tall. Her freaking blush returned. Why did she feel like the universe was shoving all these good-looking guys in her face when she wasn't interested? She started her car and got the hell out of there.

* * *

Christopher nodded as he watched the video of the encounter.

"He did well for the first meeting: casual and friendly," he commented to David, who was on speaker phone.

"I could tell she was very nervous. She didn't feel comfortable around him," David responded in a frustrated voice. But there was something else buried deep in his tone as well. Jealousy?

Christopher had spent decades of his life studying people. He often recognized the feelings they wouldn't admit to. David filmed the conversation between Alexis and his client. Did he not like seeing them together? This could be an interesting new twist.

"That will take time," Christopher said. "She just met him. He will build that trust. I noticed you have not given me updates on your interactions with her."

"They're going well so far. She seems to enjoy my company." The casual sound of David's answer was forced.

"Excellent." Christopher pretended not to notice. "The faster you build that foundation, the faster he gets the girl. Keep the pace steady for now."

"Of course. I'll keep you updated," David responded. Christopher heard both darkness and excitement in his words.

* * *

As Alexis walked toward Kassidy and Brett's cozy 1950's bungalow, she was daydreaming of what it would be like to have a house of her own. There was a little too much dreaming, because as she turned from the sidewalk onto the path leading to their door, she ran smack into someone much taller than her going the opposite direction.

"Sorry," a gruff voice said and she groaned inwardly, knowing who it was before she even saw his face.

"It's okay," she said, taking a moment to get her bearings, grateful she hadn't dropped the bottle of wine she'd brought with her.

Kruger took her in for a second before trying to edge past her. It was hard to believe the guy didn't have something against her.

"Aren't you going the wrong way?" The snarky question left her mouth before she had a chance to stop it.

Kruger stared at her in confusion, then pointed at his phone. "I have to make a call." He'd turned away from her and was already on the sidewalk before she could say anything else.

"Thanks for coming!" Kassie beamed as she opened the door, giving her a hug and grinning at the bottle of wine.

"Hey, Alexis," Brett greeted her with a warm smile.

"Hey! Thanks for the invite. Congratulations again on the house."

There were about a dozen people milling around the couple's front room, chatting and grabbing snacks from a card table covered with a cloth.

"I need to check on the pulled pork. Want to come with me?" Kassidy asked and Alexis nodded, following her friend to the remodeled kitchen. *Ah, to someday have a kitchen as beautiful as this one.*

As Kassie went about turning off the crock pot and setting up some rolls to make pulled pork sliders, Alexis grabbed a glass of water. The temperature had peaked in the high 90s and being outside felt like traveling through an oppressive cloud.

"I quite literally ran into Kruger outside."

Kassie looked up with a little cringe. "Oh, yeah, he said he had to make a call. I'm surprised he's even here. He seems really off. I hope he was nicer to you."

"I don't know if he even remembered me," Alexis answered with a shrug.

Kassie stopped what she was doing and turned to look at her. "I swear he's a nice guy, and really smart, just tends to be a little guarded about himself. But you remember, he was more supportive than Brett was when I suggested Kurt was behind those murders. Of course, Brett was pretty pissed with me at the time because of our breakup. Anyway, I don't know what's up with Luke right now, but I plan to do some snooping."

"He doesn't seem like the kind of guy who'd want someone snooping into his life." Alexis put down the water glass and upgraded to the glass of pinot grigio her friend handed to her.

"He doesn't have to know." Kassie went back to arranging the sliders.

"Seems dangerous to investigate a detective, but if there's anyone for the job, it's you." Alexis laughed.

"That's what I figure." Kassie grinned.

As they made their way back to the front room, Kassie carrying the sliders and Alexis a salad, Kruger came back in the front door, his face more of a storm than before. His dark brown, wavy hair was messy, as if he'd been running his hand through it. His chocolate-colored eyes looked almost black.

What is this guy's deal? Alexis frowned.

"Sorry, Green, I gotta go," he said, using Brett's last name. "Thanks for the invite, Kassidy. Congratulations," he said in a rush.

The couple walked him to the door. Alexis heard Kassie ask, "Everything okay, Luke?"

"Yeah, fine. Something just came up. Sorry to leave so early."

"No worries, man. See you Monday," Brett responded, his arm around his fiancée's shoulders.

Kruger nodded. Alexis saw his eyes flicker over Kassie's shoulder to her face. She pretended not to notice, joining the casual conversation of the two people closest to her.

Luke Kruger was a mystery, but she didn't have the desire or the time she would need to figure him out.

CHAPTER 3

Monday. The exact day. Five years from the night he'd found her dead in their kitchen. The scene kept flashing through his mind. The horrible, gut-wrenching scene that still stole his breath. After the day was done, things would feel better again for a little while.

Luke sat at his desk, staring at his laptop. Work was what he needed today.

Brett came in, throwing his work bag on his desk and turning on his computer. "Morning." He glanced at Luke.

"Morning." Luke knew he should explain Saturday, but he couldn't do that.

Susan had called him Saturday morning, pleading again, saying horrible things again. He was confused by her change in pattern. In the past, her second call had always been to apologize for berating him, but not this year. This was the second time he'd heard from her, but she made no apology. After the conversation, Luke had decided to start looking into Emma's death. He was still on good terms with a few confidential informants back in North Carolina. The Sunset Killers had been quiet since Emma's murder, but he was sure they were still out there. Maybe they'd let down their guard in the last five years.

One of his informants sent him a message after he'd already arrived at Brett and Kassidy's. He'd been rushing to get back to him when he'd run into Alexis. *She must think I'm an asshole.*

As the thought flashed through his mind, he noticed Brett's tapping foot.

The man couldn't hide his nervous tell. Brett glanced over his shoulder, a sheepish look on his face.

"What's up, Green?"

"Nothing. Just distracted," Brett muttered.

Luke sat back in his chair, watching his teammate's foot tap away. "I have to leave for an interview in about ten minutes. Want to tell me what you found out?"

Brett turned in his chair. "Damn my fucking foot," he said with a sigh. "Kassidy researched you."

"What?" Luke frowned. He liked Kassidy, but, being a reporter, she couldn't mind her own damn business.

"She was worried about you. You've been so pissed. She found several articles from papers in North Carolina. She told me about—your girlfriend," Brett finished the sentence in an awkward tone and waited, as if expecting Luke to open up about his past. But his face looked like he wanted Luke to do anything else instead. It was obvious he felt guilty about the way he'd gained the information.

"Don't worry, Green. I don't want to talk about it. Let Kassidy know you tried." He stood up, clocking the embarrassed look on Brett's face as it turned into a smirk. He strode from the office.

Later that morning, Luke picked up a sandwich and headed to McKinley Park. He usually ate lunch at his desk, but he couldn't do that today. He needed fresh air to relieve the feeling of constant pressure on his chest.

He found an empty picnic table on the side of the park that bordered H Street. He took a deep breath, gazing in the direction of the park's famous rose garden. He sat near multiple pathways, but they were quiet at that moment. As he took his first bite, he noticed someone walking toward him from the street. She seemed lost in thought and hadn't noticed him. *Alexis.*

She was wearing jeans and a floral top. He felt guilty for thinking how beautiful she looked with the sun shining down on her hair, bringing out the gold tone in the red. He shook his head. He shouldn't be thinking about her that way. Not today.

But he'd been such a jackass to her, and she was a good friend of Brett and Kassidy's. He wanted to apologize. Try to make it right. When she was just feet from the table, she stowed her phone and looked up, stopping in her tracks when she saw him. Her blue eyes stared at him for a moment, looking confused. He tried to ignore how pretty they were. *What the hell, Luke?*

"Hi," he said, his normal confidence replaced by a feeling of idiocy as the mediocre greeting fell out of his mouth.

"Uh, hi," Alexis answered, still not moving.

"Lunch break?"

"Um, yes. I come here for lunch a lot. I usually sit at this table."

"Oh, sorry. I normally eat lunch at the station." *Extra information, Luke.* He made to get up, but she waved him back down.

"You don't have to do that. I'll find another table." She started to walk away.

He shook his head and made himself speak again, "Sit here." He motioned across the table.

She stopped and turned around, but her eyes were looking past him, as if she were trying to find somewhere else to go.

"You won't have to find another seat." He gave her a reassuring smile.

She thought a moment longer and then put her purse on the bench opposite him, sitting down without looking at him. She unwrapped her own sandwich and pulled out a bottle of water.

"I'm not really an asshole." No need to beat around the bush.

Alexis looked up in surprise.

"I'm sorry. I know I acted like one at the coffee shop and again at Brett and Kassidy's house. This is a rough time of year for me. I don't handle it well. I guess I take it out on anyone who gets in the way of my wallowing."

"Thanks. And—I'm sorry about whatever you're going through," she responded.

Luke nodded. "I just wanted to explain. I'm more like the person you met over a year ago." He caught the faintest sign of relief in her eyes before she looked away. He wasn't sure she wanted to talk, but he found himself wanting to talk to her, so he thought he'd give it a shot. "How do you like living in Sacramento?"

She smiled as she finished a bite of her sandwich. "I really like it. I enjoy my jobs. I have friends here. My mom is here. After being away from her for a few years, I wanted to be close."

"I'm glad you've been able to create a life here." He hesitated for a moment. "I've never been in Valle Coffee before. Nice place. Brett and Kassidy never mentioned you worked there, so when you said hi to me I didn't...." He let his words trail off, annoyed at how awkward he felt.

Another smile lit her face. "Oh, it's pronounced 'Valley Coffee.' It's the owner's last name, but also meant to be a play on words for the Sacramento Valley. And it's been a while. When I first met you, I'd dyed and cut my hair and was wearing contacts. I wouldn't expect you to recognize me. I changed my name to hide from Kurt, and it's also given me a fresh start here. But I wanted to look like I used to. How I should look." She motioned toward her red hair and blue eyes.

He nodded again, distracted by her smile. He didn't want to comment on her looks—didn't want to let himself think about them too much. "You told me your birth name the day I interviewed you." He searched back through his memory, sure it would come to him.

"That's okay." She put up her hand as if to stop his thoughts. "I love that name," she said with sadness in her eyes, "but it's too tied to my past, so I had to leave it behind."

The sadness he'd seen morphed into a pained expression. He knew he needed to move the conversation in a different direction.

"You said you like your jobs. What else do you do?"

"I'm a painter. I teach classes at a few locations in the city." With these words, joy made its way back onto her face.

He hadn't known this either. He realized that although he saw Brett and Kassidy several times a month socially, it was never with Alexis, and Kassidy never offered information about her. Maybe he'd just never asked.

She was smiling ever so slightly at the surprise on his face as she said, "I'm also an instructor at a paint-and-sip studio in Midtown."

"Paint-and-sip studio?" He raised an eyebrow.

She looked shocked. "You know, where people get together, drink wine, and paint? They have a specific painting they're trying to complete. There's a professional painter who leads them through it."

"I've never heard of that." He shook his head at the idea, wondering if people really did things like that.

She stared at him with her mouth open. "You haven't? Wow. They're pretty popular. There're tons of them throughout California."

Luke shrugged, finding her shock amusing. "Doesn't sound like something I'd be into."

She'd been leaning on the table, resting on her arms, but now moved back, looking at him like he had to be from another planet. "Huh. Even Kassie and Brett have been to one of mine. I'll have to see if they'll come back and drag you along."

He wanted to laugh out loud, but didn't want to offend her. "Something I'm going to have to give Green crap for, but I'm sorry, that's not going to happen."

"Pshaw, we'll see. It's fun, and anyone can do it. You don't have to have any talent." Alexis grinned.

He knew that was meant as a jab. "I'm glad so many other people enjoy it, but I can tell you now, that will not happen."

She rolled her eyes, admitting defeat.

"How about you? Do you like your job?" she asked, waving her hand toward him, a smile still on her face.

"I love it. That job is my life. I can't see myself doing anything else," he answered without hesitation.

"You and Brett are the perfect team, then. Kassidy seems to be the only person who can slow him down when it comes to work," she said with a grin. "Do you have family around here?"

The question was innocent, but going in a direction he didn't like. He'd need to steer the conversation back to her. "No, just me. I moved here from North Carolina over four years ago."

Before he could ask her anything else, she continued with an interested look, "Oh, I thought I heard something from around there in your voice. Did you move here for the job?"

"Yeah," he answered, but looked away across the park, hoping she'd get the hint that he didn't want to talk about himself.

When he looked back at her, her face was red and she kept her eyes down. *Crap.* "Sorry, my past is a little—uncomfortable."

"I get intrusive without meaning to sometimes. It's like I still haven't adjusted to being around real people again." She gave a small smile.

"It was a normal question, not intrusive. It's just—hard for me to get into it. Is it just you and your mom here?"

"Yes, just us," she answered, but the spark in her eyes had dimmed. He wanted to kick himself. She checked her watch. "I'd better get going. Thanks for the lunch company."

"Yeah, anytime." He tried to smile as she got up from the table.

"See you around." She returned the expression, but it didn't seem genuine.

"What the hell, Luke?" he cursed at himself as he watched her make her way across the park.

CHAPTER 4

Alexis had the nightmare about Kurt that night. She woke up dripping with sweat, trying to breathe. Her nightmares were too real. It always felt like she was back there, shoved in a corner, gagged, praying he'd let her live. But afterward, she wasn't sure she really wanted to be alive.

She called her mom, but there was no answer. Eileen was probably getting ready for work at the huge UC Davis Medical Center in the heart of Sacramento. Alexis knew she should be getting ready for work too. She sighed and forced herself out of bed.

She was barely awake when she started her shift just before the shop opened. Zeke was on the register next to her. His enthusiastic personality was rubbing her the wrong way. The fear and anger from her dream were still gripping her. She wasn't sure how she was going to make it through the day.

"Good morning." That deep voice with a hint of the south made her look up. Alexis hadn't noticed that they'd opened the doors, but customers were already trickling in. Luke was so tall. It almost felt like too much work to meet his eyes.

"Good morning." She stifled a yawn and tried to give him some sort of smile.

"You okay?" His eyes were concerned, which surprised her. Their conversation had turned awkward at the park. She'd been happy to have a reason to leave.

"Yes. I just didn't sleep very well last night."

"Ah, you and I have the same problem," he responded, although she found that hard to believe based on his appearance. His hair was gelled just enough to make it look like he hadn't put any effort in. He was wearing slacks, a button-down shirt, and a suit jacket.

Luke caught her eyes and she blushed. He looked down at the jacket. "I have to testify in court today."

She nodded, giving him a small smirk. "So, an extra-strong coffee then?"

"Yes, please take all the caffeine you have and put it in my drink," he answered with what she could only call a devastating smile.

"Sure thing," she laughed and punched in his drink order.

She made Luke's drink as Zeke took orders. Their shift lead, Nora, should be in any minute. She was always a little late, which made the morning rush difficult for her coworkers.

As her mind focused and took on the mounting orders in front of her, she threw a glance at Zeke. Pre-frantic would be a good way to describe the look she saw on his face, and it confused her. His demeanor always seemed bright and collected. This rush was no different from ones he must have experienced with the big coffee companies. Maybe he was just used to a larger staff. If Nora were there, it would make a world of difference. She might often be late, but when she was there, she was one of the most efficient workers Alexis knew. *Where is she?* Alexis frowned up at the clock.

As she placed the detective's drink on the pickup counter, Zeke rushed behind her, brushing against her back. She flinched and bumped a stack of empty cups, knocking them to the ground. She felt her cheeks go red and hoped no one had noticed.

"Sorry, Alexis!" Zeke called as he made his way back to the register, where the line seemed to be growing ever longer. He motioned at the water bottle in his hand, a guilty look on his face.

At the same time, Luke asked, "Are you okay?"

When she looked up at him, she noticed his eyes were dark, and he had them set on Zeke.

"Yes, I'm fine. I still get a little jumpy when it comes to guys and touching," she explained in a low voice that made him draw closer. She tried to sound casual and was glad the place was too loud for anyone else to hear her.

He turned his eyes toward her and nodded that serious nod of his, which he'd done several times in the park. "I think he did that on purpose. He should have had plenty of room." He motioned to the area behind her.

"No," she made herself laugh. "It was an accident. He's new, so he's still learning the ropes. I think the rush is stressing him out. Don't worry, Kruger."

His dark look was replaced by one of amusement. "Kruger?"

She shrugged and tried to keep her expression nonchalant. "It's your last name, isn't it?"

"Yeah." A flash of something crossed his face, but he looked down to check his phone before she could study it. "I'd better go. See you around, Miller." He gave her a smirk, picked up his drink, and strode from the shop. Her eyes lingered on him as he left.

Wait, no! That's a bad idea. He's Kassie and Brett's friend. Brett's coworker! You are not interested in him! But thoughts of his dark eyes and slight southern lilt flited through her mind. *Oh my God. No, Alexis!*

Just then, Nora walked in the door, already tying on her apron. "I'm sorry! My car wouldn't start, and my husband wasn't home from his shift yet." She got right to work making drinks so Alexis could go back to the register.

Alexis passed Nora an empathetic smile and heard Zeke let out a sigh as the line became more manageable.

He turned to ask her, "Hey, you want to go see that French film I told you about? It's at Tower this weekend. Saturday night?"

Alexis loved the Tower Theatre's propensity for foreign and indie films, as well as its Art Deco style. She'd seen several movies there since moving to

Sacramento. Zeke had talked at length about this new French film, its director, and themes. It sounded dark but fascinating.

Now Zeke was someone she should want to date. He was thirty, a little older than she was; cute; and fun to be around. He seemed a little too honest sometimes, but that was better than being closed off, right? But the thought of sitting in a dark movie theater with him, or any other guy for that matter, set off a panic alarm in her brain. Her therapist had given her some ideas on how to date again, but taking the leap was scary.

"I'm sorry, I have a painting class Saturday." This wasn't a lie. It was an afternoon class, but she didn't want to clarify that.

"That's okay!" Zeke's grin didn't falter. "Another time!"

She smiled back, but didn't say anything. She didn't want to lead him on, but she didn't want to close the door either.

Saturday morning found her frowning over the easel standing in the corner of her front room. Her heart yearned to put a brush to it, but she had painting jobs for the rest of the weekend, so she needed to run errands.

At a stop light halfway to the grocery store, a frantic dig through her purse told her she'd forgotten her list. *Really, Alexis? The thing you need to make this trip happen. Start putting it on your phone!*

With a groan, she turned her car around. The parking space she'd had in front of her building was gone, but there was an open one across the street. She slammed her car door and sprinted over the asphalt, gripping her keys in her hand. She took the stairs two at a time and opened her door. Confusion set in as she walked into her kitchen and noticed most of her cabinet doors were open, their contents spilled on the counters.

"What the hell?" She looked around and then heard a noise from her bedroom. "Shit," she breathed.

She retreated to her front door, forgetting about the list. Her hand was on the doorknob when a dark form rushed toward her in her peripheral vision.

The person put their arms around her and dragged her from the door. She screamed, memories of the night she was dragged into Kurt's office flashing through her mind. She would not let that happen to her again. She frantically searched her memory for key points of the self-defense classes she'd taken during isolation.

As her heart slammed and adrenaline rushed through her, she thrust her right elbow back into the intruder's chest. The grunt that followed was male. Alexis whirled as he tried to regain his composure. He was taller than her by quite a few inches, but was dressed casually, except for a ski mask. She couldn't see the man's face, but decided to try to break his nose. She thrust her palm up as hard as she could, exhaling as she made contact. He grunted again but didn't speak.

She twisted, running for the door. He yanked her arm with such force she felt her shoulder pop out of the socket, but it went right back in as he shoved her against the wall. She cried out in surprise and pain as she cracked the side of her face against the coat rack hanging there.

She was dazed by this point, but realized one of her hands still had a death grip on her keys, the worn metal making dents in her flesh. She held one up as she felt the blood dripping down her face. Her arm throbbed, but she was ready to stab him with the key if she needed to. He scoffed at her, throwing open her door. She heard him running down the stairs toward the back of her building. She scrambled back to her kitchen, trying to slow her heart and her breathing. Her purse was where she'd left it. She grabbed her phone and dialed 911.

After the operator assured her police and an ambulance were on their way, she hung up and called Kassie. No answer. She tried Brett, but his phone was off. She left them both voicemails, not trying to mask the frantic sound in her voice. Alexis knew her mother was working an extra shift that day. She wanted to calm down before leaving her a message.

She rested against her counter, pulling some paper towels off the roll and getting them wet. She dabbed at her face, but the intense stinging made her gasp. She found a dry washcloth and held it there instead, just to stop the bleeding. She could feel her face swelling. Her shoulder beat in time with her heart.

Two police officers and an ambulance arrived in minutes. The officers left to search the area for the suspect, calling for backup as they went. The two EMTs went to work checking her injuries just as her phone rang. Kassie's name popped up on the screen.

"Alexis, are you okay?" Kassie's voice was anxious. "I just got your voicemail. I'm so sorry. We're meeting with our caterer, and my phone was on silent."

"It's okay, don't worry. I just freaked out," she responded.

"Hold that gauze tight for a second," one of the EMTs said right next to her face.

"Um, gauze? Are you hurt?" Kassie sounded like she might be pacing.

"Just a little. Don't worry about it."

"Ma'am, you'll need to go to the hospital. This needs stitches," the same EMT commented.

"Stitches?" Kassie's voice went up an octave.

"I just cut my face a little in the scuffle," Alexis responded.

"Right." Her friend's voice was full of disbelief. "We're up in the foothills, so it'll take us a while to get there, but Brett is sending someone."

"What? Who?"

As she said this, another female officer arrived, walking toward her through the mess that was Alexis's apartment.

"Sorry, I have to go. They have more questions."

"Okay, we're on our way down there. You'll go to UC Davis Med Center?" Kassie asked.

"Yes. See you soon," Alexis said in what she hoped was a positive tone. Then she ended the call.

As the officer introduced herself and began her questions, there was a knock on her door frame.

She looked up to see Kruger standing there. Although his height made him appear formidable as always, he was dressed in a gray short-sleeve T-shirt and dark jeans, a striking difference from the last time she'd seen him. His eyes were troubled as he surveyed her apartment and studied her wounded face. Her heart, which had calmed down, picked up its pace. *Seriously? Just stop!* she told herself.

The uniformed officer gave Kruger a nod and stepped away to listen to her radio. He hadn't shown her a badge, but Alexis wouldn't be surprised if Kruger knew everyone in his department.

"You okay, Miller?" he asked, crouching down to look at her, a caring tone drifting through his words.

"That's becoming somewhat of a theme question, Kruger," she answered with a sigh, and she could tell he was trying not to smile.

"They'll need to do some imaging of your arm as well," the second EMT said with a gentle nudge in his voice, reminding Alexis that the hospital was in her future.

Kruger nodded. "Let me just make sure there's nothing else they need from you right now. Then you'll be good to go."

He turned back to the uniformed officer. "They didn't find him," she explained, "but we have more units searching the area. They knocked on some doors as they were going through the building. Sounds like he hit one other apartment here, but the renters just got home. He took a few things from them. Simons and Gordon are heading to the neighboring buildings."

As she was filling Kruger in and the EMTs were gathering their supplies to head downstairs, Alexis inched toward her bedroom. It terrified her that he'd been in there, but she had to see if he took anything.

The diamond earrings her mom had given her for her sixteenth birthday, which usually sat in a small dish on top of her dresser, were gone. Her tablet was no longer on her nightstand. Things looked riffled through, but she couldn't tell if anything else was missing. The tablet pissed her off, but the earrings crushed her. They'd meant so much to her mom.

Kruger and the officer were waiting for her in the front room.

"Did he take anything?" Kruger asked, knowing why she'd disappeared.

"Yeah." She fought back the angry tears that threatened to spill. "He took my tablet and a pair of diamond earrings."

The female officer nodded, writing the items down.

A wave of exhaustion and anxiety hit Alexis. All she wanted to do was sit down.

Kruger noticed. "You need to go to the hospital." There was a finality to his voice. She had no choice.

The anger, fear, and sadness sweeping through her brain, and the pain in her body, manifested in several choice, but silent, words hurled his way.

"We'll get in touch if we need anything else," the officer said and stepped aside. Alexis made her way out the door. When she got to the bottom of the stairs, she stopped.

"I'll drive myself," she said to the EMTs.

"Uh, no." Kruger frowned. "Take the ambulance, Miller."

"Ambulances are expensive, Kruger." *And those EMTs are both men.*

He sighed and looked around. "Brett and Kassidy won't be back for a while. Did you call your mom?"

"She's working right now. She's a nurse at UC Davis."

He didn't hesitate. "Okay, I'll take you."

That wasn't going to work. She barely knew him. As good of a person as he seemed to be, a vehicle was too small of a space to be alone with him. She knew where her anxiety would take her.

Looking confused by her hesitation, he said, "Miller, it's either me or the ambulance."

Breathe. You can trust him. She nodded and thanked the EMTs. Luke motioned across the street to his black Chevrolet Colorado. Alexis forced her legs to walk to it. He opened the passenger door, closing it after she climbed in. Alexis kept her breathing steady as he rounded the front of the truck and climbed in. She scooted herself as close to the door as possible and kept her gaze out the window.

"Doing okay? You look like you're ready to perform an escape maneuver." There was the smallest amount of amusement in his voice.

"Yeah, I kind of am. I—have some trouble being alone with men in small spaces." She tried to make her voice louder as she said the words, but it still sounded like a whisper.

She hated making people uncomfortable by reminding them what she'd been through. She knew rape would always be an unsettling topic, but she despised that it was so attached to her, especially with how much her story had been in the news after she'd come out of hiding.

She watched realization dawn on his face and then guilt as he cast her a glance. Now it was time for yet another awkward conversation.

CHAPTER 5

Luke felt like an idiot and then a jackass all over again.

"Which is why you wanted to drive yourself. Alexis, I—"

"You didn't know." She waved his words away before he could finish them.

"I know what you've been through. I should've thought about why—" he started again.

"I don't like to have the conversations where I explain why. I don't like making people uncomfortable. My therapist says people should be able to—"

"Deal with it," he finished the thought. "I agree. If people care about you and want to support you, they should deal with the discomfort they might have. If you're willing to talk about something, they should be open to that."

As Luke dealt with the Midtown traffic, he felt her gaze on him and sent her a quick glance. She looked surprised, but her eyes showed something deeper.

He cleared his throat. "My past, my grief, has been awkward for other people too. It's been awkward for me, because I don't like to talk about myself to begin with. But *my* therapist, who is probably friends with yours," he smiled and she let out a small laugh, "has told me many times that conversations about grief—and maybe traumatic experiences—are not going to be comfortable, so we just have to let them be how they are. But that's why I try to avoid talking about my past. I don't like dealing with discomfort."

She nodded, seemingly fine with his honesty. "It's not easy." She paused for several moments, and he started to think she didn't want to talk anymore.

Then she took a breath and continued, "I feel like my life is another definition of that phrase, 'withstanding the test of time.' But my definition doesn't mean something that holds up well as time marches on—it means how well I'm doing at keeping my head above water as time crashes by me, often almost crushing me as it goes. Sometimes I think the universe and society are saying, 'This much time has gone by, so how healed are you from your trauma now? Can you handle being alone with a man? Can you handle a man accidentally touching you or staring at you for too long? You should be doing so much better than you are now. You should be moving forward.' It's always a test of time. I don't want to seem like I'm failing."

Alexis looked over at him, guilt flashing across her face, as if she felt she shouldn't be saying all of this to him.

He sighed, staring out at the road. "Another thing my therapist likes to remind me of is that grief is not linear. It doesn't ease every day or go away after a couple years have gone by. It stays. And it goes back and forth, up and down in intensity. Really good days, horrible days, just normal days. They're mixed together. And it's triggered by so many different things. And I think a lot of people say it gets easier with time because after a while you just have more experience dealing with it. And, I don't know, maybe trauma is similar? I don't think you can judge yourself in a linear way."

She looked full-on shocked now. He laughed at her expression. "What?"

"You sure you're a detective? Not a therapist?"

This caused Luke to laugh even louder. "Uh no. I couldn't do that."

"I'm not so sure," she smirked back. "And thank you. This is the nicest conversation we've had."

He took in her expression. Even though he was trying to ignore how much he was enjoying her company, he felt a slow grin spread across his face.

Alexis checked in at the emergency room, was triaged, and told to wait, but she didn't seem to want to sit down. She hugged herself with her arms, her face a little white. Luke didn't feel right sitting if she wasn't going to, so he stood next to her, leaning against a wall. A quick text to Kassidy garnered an immediate response.

"You can go if you want." Her voice was quiet. He looked down to meet her eyes. They were darker and troubled, but still beautiful.

Shit. As long as it doesn't go any further than admiring her. She needs someone more stable.

He tossed a look at the door where he'd seen other patients being led back for exams. The waiting room wasn't that full at the moment, so it shouldn't be long.

"I'm not leaving you here alone. You look like you're gonna jump out of your skin." He shook his head. Then realizing she might be more comfortable if he left, he added, "I got a text from Kassidy. She and Brett are meeting us here. I'll wait till then."

"Thanks, Kruger," she said, and he smiled to himself. He was enjoying the last name banter.

When their friends arrived, a doctor had stitched the gash on Alexis's face, and she was in radiology for X-rays.

"Thanks so much for getting her here and waiting. Is she doing okay?" Kassidy's voice was full of concern. Brett was clearly pissed about the attack and was scowling around the hospital as if Alexis's attacker might be there. Luke resisted the urge to tease him. He understood how Brett felt.

"She's in pain, but she seems pretty stubborn about it."

"Sounds like her," Kassidy said with a weak smile. "I got a text from her mom. She's coming down from whatever floor she's on."

"I'll get going then." Luke looked back in the direction Alexis had gone for her scans. He didn't want to leave, but he needed to. He needed to distract himself from thoughts of those blue eyes. "Tell her I said she needs to rest."

"Thanks, man." Brett, his face still a storm cloud, shook his hand.

Kassidy narrowed her eyes at Luke, like she was reading his thoughts. "I'm guessing things are better between you and Alexis now?"

"Yes, thanks to you," he grinned, fishing his keys from his pocket and motioning around the room. He loved giving her a hard time.

Kassidy looked like she wanted to say something else, but stopped herself. This time Luke was the one reading her thoughts.

"Don't worry about it, Kassie. I know I haven't been open with you guys, but Emma's not easy for me to talk about. I'll try sometime. But please don't make me the subject of any more research."

She nodded with a sigh.

As he left, he gave her a smile to take any sting out of the request.

* * *

Berlin was warm, but the sky was full of clouds. The forecast called for rain that night, a very common occurrence in June, and Christopher welcomed it. He had always loved rain, especially when those around him moaned about it. To fellow rain-lovers, it might seem like a cleansing, refreshing beacon of change. To him, rain felt mysterious and cold—like something sinister was just around the corner, waiting to challenge him. It was the challenge he yearned for. He never felt the need to chase it. It always made its way to his doorstep.

The streets were teeming with life as he strolled toward the Sammlung Boros art gallery in the city's Mitte district. He'd booked a tour at the beginning of the month to see the converted war bunker's current collection. The history of the building fascinated him. He imagined darkness living there, crouched amongst the art.

His cell phone buzzed in his pocket. He checked the screen, a feeling of satisfaction flooding him. He'd spoken to David's client, Thomas, an hour ago. The man had been quite livid.

"Good morning, David. I understand it's very early in California, but I thought we should talk."

"So you said," David muttered in response.

"How is your face?" If Christopher were the grinning type, he would have done so in that moment.

David was silent for a moment. "I don't know what you're—"

"You should know that trust doesn't come easy to me. I always provide myself with certain methods of insurance, just to make sure those I work with are doing what they should."

"You're having someone watch me?" David's frustration was clear in his question.

"Don't worry, you're not the only one. Thomas as well, although I didn't tell him as much. He seems intelligent, so I am sure he can reach that conclusion on his own."

David said nothing, but Christopher could hear him breathing.

"In my opinion, you haven't done anything wrong, and I didn't tell Thomas what I know. He was very angry, though, that whoever broke into Alexis's apartment and wrestled with her might have scared her enough to make her go into hiding. Is this something that will be a—problem for the project?"

"Of course not!" David snapped. "I was trying to get more information on her!"

"We could have paid someone to do that," Christopher noted. "And your broken nose and black eyes are a little too obvious. How are you going to explain that to her at work?"

"I'm going to take some time off. Then I'll figure it out. Zeke is an avid bike rider. Maybe he had a fall," David responded in a casual tone.

Christopher shook his head, not saying anything for a moment. "Try not to take too much time. Use some makeup if you need to. Thomas is angry. I'm sure he wouldn't like that you deviated from the plan."

"He's not doing half the work I am," David growled back. "It'll be fine."

When he hung up the phone, Christopher took a deep breath. He hadn't been wrong about the frustration this project would cause, but David was providing an interesting new twist. As he made his way to the gallery, he couldn't help but feel anticipation for the days to come.

* * *

Sunday started off with thoughts of Alexis floating through his mind. Her red hair in the sun, those flashing blue eyes, the teasing tone she used to say his name. *Damn it.*

He hadn't thought this much about a woman since Emma. When she died, he'd decided he didn't want to make that kind of emotional investment again. He stuck to very casual dating now. He needed to stop thinking about Alexis. But there wasn't anything wrong with making sure she was okay.

How's Alexis? He sent a quick text to Brett. He didn't want to keep bringing her up to Kassidy, because the reporter was always able to read between the lines.

Pretty sore. Arm was sprained. She might have some issues with that shoulder in the future, so she has to follow up with her doc. She's gonna stay at her mom's for a few days, take time off work, Brett responded.

Glad she's taking it easy. Haven't heard if they found the guy.

Not yet. He hit two other apts. in the neighboring building. No one else was home. Thanks for taking her to the hospital, Krug. Kass says thanks too, Brett sent back.

No problem.

Luke put his phone down on his nightstand and rubbed his hands down his face. He wanted to see her. *Nope. That wouldn't help,* he reprimanded himself.

When he got out of the shower, he had a voicemail waiting for him from a blocked number.

"Kruger, it's Sheridan. Call me."

Cormac Sheridan was one of his confidential informants from his days as a detective at the Charlotte-Mecklenburg Police Department. Luke had been getting in touch with those he still had numbers for to see if there'd been any recent whispers about the Sunset Killers. Sheridan had always been one of his most reliable sources.

Luke knew Sheridan's number by heart. He punched it in, pacing his bedroom until the man answered after the third ring.

"Kruger."

"Sheridan. What'd you find?"

"Freeman's dead. Murdered about nine months ago. He was living in a shitty place in downtown Charlotte. Not sure if Crawley did it. Whoever killed him managed to keep it quiet for a while, but there's always someone with loose lips. Local cops and feds found out a few months back, but they never found the body. They've been waiting to tell the public until they had more information to release. Sounds like some journalists have caught wind of it. It'll be a breaking story soon."

Joshua Freeman was one half of the Sunset Killers. Will Crawley was the other. It pissed Luke off that Freeman had been living in Charlotte. But who knew how long he'd been there? Now that he was dead, what would Crawley do?

"Any idea where Crawley is? Is he still in the state?" Luke ran his hand through his still-wet hair.

"Either North Carolina or one of its neighbors. From what I heard, he's never wanted to go far. He's good at hiding—staying off the grid. Heard Freeman got lazy, tired of all the work it took to hide. Maybe that was why Crawley offed him—if it was Crawley."

"Can you keep digging on Crawley?" Luke asked.

"You coming back to the state?" Sheridan sounded curious.

"If I need to at some point, but not to stay. Just trying to get a handle on this guy."

"This about your woman?" Sheridan knew about Emma's death. Everyone in that area did. He never talked about his personal life with his sources, but this wasn't something he could hide.

The FBI had worked with his and Emma's former departments to investigate the Sunset Killers. He knew the Bureau was still searching for the pair—although, it would just be Crawley now. There was no statute of limitations for murder in North Carolina, so it was possible Emma's killer could still be brought to justice. He had to know if it was Crawley or not.

As a deputy with the Mecklenburg County Sheriff's Office, Emma was one of the first to respond to the scene of three of the murders. She wanted nothing more than to locate the serial killers, but as one deputy, she'd couldn't have been enough of a threat to get Crawley and Freeman's attention. Her death had always been loosely attributed to them, and it was true that she fit the victim profile, but the pair had never killed a cop before. But it also seemed like too much of a coincidence for her murder to be random. Luke's thoughts were a jumbled mess. For now, he had to focus on Crawley.

"I appreciate your information, just like I always have." Luke decided not to answer Sheridan's question. He trusted the man for information, but Luke wasn't the only cop Sheridan worked with. "Can you keep looking for Crawley?"

The informant was silent for a second. "Yeah, of course. I'll be in touch soon."

"Thanks." Luke ended the call.

It was too late to punish Freeman. But if Crawley so much as dreamed about letting a fraction of his guard down, Luke was positive Sheridan would find him.

By Monday, Luke was exhausted. His brain had betrayed him overnight with a dream of kissing Alexis that became a dream of making love to Alexis. But someone else was there too. They grabbed her from him and pulled her away. She became like a ghost that he could sense, but he could no longer reach her. He woke up with a pounding heart.

The nightmare made him want to ask about Alexis, but he resisted checking in with Brett and Kassidy. His therapist was who he needed to talk to.

He was eating a protein bar and gulping a cup of coffee when Brett got to work.

"How was the rest of your weekend, Green?" he asked, flipping back and forth through a few emails for one of their cases. *Not going to ask about her, but if he volunteers the information—*

"Good. Got some stuff done around the house. We also visited Alexis at her mom's house." His voice sounded too casual.

"Oh yeah?" Luke didn't look away from his screen.

"Yeah. You know what's funny? Kassie thinks you're into Alexis."

Damn that journalist. "What? Why?" Luke tried to laugh, but it sounded fake.

"She said she 'just has a feeling,'" Brett answered with air quotes. "Something about how you acted at the hospital, then checked in about her yesterday."

"You know, Green, I try to be a friendly guy most of the time," Luke said in a joking tone, making eye contact with his colleague as he leaned back in his chair and steepled his fingers, as if beginning a relaxed political speech. "Maybe I just wanted to follow up about someone I took to the hospital?"

"Maybe." Brett grinned back. "Or maybe you're into her." Then he leaned forward in his own chair. "Look, Kass is going to expect certain things from this conversation, so can we just get them over with?"

Luke rolled his eyes, but gave a wave of his hand. "Go ahead."

Brett let out an evil laugh and rubbed his palms together. "She's too young for you. She's twenty-nine. You're thirty-seven."

"Eight years younger is too young? That seems like a stretch." He raised an eyebrow.

"Quick math, Krug." Brett rolled his eyes. Then he lowered his voice, and his face became much more serious. "She's been through—really traumatic shit. Her rape and isolation—she still deals with them. Do you remember how timid she was when you interviewed her back then? Remember she had to have a female detective present? It took her a long time to even be comfortable around me. She's come a long way, but—"

"I understand that. I also think she wouldn't be okay with us having this conversation," Luke said. "If I were interested in pursuing her, her comfort level would be the most important thing."

Brett cleared his throat. "So, you're keeping that at a solid 'if' then?"

Nope, it's not a good idea, so it's not gonna happen. "Yep! Tell Kassidy I enjoyed this." This time it was Luke's turn to grin as he clapped his friend on the back and turned toward his computer screen.

He loved giving Brett crap. But as he turned his attention back to work, he couldn't ignore the pair of blue eyes drifting through his mind.

CHAPTER 6

Alexis heaved a sigh as she stared out the passenger window of the late-90's Toyota Corolla while her mother searched for a parking spot. She always found it amazing that her mom still had this car.

She'd planned to stay at Eileen's house for a couple days, but when it was time to go home, her anxiety was there to greet her like an old friend. She reminded herself that confronting fear was part of her new life. But she'd stayed until Thursday anyway.

One burglar isn't going to take away all my progress, was the mantra floating through her head. It didn't hurt that her landlord now promised to install security systems in every apartment.

Since her injured arm was still tightly wrapped in an ACE bandage, Kassie had helped clean up her place. When they'd tidied her bedroom, Alexis had noticed several pairs of her underwear and two bras were missing. She shuddered while reporting it to the police. Maybe this guy had something on his mind other than just making a quick buck off stolen valuables. She felt sick if she thought about it too long.

"You can always come back to my house if you don't feel safe." Her mother reached over and squeezed her hand.

"Thanks, Mom. I really appreciate it. I'm going to try my hardest to stay home. I go back to work on Monday. I just want to get back to normal."

"I know, babe. I think you should. But this could be hard for you. A break-in feels violating enough when someone hasn't been through the trauma you have. So, you know I'm here if you need anything."

Alexis turned her gaze to study Eileen's face. She could see stress and exhaustion in her eyes, but her mother always hid those things well. She was sure working as a nurse at a hospital was helpful for keeping emotions in check, but Alexis knew her mother too well. She was worried. She must be afraid she would lose her daughter again.

Her isolation had been difficult on her mother. Alexis knew this, but Eileen would never admit it. She'd always tried to be calm and supportive. The only obvious thing she had a problem with was Alexis's name change. It was as if she couldn't make herself say it, so she called Alexis pet names instead.

Growing up, Alexis had often heard the story of her mother agonizing over the perfect Irish name when she found out she was having a baby girl. Both her mother and father had Irish lineage, hence her father's last name of Kelly. As fate would have it, both families originated from County Galway.

Alexis had chosen the name Alexis Miller to get as far from the sound of her birth name as possible. When she was a child, she'd hated the fact that no one could pronounce or spell her name, but when she'd had to give it up, she'd grieved her loss––and her mother's. But she knew the name change had kept her alive when Kurt was ordering the murders of his victims. He couldn't kill who he couldn't find. And now it felt like Alexis Miller was who she needed to be. Her former name was shrouded in too much pain.

Her mom walked her into her apartment, which Kassie had made sure was spotless and as cozy as possible. The anxiety was still there, but Alexis tried to feel grateful for her friend. Eileen stayed for coffee and several hours of home improvement reality shows, which they both loved.

"I'd better get some grocery shopping done. Do you think it's lame to thank someone with cookies for driving you to the hospital?" Alexis decided to ask. She wanted to show Kruger her appreciation, but she was also trying to ignore how much she wanted to see him again.

"Not lame at all. Who doesn't like cookies?" Eileen smirked.

Alexis nodded. "Not anyone I care to know."

She'd pilfered Luke's phone number from Kassie's phone and texted him on Friday morning. Her heart was slamming, but she forced herself to send the message before she lost her nerve. She told herself she just wanted to deliver the cookies.

Hey, Kruger, it's Miller. Lunch at McKinley Park today?

It took a minute for him to answer, *I like this whole 80s vice cop vibe we've got going now. You ok? I'll be there at 11:30. Same table?*

His comment made her grin. *It works well when one person is a cop. I'm doing much better. Same table!*

Yeah, guess that helps. Glad to hear! See you then.

Alexis couldn't find any parking on H Street, so she parked right next to Lake Kiesel around the corner on G Street. She swore under her breath when she almost dropped both containers of chocolate chip cookies and her lunch as she got out of her car. When she got everything balanced, she started onto the path that rounded the lake. She smiled at a little girl who stood on the shore nervously eyeing some nearby geese. Her mother squatted down next to her, speaking soft words about the creatures, but the girl shook her head with a frown. Her mother scooped her up with a kiss and they retreated to a nearby picnic blanket.

Alexis was lost in the moment for a short time. The far-off idea of having children flitted through her mind sometimes, but she had so much of herself she wanted to develop and strengthen before she got there.

Luke was waiting for her at the picnic table. She saw him frown from a distance. He jumped up and used his long legs to stroll to her in a matter of seconds.

"Miller, I have every faith in your capabilities, but this is a little much," he said, plucking both cookie containers and her lunch bag from her arms, making sure not to jostle the sprained one.

"I was doing fine." She laughed. "I definitely did *not* almost drop everything when I got out of my car."

He shook his head with a smirk as they sat down. "What is all this? Are those cookies?" His eyes seemed to get just a little wider.

"They are. Homemade chocolate chip, in fact." She grinned, looking down at her lunchbox to hide the blush that emerged as she noted his slow smile and the dark eyes that found hers. God, he was handsome.

Calm down, Alexis. He probably knows that and uses it to his advantage. Someone that good looking doesn't stay single. Geez, why are you making him into such a villain? It doesn't matter, because you're not interested in him! Could you even touch him without having a panic attack?

"Uh, everything all right?" he asked, the slight scrunch of confusion around his eyes pulling her back from her thoughts.

Oh God, did I say any of that out loud? No, no, I couldn't have. Stop acting like a teenager! "Yes, sorry, I'm just tired. The smaller container is just for you. The bigger one is for your coworkers. I figured they'd like some too."

"Yeah, these will be gone in a matter of minutes." He grinned. "Thanks, Miller."

"No problem," she responded, feeling pride at keeping her voice so casual. She took a bite of sandwich to take more time before the rest of her thought. "I appreciate you being there that day."

He nodded and studied her face for a moment. It made her pause before taking another bite.

"That looks a lot better." He motioned toward the healing cut on her cheek, then moved his eyes to her arm. "How long for the bandage?"

"Another few weeks. It's annoying to drive with, but luckily not my dominant hand. I'm taking another week off from my classes to minimize activity. I'm grateful Valle Coffee is an easy walk from my place."

"When are you starting back there?"

"Monday. My manager's letting me work half-days for two weeks. I won't know what to do with all my free time!" she laughed. "It's not too strenuous, and they'll have me on the register a lot. They finally filled another one of our open positions, so I'm sure that will help."

"I'll have to stop by for a cup of pure caffeine then." His grin stayed. She couldn't help but return the expression.

His phone beeped, and he pulled it from his pocket. A frown replaced the smile. "Sorry. I've gotta make a call."

"No problem!" she said as he stepped away.

"Hey. What's up?" she heard him say.

Alexis was starving, so even though she felt a little guilty he hadn't touched his lunch, she continued to eat her sandwich. She looked back in the direction of the lake as she heard children's laughter. She wondered if the little girl felt more comfortable about the geese. As she turned to look back toward Luke, an uneasy feeling made its way up her spine. His back was to her. He was still on his call, but she felt like someone was watching her. She whipped her head around, gazing in all directions, but she saw no one. The laughter from the lake continued. She heard people chatting by the rose garden. Her eyes scanned nearby trees. For just a moment, she could have sworn she saw a flash of movement.

"Sorry about that." Luke's deep voice shook her back to the picnic table. "There was a development in one of my cases. I have to get going." He looked anything but happy about said-development.

"Oh, okay," she said, her tone sounding strange in her ears.

"Are you gonna stay a while?" he asked, gathering up the containers and his lunch.

"Um, no. I think I'm good." She tried to look satisfied with her partially eaten meal. No one could have paid her money to stay there in that moment, even though she had no idea if she'd actually seen anything.

"Can I walk you back to your car?" His offer was sincere, but his eyes were impatient.

"No, it's fine!" She waved him away, trying not to look rushed as she collected her own things. "I'm not far."

He nodded. "See you soon, Miller."

And it sounded like a promise.

* * *

Wednesday morning, Luke's phone rang at five-fifty-two.

Susan again?

He grabbed the annoying object, willing his brain to work. "Hello?"

"Morning, sunshine." A familiar voice came over the line.

Alan Langley was a detective with Luke's former department. He and Luke had worked countless cases together, and they'd become close friends. Alan had been there for him after Emma died. He always called Luke around the anniversary of her death.

"Langley. How the hell are you?"

"Doing good. Sorry I didn't call you until now. Things are crazy."

"I get it. Lots of cases?" Luke rubbed his hand over his eyes in an attempt to keep them open.

"Yeah, and I'm training a couple new detectives. But I'm also having this problem with a former coworker."

"Who is it?" Luke yawned. His body begged for more sleep, but he knew that wasn't going to happen.

"It's you, Krug." Langley's voice was low and serious.

Luke was silent for a moment. There was no point in denying he was trying to find Crawley. Langley already knew.

"How'd you hear?" He sat up.

"An informant told us you were having Sheridan and a few others digging around. You can't be doing that, Luke. You don't work here anymore. Even if you did, you know you wouldn't be assigned to that case. It's been *five years*, and Crawley is like a ghost. And I know you heard about Freeman in the news. With everyone sure Crawley killed him—" He cut himself off. "I'm sorry—I'm not trying to be an asshole. I know you of all people understand all this. We're still working with the FBI...."

"I know that." Luke heaved a sigh and was quiet for a moment before continuing.

Langley waited.

"Susan's desperate. She feels like everyone's given up. Time passes, Langley. Pain doesn't."

"I know. I'm sorry. Susan calls us all the time. We try to explain that we're still looking. That the FBI is still looking. She doesn't want to hear it. She wants us to do something. What can we do until we find him?"

"Yeah, I get it." Luke sat up and ran his hand through his hair. "I know you're trying. I guess as time moves on like normal and the anniversary number gets bigger, so does the panic that there will never be an answer. Susan was angrier and more accusatory this year than I've ever heard her."

Langley's tone was empathetic when he spoke again. "It's shitty that she does that to you, Luke. She shouldn't. She should be offering you the same support you've given her over the years instead of making you feel like crap. You need to stop answering her calls."

He shook his head as if Langley could see him. "It'd feel like a betrayal to Em not to talk to her mom. You know how close they were. I'm the only connection she has left to her daughter since Nicholas left."

Langley sighed. When he spoke, his voice was understanding but firm. "I know you have your own crap to deal with in your job there. And you must want to move on with your life. From now on, just refer her to us. To me, specifically."

Luke listened to the sound of his ceiling fan racing in a never-ending circle, just like he was doing. Year after year.

"I'll think about it. And I'm sorry if I caused any problems. Thank you for the call."

"Of course, brother. I'm always here for you."

The call ended. Luke forced himself out of bed, shutting off his alarm as it started to buzz. Langley was right. He should let them handle it. He shouldn't take the words Susan spewed at him every year. He should try to move on. He thought of Alexis again. Maybe he'd try to move on, but he could never give up on the past.

CHAPTER 7

On Monday, Alexis got up early, inspired to paint. She found a field of wildflowers in the recesses of her mind and got started. Maybe it was somewhere she'd been in childhood? She couldn't remember, but it felt perfect and peaceful for the new morning.

Fifteen minutes before Valle Coffee opened its doors, Zeke stepped up to the register next to hers.

"Heard you had a break-in? Are you okay?" he asked, nodding toward her wounded arm.

"I'm fine. Nothing too serious." She didn't feel like elaborating. "It's just nice to be back at work. Nora told me you were out last week too. A biking accident?"

She gazed at his face. It was clear he had a couple black eyes, although they seemed to be healing. It also looked like he was wearing makeup. Why would he be trying so hard to cover up his injuries?

"Yeah, I was out riding with a couple friends. An SUV cut me off at an intersection. I managed to get myself out of the way but had to swerve so hard I lost control and face-planted into a parked car. I got pretty bruised up, but luckily I wasn't alone. And it's my ego that hurts the most." He said all this with a sheepish smile. She felt bad for him.

"Well, I'm glad you're okay and that we're both back. I know Nora was pretty stressed while we were out, although she didn't want to admit it."

"Maybe not to you," Zeke answered with a smirk. She laughed as he rolled his eyes toward their shift lead.

At seven-thirty, the morning rush was under way. Her anxiety was rising right along with it. She felt thrown off by her days out of work, and her bandage was annoying her. She was glad to be on register duty, but it was Monday. Customers who had not yet had their coffee on a Monday meant sleepy, stressed, and cranky customers. She knew they were all picturing those soul-changing first sips, and the fact that they had to wait for them was too much.

But it was impossible to miss Luke coming through the door with his staggering height and charismatic presence. When she saw him, she felt an instant sense of both excitement and calm. *Yep, this whole not-being-into-him thing is working out well,* she rolled her eyes at herself.

"Morning, Miller," he greeted her with a charming grin.

"Morning, Kruger. All the caffeine today?"

"Yes, please." His smile grew as he gave her his usual order, studying her face. "A couple days has done wonders."

"Yeah, it's coming along," she answered, although she was sure the cut on her cheek would leave a scar.

Zeke, who had a quick moment in between customers, said in a low voice, "I hope you're doing something to find the shithead that did that to her."

Alexis couldn't help but pass him a surprised look. He hadn't seemed that angry about it when they first talked.

Kruger frowned and opened his mouth, but Alexis interrupted before he could speak, "It's not his job to find the guy, Zeke. He's not assigned to the case."

"I'm sure your colleagues will find him," Zeke said. His tone sounded like he was trying to insinuate something about Luke's competence.

"I don't like that guy," Kruger muttered as Zeke turned away to talk to Nora.

"He's harmless. He got into a bike accident recently, so I'm sure he's having a rough time right now. And Mondays suck for everyone."

Luke shrugged, looking unconvinced. "Talk to you soon, Miller. Have a good day."

"You too!" she managed and took a deep breath as he turned away to get his drink.

When things slowed a bit and she was tidying the back counter, Zeke came up next to her. "That cop's into you."

She turned away from him. His attitude about Luke was starting to get on her nerves. "No, he's just a friend. He works with my best friend's fiancé."

"Not sure that's how he sees it. Just be careful. He doesn't seem like an easy guy to be around."

What the hell is happening? I don't know him well enough for him to be giving me dating advice.

"I'd still like to take you to see that French film," Zeke said, breaking through her thoughts. "I don't know how much longer it'll be at Tower."

Something about him was off, and it was making Alexis uncomfortable. Maybe he was still in pain or just bitter after his accident, but her intuition was giving her strong "stay away" vibes. There was no point in her living this new life if she wasn't going to be true to her feelings. But how should she tell him?

"Thanks, but I'm not dating right now. I'm still dealing with some trauma from my past, and I'm just not ready," she said, trying for confidence. It wasn't a lie, although she wasn't sure her answer would be the same if Luke asked.

"Oh, okay. No problem. Although friends do see movies together." It was like he was going for a joking tone, but didn't quite cover up the frustration he felt at her rejection. In the end, he turned away before she could say anything else.

She sighed. She had to remember the boundaries she and her therapist talked about so often. If she didn't feel comfortable doing something, she didn't have to. But it didn't make the situation any less awkward.

In the first week of July, Alexis met Kassie at Miosa Bride on J Street in the heart of downtown. Kassie and Brett's wedding was at the end of August, and Kassie's dress seemed right on schedule with her second fitting. But Alexis could see her friend felt anything but calm, cool, and collected.

"Kass, you're gorgeous!" Alexis breathed as she took in the dress's white A-line cut with sweetheart neckline, delicate straps, and sprinkling of lace that started at the bodice and flowed through the skirt.

"Thanks! I'm happy with it," she answered, even as she fidgeted in front of the mirror. "Your dress will be ready at the beginning of August?"

"Yes, can't wait to see it again! All of your bridesmaids have our shoes and jewelry lined up. And you said everything is good with the venue, right? Smart of you guys to find a place that works with certain vendors. It's got to be better than searching all over the place for the things you need."

"Yes, everything's good there." Kassie sighed. "Am I a horrible person for wanting it all to be over?"

Alexis almost spit out the sip of water she was taking, but she knew what her friend meant.

"You mean so you can be done with people asking you to make decisions, then staring at you as you walk down an aisle and just be married to the love of your life?" Alexis grinned. "No, you're not a horrible person!"

Kassie smiled back. "Okay, good. I'm sure it'll be a beautiful day. I'm excited—but it's exhausting. And yeah, the staring! As a reporter, I'm supposed to be the one staring at people!"

Alexis laughed at this, knowing her friend's job entailed a lot more.

"It's going to be amazing, Kass. You have beautiful taste, so I know everything will look flawless. You two love to have fun, so everyone's going to have a great time. And at the end, you'll be married to Brett, and you will never have to plan a giant ceremony again."

"Thanks, Lex." Kassie was now grinning from ear to ear. "You really do know the right things to say. You can still bring a plus-one, you know. We'll have tons of food. So, if your mom wants to come. Or maybe—" she hesitated, "Maybe that cute guy from the coffee shop?"

Alexis knew Kassie was trying to be careful. Everyone tiptoed around the topic of her dating life. She understood, but this time she had something she wanted to say about it. She just wasn't sure how it would be received.

"I was starting to consider that, but ever since we both came back from our medical leaves, he's been acting weird—kind of intense, I guess. And he asked me to see a movie with him, but I said no, because he was making me feel uncomfortable. But there's someone else I've been thinking about."

"Oh! Who?" Kassie regarded her in the mirror. Alexis thought her smile became a little forced and knew her friend had already guessed.

"Luke," Alexis said in a quiet voice.

Kassie turned to look at her. "Honestly, I saw that coming with some of the things you've said about him."

"And?" Alexis persisted.

"And, if he makes you feel happy and safe, then I can't see anything wrong with it," Kassie responded. "He's a good guy, although sometimes brooding, but I guess we can all get that way. He has some pain in his past that he doesn't seem to want to talk about with us, but maybe he'd open up to you."

Alexis nodded. "He kind of mentioned that. You still don't sound convinced. Your opinion matters to me."

Kassie sat down in the chair next to her, trying to maneuver the layers of dress. "I don't know what it is. I think I'm just too protective of you. I just want you to be safe. And you deserve to be so happy. I have a good idea he's interested in you too. And at least I wouldn't have to run the typical background check."

Alexis laughed out loud. "And if things don't work out? Would it be weird for you and Brett?"

Kassie smirked. "Brett could feel weird about it all he wants. You know whose side I'd always be on."

Alexis smiled, but then a sigh escaped her.

"What else is up?" Kassie patted Alexis's arm.

"How did you do it, Kass? How did you move on from what Kurt did to you? I want to move on, but sometimes it seems—impossible. I'm in awe of this life you've made for yourself."

Kassie looked shocked. "You've made a great life for yourself, Lex! And I didn't go through anything close to what you did. I was just a naïve girl-friend. I wasn't—"

Raped. Alexis knew Kassie didn't want to use the word—didn't want Alexis to have to think about the experience. Alexis wished it were that easy. "Sure, but when he came to Sacramento, Kurt cut you off from everyone you knew—forced you to break up with Brett. You had to be brave enough to go to the police when you weren't sure if he was still stalking you. That's a big deal. How have you moved on from the trauma he caused?" Alexis also didn't want to bring up painful memories for her friend, but she needed Kassie to give herself more credit.

"I'm not sure," Kassie responded with a weak smile. "Lots of therapy, Brett's support, your friendship. Having a job I love helps. I guess I just take it day by day. You may not see yourself moving forward, but I do."

Alexis nodded. She was glad to have another perspective to keep her grounded. Sometimes it was so easy to forget how far she'd come. "Thank you."

"Always, friend," Kassie said. She gave Alexis a quick hug and stood up from the chair to go take off her dress.

A few days after the Fourth of July, she woke up to views of the real estate guy hanging around outside the neighboring building. What was his name? Geoff? She checked the business card she'd discarded in the corner of her kitchen counter after she'd looked up his license. Geoff Morgan, yeah. This time he was talking with two other men, one in a suit, one in more casual clothes. His license was real, but this made him seem more legit.

Alexis peeked through her curtains as she ate a bowl of Cheerios and sipped some black coffee, which she'd developed a taste for in recent days.

A knock at her door made her jump. Geoff wouldn't have seen her, right? It was sixty-thirty in the morning, and she had to leave for work.

She took a cautious glance through the peephole and was surprised to see Luke.

"Um, Kruger?" she questioned as she opened the door.

"Hey." His face carried the slightest awkward expression, something she wasn't used to from him. "Sorry it's so early, but I thought I might catch you before work. I had dinner with Brett and Kassidy last night. She said you needed this right away. Since we live closer, she asked me to drop it off. She said she wasn't sure when she'd see you again since they're going out of town this weekend to see Brett's family."

"Oh, uh, okay." She took the small box he held out and opened it. Inside was the hair comb Alexis would be wearing in the wedding.

"Yeah, she said she had this—" Alexis murmured, wondering why Kassie couldn't have just given it to her when she drove the couple to the airport on Saturday.

"She said you had to have it before she lost it," he offered, now looking confused at Alexis's reaction. "I'm working late tonight, so I wasn't sure when I would get it to you other than now...." His words trailed off as if he was realizing something.

But Alexis already understood. Kassie was one of the most organized people she knew. There was no way she would have lost something like this. Her friend was playing matchmaker.

"This wasn't a hair emergency, was it?" Luke asked, smirking now.

"Not exactly." Alexis laughed. "Kassie likes to 'help out' sometimes."

"Yeah. I have a different thing to call it, but yeah." He rolled his eyes, which became a little more intense, as if he wanted to say something else.

"I'm heading out to work," she said when he didn't continue. She left her front door open with him standing there as she rinsed out her bowl and grabbed her shoes.

Once again, she marveled at his height as she sat on her couch to tie her laces. He must intimidate a lot of people, but she found his presence comforting. Of course, she wasn't on the wrong side of an interrogation.

"Oh. I'll walk you out. I parked my truck right in front of your place. I'd drive you, but I'm going the opposite way. But I can—"

Wow! Luke Kruger flustered! Well, if I didn't know how he felt before, at least I can guess now. "That's okay! I like to walk, and I don't want you to be late for work." She grinned, feeling a little bad about her enjoyment of this moment.

He nodded.

She stepped past him to close and lock her door. She felt him watching her, but when she looked up at him, his face was stormy. *So much going on in that head*, she thought and started down the stairs.

She saw his truck and stopped to wait for him to catch up.

"Good morning!" Geoff Morgan called from down the street, waving. She could have sworn she saw his expression falter when he clocked Luke, but it was back to its previous cheer the next second.

Without thinking too much, she waved back and turned toward Luke. "Thanks for bringing it by. Have a good day, Kruger."

"Yeah, no problem. Talk to you soon, Miller."

She'd have to tell Kassie that her ploy was a little too obvious, but at least seeing him had put her in a good mood for the morning. She pulled out her phone to check her email, looking both ways before stepping off the corner to cross the street. Then she heard the squeal of tires. Her eyes flashed up from her screen to see a car barreling straight toward her.

CHAPTER 8

Luke had still been watching her from his truck, wondering how Kassidy had slipped that one by him. When he saw the car pull away from the curb and speed forward, he wrenched his door open and ran.

"Alexis!" he yelled, sure the car was going to hit her; sure he would lose her in that moment.

Somehow, she propelled herself backward and fell into a sitting position on the sidewalk she'd stepped from seconds before. He forced his eyes toward the black Mercedes-Benz and tried to get the license plate, but only managed the first three digits before it turned left, still going a high rate of speed. He called dispatch. There had to be a traffic or patrol unit nearby.

He finished the call as he ran toward her, noticing the guy she'd waved to was just standing there staring, his two cronies doing the same. He wanted to tell them to close their fucking gaping mouths and help, but knew that wouldn't make the situation better.

"You all right? Are you hurt?" The words flew from him as he kneeled down beside her, inspecting her for injury. He pushed some of her hair, which had fallen in her face, back behind her ear so he could see her eyes.

"No, I'm okay." Her voice was shaky. "I didn't look well enough. I—" She started looking around. He knew she was wondering where her phone ended up. He retrieved it from where it sat about six feet away and put it in her hand.

"No, that asshole was going way too fast," he responded in a firm voice. "Like he didn't see you."

"Or didn't care," she mumbled, still looking dazed, but pushing herself to her feet. "What is happening in my life right now? Is this like a *Final Destination* thing?"

He was confused for a moment and then remembered the movie. "Jesus, that's morbid, Miller. No, that's just a shitty movie with a million sequels. This was just a couple weird coincidences."

"I think it was pretty popular, actually. I think you'd be offending a lot of people." She gave him a weak smile. He rolled his eyes when he realized she was still talking about the movie.

"No accounting for *their* taste," he responded. "Come on, I'll get you home."

"I'm not going home. I'm going to work." She frowned.

"You were almost hit by a car. You're going home."

"No, I'm not." She moved away from him. "It was a stupid mistake on my part, Luke." Although it didn't appear she believed her own words. "I've spent enough time at home. I'm done with that."

He knew this wasn't just about today anymore. She was referencing the last few years of her life.

"I'm fine," she insisted as her eyes flashed. He knew his face didn't look friendly. He was a master of dark expressions when he needed them at work, but it was clear Alexis couldn't care less about this tactic.

"Okay, I'll drive you." He threw up his hands.

"No, you have to get to work." She gave him a light shove, which surprised him. He wished he could pull her close instead of letting her push him away. "I'll be fine."

"Whatever you want," he sighed, putting more space between them. "But I'm going to call you later."

She gave him a wave, but her back was already turned toward him as she started off down the street. He had a feeling she would have liked to flip him off instead. Was it weird that he was even more attracted to her when she stood up to him?

He turned on his heel, heading back toward his truck. She couldn't stop him from following her to make sure she arrived at work in one piece.

"Is she okay?" The guy on the street asked with his hand outstretched, as if about to introduce himself.

"Maybe if you'd helped instead of gawking, you'd know the answer to that question," Luke couldn't help but growl back, brushing past the man's hand. Truthfully, he wouldn't have wanted the guy anywhere near Alexis, but the harshness of his words eased his frustration a little.

Luke slammed his truck door and started the engine, letting her get a little farther ahead of him. When she reached Valle Coffee, she turned to look at him with a frown as he drove past. He grinned at her and was sure he saw her roll her eyes as she went inside.

As he made a couple turns to head back in the other direction, Luke thought about the panic he'd felt when he'd seen the car heading for her. The way he was sure she'd die—like he could see it happening, even though she hadn't. He knew it was easy for these thoughts to infiltrate his mind because of what happened with Emma. Up until now, Luke would have convinced himself that this was why he shouldn't be in another relationship. He hadn't wanted to risk losing someone else. He also hadn't wanted to tinge a new relationship with the trauma of his past.

But with Alexis, time felt important. It felt steady. But it was still rushing by like it always did. And right now, it felt like he was wasting it. Based on Kassidy's meddling, he could assume Alexis was interested in him, so it was time to take a chance.

A call rang through his Bluetooth, clearing his mind. The words No Caller ID came up on his center display. It was just after seven, a little early for most people to be calling. He hoped his guess was right.

"This is Kruger."

"It's Sheridan. I think I might have a reliable lead on your man. Couple guys I worked with a few years back were approached by Freeman before he died. Said he was recruiting for some work in Alabama. They said he mentioned his partner. He never contacted them again, but they said they have more information they're willing to give in person. Might lead to something."

"Alabama. I think I remember Crawley having some family there. I'm sure the feds have checked—" Luke said, mostly talking to himself.

"Sometimes it's easy to hide in plain sight, if you do it the right way," Sheridan responded.

"Yeah, you're right," Luke said, already fuming at the possibility of Crawley being in such an obvious place all these years. "Worth checking out."

"Yep. I'll get back to you when I know more."

"Thanks," Luke said, trying to convey his gratitude in the one word.

He didn't have much time to think about it as he approached the house where he and Brett would be serving a search warrant, but he hoped he'd hear from Sheridan soon.

* * *

"And you thought it was appropriate to run her down with your car?!" Thomas screamed into the phone.

Christopher couldn't help but smile as he listened to Thomas and David converse. He was glad both men were in California while he stayed tucked away in Berlin. He could enjoy the drama without being near them.

"I told you that was an accident. When I saw her outside her apartment, I panicked. I was trying to get out of there as fast as I could so she wouldn't see me. I didn't notice she was already crossing the street when I pulled away from the curb," David seethed, as if he had done nothing wrong.

"I was standing there! That's not how it looked!" Thomas seemed to have one volume for this phone call. "If she's dead, what good is her body to me?"

Truly, no conversation had ever entertained Christopher this much.

"And you said she turned you down for a date? I know my part in this was supposed to be introduced slowly, but I think I need to get more involved. David, maybe you can move more to the background." Thomas seemed to be calming down.

David said nothing.

"We can make some adjustments to the plan," Christopher said when the silence stretched on.

"I look forward to it," Thomas replied and left the call.

David still said nothing.

"I think you need to get this under control," Christopher said with a sigh. *"You saw her with the cop, didn't you? That caused your reaction? You are trying to procure this woman for Thomas, not yourself. When I first spoke to you about this project, I didn't know we were going to have these—problems."*

"It really pisses me off that you're having me watched. You know everything, like you're standing there when it happens," David grumbled. *"And I've never seen who the hell is watching me."*

"There were more than enough people to witness your actions this time. I received most of the story from Thomas himself. He hasn't made the connection about your feelings for the woman, but he was the one who told me she was with the cop before you almost ran her over."

"There will be no more problems. Let's move forward." David's voice had become more of a growl as he said these words and ended the call.

* * *

Luke called Alexis Friday after work, hoping he'd catch her before a class. He'd called her the night before to make sure she was okay, but she hadn't picked up.

"Hi, Luke," she answered. He couldn't figure out the tone in her voice. He didn't hear any of her usual playfulness. "Sorry I didn't get your call last night. I went to bed early." She still sounded exhausted.

"No problem. How are you feeling?"

"Sore—and embarrassed."

"Why embarrassed?" He opened his refrigerator to find something for dinner, but it was barren.

"I think that should be obvious," she laughed.

"Because you saved yourself from being hit by a jackass in a car?" He found a frozen pizza in his freezer and decided it would work.

"I'm glad you see it that way," she mumbled.

"Because that's the way it was. I was watching you, Alexis," he used her first name to let her know he was serious, "and there was no one coming when you stepped off that sidewalk."

She made a sound that could have been an agreement. "Watching me, huh?"

He chuckled. "Yeah. Miller, I want to spend more time with you."

"I'd like that," she said without any hesitation. He felt relief flow through him, realizing he'd been nervous to put his interest out there.

"If you're feeling up for it, are you free on Sunday?"

He heard her shuffling something around. "I have a painting class at three, but other than that, yes. Can I pick the place? Around ten?" she asked.

He smiled to himself at the excitement in her voice. "Yeah, sure. What am I in for?"

"Somewhere beautiful," she responded.

CHAPTER 9

Alexis had the dream again that night. It seemed to come in flashes. Working late. Kurt knew that. He called her to his office. He was the only one there, but no, he wasn't. There was another person in the shadows. She was trying to run. Kurt overpowering her. She screamed in the dream and woke herself up screaming. She'd gotten better at forcing herself awake.

At least she shared a living room wall with her neighbor and not a bedroom wall. She always worried she'd scare people with her screaming. She didn't know if the neighbor below her would hear. Those neighbors never spoke to her, so maybe that was her answer.

The FBI believed there had been someone else in Kurt's office that night, and every night Kurt claimed another victim. But they'd never been able to identify who it was. Her subconscious mind seemed to have memories of that person, but they were never very detailed.

Her mind buzzed and tripped along with dark thoughts. It was just after two in the morning. She wanted to go back to sleep. It was Sunday, and she wanted a fresh mind for her date with Luke, not that of a zombie. But as she could have predicted, sleep eluded her.

She finally got out of bed at six-thirty. She'd had two cups of coffee by the time Kruger got there promptly at ten, but she was still exhausted.

"Good morning," Luke said as she opened the door. Then studying her face, he asked, "How'd you sleep?"

She knew he already knew the answer based on his expression, so she decided to be snarky. "It was the best sleep of my life!"

"Wow! Then I'm sorry," he smirked back.

She felt such a strong connection to him in that moment that it made her pause. Besides Kassie, she couldn't remember feeling like anyone "got her" the way Luke did, cliché as it might sound.

It was somewhat fascinating to watch Luke climb into her little sedan. She'd insisted on driving, because she wanted to surprise him with their destination. But he didn't complain, just pushed his seat back and then stretched his legs out in front of him as much as possible.

As Alexis drove to the place she'd been countless times, it was easy to think back on the dream and the feelings she'd been having. Her flight response was nudging her from a corner of her brain. She'd been working hard with her therapist, but that didn't make it go away. Still, a couple weird incidents weren't enough to make her give up her life. She had to keep moving forward.

When they'd parked and walked up to the Crocker Art Museum, Luke nodded with a smile. "Okay, this makes sense."

The museum's original mansion and gallery buildings had graced the corner of 3rd and O Streets since 1872. It was one of Alexis's top places to go for artistic inspiration. Her heart picked up speed and her mind charged with anticipation every time she walked through its doors.

Art had been her first love, but thinking there was no way she could make a viable living from it, she'd gone into technology instead. The inner workings of a gigantic technology company were fascinating to her, and tech had helped her survive when she left San Francisco. But it wasn't what she loved. Every day she was grateful to have the chance to create art again.

"Have you been here before?" she asked as they explored a collection of American art created before 1945.

"No. I guess I haven't taken advantage of what the city has to offer, except for restaurants. I can cook, but prefer not to," he grinned.

"I'm the same, but I try to force myself to most of the time," she smiled back.

She tried to study Luke as he stared at the oil painting in front of him. He looked to be searching for something less obvious in the colors and brush strokes. She wondered if that was the detective in him or just part of his nature. There were darker circles under his eyes, which confirmed his lack of sleep. But long laugh lines extended from his eyes when he smiled, so he must have had his fair share of joy. His skin was olive-toned, and she wondered about his heritage. She had to assume German, because of his last name, but also maybe Italian?

His hands were in the pockets of his slacks. She sensed a certain vulnerability from his posture, his eyes moving back and forth and up and down in his inspection of the piece. He seemed open to whatever the painting was trying to tell him, much like she felt when in the presence of any work of art.

"It's beautiful, right?" she asked after giving him peace for several minutes.

"Yeah." He smiled down at her, his eyes lingering for a while. "I understand why you'd rather come here than go somewhere for a swanky brunch."

"Yeah, that's not really my style. I'm more of a burger and fries gal."

His eyes lit up. "Any place specifically?"

"Burgers and Brew is one of my favorites."

"Good taste, Miller. A quick lunch after this?"

"I'd love that." She turned her gaze to the wall closest to her as they started walking. Then she felt his fingers touch those of her good hand. She was surprised she didn't flinch or pull away.

"Is this okay?" he asked.

"Yes," she murmured with a nod, and he laced his fingers with hers.

"Okay, so your brother lives near Raleigh and your parents live outside Charlotte," she said later when they were eating their burgers. "But no family out here? That's a big move to make by yourself. Just needed a change?"

"Um, yeah, something like that," he answered. She could tell there was more he didn't want to say. "My brother's married, works a lot, and has his own circle of friends, so I wasn't seeing him much anyway. And my parents drive me crazy, so it's worked out pretty well."

She laughed at his honesty.

"You said you grew up in San Jose? Any extended family around there?" he asked, munching on a fry.

"Yes, on both my mom's and my dad's side. I lost touch with most of them during—my isolation. My mom still talks to her siblings a lot. Sometimes I'm at her place when she does, so I talk to them a bit then."

Luke nodded, glancing at her eyes. Alexis was sure he saw the sadness there and wondered if he'd question it.

"You've never talked about your dad," he murmured.

There it was. She took a deep breath, transported back to another painful time, well before Kurt Leonard. "My dad passed away from colon cancer when I was twelve."

"Jesus, I'm sorry," he sighed, holding her eyes with his.

Alexis gave him a weak smile in acknowledgment of his condolence. "It was very quick. My mom tried to shield me from a lot of it, because he was in a lot of pain. But he was my favorite person, so I always wanted to be around him. I have so many good memories of him. I try to remember those over the painful ones. That's what I think he'd want." She took a sip of her Coke to give herself a break.

"Losing him did inspire my mom to become a nurse. When I went to college, she got her degree at San Jose State and moved to Sacramento when she got the job at UC Davis. That's why when I went into hiding, I lived outside Sacramento. I couldn't see her, but I had to be closer to her. Luckily, Kurt never went after family members. He could've found her without much effort."

Luke didn't say anything, but he took her hand. Once again, she was calmed by his presence.

At her apartment door, he was still pretty quiet. She wondered if he'd lost someone too. She wanted to give him a safe space to talk about it.

"If you ever want to tell me about what happened—in your past, I'm here to listen."

He looked at her in surprise. "Kassidy didn't tell you?"

This was the first time she'd heard of Kassidy knowing anything, but since he was good friends with Brett, it made sense.

She shook her head. "I'm guessing she didn't think it was her information to tell."

He nodded. "It's hard for me to talk about. I've never talked to her and Brett about it. She found out through—other methods. I will tell you—"

"When you're ready," she finished after his words faded away.

He gave her a small smile. "I had a good time, Miller. Thanks for taking me out."

"Anytime," she chuckled.

He paused for a moment, and she thought he might try to kiss her. The idea was exciting but scary. She wasn't sure how her mind and body would react.

"I better go so you can get ready for your class. I'll see you soon." His words broke the moment.

She nodded, and he made his way back down the stairs after giving her one last smile.

She let herself into her apartment and leaned against the door. Just weeks ago, she hadn't been ready for a relationship, but time with Luke felt so easy. She'd dealt with so much sadness, pain, and grief over the years. She was due an extra bit of happiness.

* * *

Luke was parked down the street from her apartment. He put his hands in his pockets, staring ahead as he walked, lost in thoughts of her. He'd wanted to kiss her, but he didn't know if she'd be comfortable with that. The last thing he wanted to do was push her away by expecting anything too fast. But it'd felt good to hold her hand, and he'd definitely never enjoyed a museum so much.

He remembered the many times his mom had dragged him and his brother to museums when they were growing up—trying to force some culture on them. Somehow his dad almost always got out of it. His brother whined through most of their trips. Luke had hated it, wished to be anywhere else. But he'd loved this experience with Alexis. The art interested him, and Alexis's breakdown of the building's history had fascinated him. He'd go again tomorrow if he could go with her.

"How is your friend feeling?" A voice shattered his thoughts. He felt like someone had snuck up on him, and he didn't like it. The same man he'd seen the day Alexis was almost hit was standing in front of him now.

"Sorry?"

"Oh, my apologies! I'm Geoff Morgan." The man stuck his hand out. Luke shook it after eyeing it for a second. "I'm one of the real estate agents for this building." He motioned toward the set of apartments neighboring Alexis's, then handed Luke a business card. "I saw you walking her to her apartment just now. I met her once, but didn't get her name. I was hoping she's feeling okay. And, I'm sorry. You had every right to call me out on not helping her that day. I think I was just in shock."

Something about the guy made Luke wary. He didn't plan to give him much information.

"She's fine."

"Glad to hear it. We have a buyer for this building, but she's not happy about the recent break-ins. She's planning to install an alarm system in each unit, as I believe your friend's landlord is too." He motioned toward Alexis's building.

"Not a bad idea. Burglaries happen sometimes." Luke nodded.

"And what do you do, Mr.?"

"I work for the city," Luke answered, making a show of looking at his watch. "Sorry, Mr. Morgan, but I have to go."

"No problem! I'm sure we'll see each other around!" He gave Luke a wave as he walked off.

Awkward, Luke thought to himself, putting the business card in his wallet. He'd be checking on the guy's license later.

His phone rang just as he got to his truck.

"Hey, Kruger. It's Perez. CHP found the car believed to be the one that almost hit Ms. Miller the other day. It was on the side of I-5. Stripped. Reported stolen the day before the incident. They think the driver was taking a joyride before cleaning it out."

"Thanks, Perez. Not a surprise, I guess," he responded. He could still see the car hurtling toward Alexis as she stepped into the crosswalk.

"No problem," Perez said, ending the call.

Why did it feel like life was full of so many unanswered questions? They'd never found the asshole who broke into Alexis's apartment, and the person who'd almost run her down was a complete mystery. And in terms of Emma's case, Freeman was dead, and Crawley was maybe in Alabama.

As he got to his truck, the Sacramento sun beat down on him, filling every part of him with heat. It felt like too much. He didn't like feeling stuck, feeling overwhelmed. He wanted some sort of control.

Luke went for a drive through the city. He'd memorized these streets—and many of the landmarks and businesses they housed—during his first few months in Sacramento, and liked to think that even though he had no desire to be on patrol again, it would be easy for him to get anywhere if he ever needed to.

He picked up sushi for dinner on his way home, but before he could eat his first piece of roll, there was a knock on his apartment door. He looked through the peephole and threw the door open in surprise.

"Langley?"

"Hey, Kruger!" His former colleague grabbed him into a hug, giving him several resounding pats on the back.

"What're you doing in Sacramento? Hell, what are you doing in California?" He moved to the side so his friend could enter the apartment.

"I'm on my way to LA. I've had this vacation planned for months, but wasn't sure I'd be able to stop here. Got a hotel room in the Embassy Suites. Thought it'd be cool to hang out for a few days if it's okay."

"Yeah, that'd be great." Luke went to his fridge to get Langley a beer, not having to ask if he wanted one. "Checking on me?"

Langley laughed. "Naw, just wanted to see you, man. It's been a long time. Thought I might have pissed you off when we talked on the phone."

"No, I get it. It's not my place. Guess I've been feeling just as desperate as Susan."

Langley nodded. "Trust me, I want nothing more than to find Crawley and watch him rot in prison. I promise we'll keep looking. There's some talk he could be in Alabama, even though I know the feds looked there. But it's something."

Luke nodded. "Sheridan told me about that."

Langley took him in as if he hadn't heard him right, his frown turning into a smirk. "Sheridan always was one of the most reliable ones. And you were going to tell me Sheridan told you this?"

Luke sighed. "Yeah, I'm sorry. I know you're busy. I know the department is trying. I just figured if he found something more concrete, I could bring it to you."

"Luke, this is what I'm talking about. Please let us do our jobs. Getting too many people in the mix might make things worse. What if Sheridan tips off Crawley and he runs somewhere else? If he even is in Alabama."

Luke nodded, but he didn't want to call Sheridan off. The man was the best there was. Crawley wouldn't know Sheridan was around unless he wanted him to.

"Wanna join me for sushi? I bought a few rolls and some gyoza," Luke said after a few moments of silence, motioning toward his dinner.

Langley sighed at the change in topic, his frustration with Luke still evident. "Naw, I better go. I'm beat. Can we meet up tomorrow after your shift?"

"Sure, but call me when you get up. You can come meet some of my team."

"Sounds good, man. Call you tomorrow." Langley looked only somewhat satisfied as he shook Luke's hand and left.

Luke knew he hadn't heard the end of it from Langley. Luke also knew he should listen to Langley and bow out of the search for Crawley, but Sheridan could be close to finding the killer. Luke wasn't going to call him off now.

CHAPTER 10

On Monday, Alexis woke up feeling light and peaceful. It matched the peace she felt while painting, so she was determined to hang onto it. But when she walked into the shop and saw Zeke, guilt coursed through her. *I don't owe him anything. Even though I turned him down, I'm allowed to date.*

Valle Coffee was swamped like it always was on Mondays, so there wasn't much time to talk to her coworker anyway. She went to lunch feeling better about things. When Luke walked into the shop just after one, she couldn't help but send him a grin. He was flanked by another man with black hair and dark blue eyes. The color almost appeared to glow against the backdrop of his dark skin. Those eyes held the same confidence as Luke's.

"Hey, Miller." Luke's smile was even more charming than normal.

"Hey, yourself." She told herself not to blush. "The usual?" She was already punching in his order.

"Yes, please. But I also wanted you to meet someone." He motioned toward the dark-haired man, who stuck his hand out to Alexis. "Alexis Miller, this is Alan Langley. We worked together in Charlotte. We've known each other since our patrol days."

"Nice to meet you." The man grinned like he and Alexis were old friends as well, and Alexis took his hand.

Too tight! Too tight! Her mind screamed. His grasp was like a vise. Maybe

Alan Langley was a little too confident. It was a fight to keep herself from pulling away from him.

"Nice to meet you too," she said instead, hoping the smile she planted on her face was convincing. She wanted to rub her hand as the hold broke, but stopped herself. "Are you in Sacramento for a visit?"

"Yeah, for a few days. I'm on my way to Los Angeles, but wanted to stop and annoy this old man." Langley laughed and slapped Luke on the back.

Luke rolled his eyes. "You always do a good job of that. Order your coffee, jackass, so she can get back to work."

Langley smirked and gave Alexis his order. Then he moved to the side so Luke could have a moment with her.

His voice was a murmur and she felt her heart picking up speed. "He's in town until Thursday, but can I take you out again this weekend? For dinner, if you have any nights free?"

"Sunday night's free for me," she smiled back, running through her schedule in her mind.

"Sunday it is. I'll pick you up at six."

He moved away to wait for his drink. She hoped she was successful in forcing a composed look onto her face as she took the next customer's order.

There was a lull about half an hour before her shift was done. She felt someone at her side as she cleaned the back counter. She looked over to find Zeke watching her.

"Hey!" she said with a smile, hoping to keep their relationship friendly. "It's been so crazy, I didn't get a chance to talk to you." She noticed then how dark his expression was.

"You went out with the cop?"

"What?" She'd heard him, but it felt like her brain skipped a beat.

"I heard him before. You went out with him. You're going out with him again. I thought you weren't ready to date right now? Or was that just a line you fed me? And that arrogant guy, really?"

She was so shocked, she had no idea what to say. She'd hoped this wouldn't come up. But she reminded herself that she barely knew him. She didn't have to explain anything.

"Forget it." He waved his hand toward her, as if he didn't have time to wait for her response. As soon as they'd finished cleaning up and made sure the closing shift had what they needed, he was gone.

On her walk home, she kept her eyes from everyone else, shoving her ear buds in her ears and cranking her music. She tried to let her mind drift, focusing only when she had to cross the street. As she was just about to cross for the last time, a bicycle whipped by her on the sidewalk, the rider flipping her off. She all but jumped out of her skin and ripped the ear buds from her ears.

"What the hell?" she called after him. What was he doing on the sidewalk? She squinted after him, and something inside told her it was Zeke. "That's ridiculous. He doesn't come this way," she said out loud, trying to slow her heart.

It was hard not to flash back to all of the random things that had happened since the beginning of June. *Run! Run! Run!* her blood seemed to say as she heard it pumping in her ears. "No," she muttered and forced herself to keep walking. Her steps became stomps as her mood spiraled downhill with her thoughts.

She stormed into her apartment, tossing her purse on the couch and slamming her keys on the kitchen counter. She needed to figure out how to turn her attitude around. She had a wine and paint class that night. Right now the last thing she wanted to do was deal with a bunch of tipsy customers.

Without letting herself think too much about it, she picked up her phone and composed a text.

Hey, Kruger. Tell me something funny.

He was probably still at work, so she didn't think she'd hear from him, but her phone dinged a few minutes later.

I saw a woman pushing her dog in a baby carriage today. One of those old-fashioned carriages.

She laughed and sent a response. *That's pretty normal these days.*

The dog was wearing a tutu, and I swear I saw it smoking a cigar.

She rolled her eyes, but laughed out loud. *Now, that's just animal cruelty.*

He sent back a shrugging emoji and then, *Doing okay?*

She sighed. *Just a shitty day, but you helped. Thank you.*

Anytime, Miller. I'm here to help, annoy, or distract.

You have all three down to an art form, she replied.

Good. I hope to focus on the distracting from now on, he sent back with a winking emoji.

She put her phone down and closed her eyes, taking a breath. She didn't want to tell him he was already an expert at distraction.

The Painting Palate was located in a mid-sized studio in East Sacramento. The large windows at the front of the building allowed for an incredible amount of natural light, and there was still plenty of sunlight to be had when her class started at six-thirty that night.

The class was booked for a retirement party. It was clear the honoree, a kindergarten teacher who'd worked in a Sacramento elementary school for over thirty years, was loved. The room was packed. There were stories, laughter, and some tears before the event even started. It warmed Alexis's heart.

She was leading the class through an event-appropriate painting of the Old Sacramento Schoolhouse Museum, when she looked over at the windows, a shadow catching her eye. The sun bathing the room and a glare off the glass confused her vision for a moment. Then she saw someone standing at the corner of the building farthest from the door, staring in. She couldn't make out details of the person's face.

It wasn't abnormal for people to stand outside watching the class work, but this person was all alone. Something about the way they stood statue-still sent a chill down her spine. Her breathing quickened and her heart thumped in her chest. Alexis took several small gulps of air, trying not to bring attention to herself.

You're safe. You're safe. You're safe. So many weird things going on. It's easy to make something out of nothing. You're safe.

"Excuse me. I think I did something wrong with the overhang. Can you take a look?" asked one of the women in the room.

Alexis gave her a nod and a smile. As she made her way over to the woman's chair, she glanced back at the windows. The figure was gone. She faked a smile and happy tone until her heart slowed to normal speed.

Maybe you're just getting paranoid—seeing things that aren't there, she thought, but thank God for her therapy appointment the next day.

The rest of the week dragged. Zeke didn't speak to her.

How can he be taking this so personally? I can't mean that much to him after a month of working together.

She had a few more painting classes sprinkled throughout the nights. Those, a couple video chats with Kassie, who was still in Orange County, and a long phone call and text conversations with Luke helped take her mind off her coworker.

Her therapy appointment had helped with managing the fear that was becoming more prevalent in her mind. Her therapist also gave her some ideas on approaching a more positive relationship with Zeke. But she couldn't wait for the week to be done. The next one had to be better.

Friday morning, she was greeted by a peppy face, and she groaned silently. The real estate agent. It was only six-thirty. How could he look so happy?

"Hi! I didn't get your name the first time we talked." He was standing near her car, which was parked in front of the neighboring apartment building.

"It's Alexis. You're here early," she answered, trying to sound cheerful.

"Nice to properly meet you, Alexis. Yes, the buyer and her agent are meeting me at seven. I needed to make sure everything looks good." His smile never left his face.

"She's letting everyone stay, right? I think most of the tenants have lived there for years."

Geoff nodded. "Yes, she wants to keep the tenants. She's just hoping to spruce the building up a bit."

"That's good to hear." Alexis responded, letting her mind wander a bit. She was driving to work today, so she could make it to a painting class right after. She had more time than usual.

"I think her ownership will be good for the place." He studied her for a moment, his gaze traveling to her injured arm.

Her doctor expected her to be done with her splint next week, and she'd been strict about her physical therapy. Soon, she hoped to call this sprain a memory.

"I heard about your break-in. They hit some of these units as well. Did they catch the person yet?" Geoff asked.

"No. I hope they do." She sighed, looking down at her arm and thinking of her diamond earrings. She was sure she'd never get them back, but if they could at least get the burglar—

"Hey, would you like to have dinner with me sometime?"

The question stunned her. The answer was out of her mouth before she could think about it. "No."

He didn't try to mask his surprise. "No?"

She felt horrible, but why the hell were all these guys coming out of the woodwork? Before Kurt, she'd loved to go out with guys. She'd had several boyfriends in high school and college, casually dated a few others, and even had a one-night-stand her first year working at Reliant. Finding a guy never seemed to be a problem, and she'd loved it, but Kurt had changed all that. Now she was starting to feel comfortable with one man and another one hated her. She didn't need any more men in her life.

"I'm sorry. I wasn't trying to be rude. My life is a little crazy right now, and I'm already sort of seeing someone."

"Oh, okay. No problem." He wasn't entirely successful at erasing his surprised expression, but she could tell he was trying to sound gracious.

"I'm sorry," she scrunched her face and motioned toward her car, hoping she sounded sincere. "I have to get to work."

He looked behind him, then made one jerky movement away from the sedan. "Of course. Well, nice to meet you, Ms. Miller."

As she closed her car door and he turned away from her, a thought went through her head. Did she tell him her last name? She couldn't remember, but she didn't think so. He must have learned it when he heard about the break-in.

CHAPTER 11

Luke saw his therapist on Friday night. It wasn't normal for him to have so many nightmares this far into the summer. For the last couple weeks, they'd been a jumble of North Carolina and California. And they seemed to involve the full cast of characters from his life.

Seeing Langley had been comforting. They'd been able to talk over a couple beers. Luke felt their friendship slip right back into place. It felt like going back in time to the days before Em's death. When Langley left, there was nothing Luke could do but return to the present. He reminded himself that he felt more positive with the lead on Crawley.

Alexis continued to race through his thoughts. The sight of her turned him on, but he was also genuinely excited every time he got to talk to her. He'd forgotten what it was like to feel such a strong connection with someone.

On Sunday, he went to the gym and the grocery store—one of his more hated tasks. He took his truck to get washed and watched some of the newest season of *Stranger Things*. He thought about trying to do more research on Crawley, but stopped himself. He didn't need to bring that energy to his and Alexis's date.

When Alexis opened her door just before six, her beaming smile put him in a momentary daze. She'd curled her hair and was wearing a blue and white dress that made her eyes shine even brighter. God, he wanted to kiss her in that moment. He wanted to kiss her and do so much more. To back her up against a wall and run his hands through her hair and then all over her body. But he wasn't going to do anything more than hold her hand until she was ready.

A blush torched her cheeks as she watched him admire her.

"You look really nice," she said in a hushed voice.

He was wearing a collared shirt and dark-wash jeans. He was very secure with the way he looked, but he doubted he looked half as good as she did.

"Thanks. You look beautiful," he responded. Her blush deepened as she turned to grab her purse.

"I thought maybe Mikuni for dinner and then a walk in Old Sac?" he suggested as they climbed into his truck.

"Sushi is always a yes for me," she grinned back.

"Yet another reason to like you, Miller," he said, returning the expression.

Luke decided to ask about something he'd been thinking about, hoping she'd be okay with it. "Hey, so, knowing you as Alexis Miller has me thinking about your birth name. I know your last name was Kelly, like your mom, but I don't remember your first name—just that it was something unique. I know you told me back when I interviewed you, but I don't remember the media using it after that. Is it okay to ask about it?"

Alexis frowned, but didn't seem offended. "Yeah, it's okay, but it's not something I like to talk about. The name meant a lot to my mom, and it was painful to give it up. But it still feels so attached to everything that happened with Kurt. And I've been Alexis Miller for years. That's who I am now. I just don't feel comfortable voicing that other name." She looked over at him. "Does that seem weird?"

"No, not weird. You experienced serious trauma, so I can see how you'd want to separate yourself from that."

She turned even more in her seat. "Don't get me wrong, I do a lot on a daily basis to work through it. I'm not ignoring any of it."

"I understand." He gave her a reassuring smile. Not wanting their conversation to stop, he asked, "Why did you pick Alexis?"

"It was a popular name when I was born, so it would make sense. It means helper and defender, so it made me feel stronger, I think. Like I was keeping myself safe." She gave him a small smile and then was silent.

When he'd found a parking spot not far from the restaurant, he turned off his truck and moved to face her in his seat. "The pain from my past is different from yours, but I understand how it hangs on. I get that you can be having a great day, but by the end of it, feel lost in sadness, anger, guilt. You're an amazing person, Alexis. The things you've had to do to keep yourself safe, alive. Just know that I think you're amazing."

She was beaming as his words ended. "Thank you." Then her voice became more cautious. "Do you think you'll ever tell me about your past?"

He studied her eyes and nodded. "I will, but now—"

She spoke again, "Now we have some sushi, and you can tell me about your awkward teenage years. Even you must have had those."

He laughed out loud. "I did, but I can't ruin your image of me."

To his surprise, she gave him a playful push. She looked proud as she let herself out of his truck. As they walked toward the restaurant, he intertwined his fingers with hers.

* * *

After dinner, they strolled on the boardwalk in Old Sacramento, looking out at the river and across to West Sacramento, where the Ziggurat and CalSTRS building were lit up before them. When they stopped to lean against the railing, she moved her side close to his, nervous and hopeful that he would put an arm around her.

Alexis's heart pounded. She knew he wanted to move forward based on her comfort level. To be honest, she liked having that control. So, before she could stop herself, she turned to him and said, "I'd like you to kiss me."

Luke's eyes held hers as his hand glided to her arm and the other made its way around her waist. "You're sure?"

Yes. I don't want my body to jump away from you. I don't want my mind to go into a panic. But do I want to kiss you? Oh, yes. She nodded with conviction.

He moved his hand from her arm to tip her chin up. His lips brushed hers, and he kissed her softly. Every nerve in her body seemed to flare to life. She held onto his arms, trying not to think about a panic attack. She didn't need to send herself into one. She just had to focus on him.

She was so much shorter than he was, she had to stand on her tiptoes so as not to strain her neck. For a brief moment she wondered if it looked comical, but she brushed that thought away. He was going slow, being cautious. She was grateful, but part of her was frustrated that it was even necessary.

"Is that okay?" he asked as he pulled away from her, his voice low.

"Yes," she murmured. "More than okay." So many thoughts and emotions swirled and fought in her mind, but the overarching one was that she wanted this. She wanted to be able to move forward with a relationship again, and she wanted it to be with him.

He gave her a small smile, his eyes heated but soft as they looked into hers. "You're beautiful. You deserve to be happy, Miller." It was almost like he was reading her mind.

"So do you, Kruger," she said. He looked unsure. There was a hint of the vulnerability she saw in him at the museum.

She didn't know how to comfort him for a pain she didn't understand, so instead she pulled him toward her for another kiss. This time he kept both arms around her.

"I haven't been in a serious relationship in a long time, but there's no way you'll be casual for me," he said, and her heart leapt. "And I want to make sure you always feel safe."

"We're in agreement there. And I do feel safe with you." Alexis took his hand again.

He looked out toward the water, his eyes dark. "You never asked Kassidy about my past. I thought you would. I understand now that that's not who you are."

"My past became front-page news when I came forward about Kurt. It was a shock after multiple years in solitude. It's not that I'm not curious, but you deserve your privacy if you want to keep it."

"I do want to keep it when it comes to most people," he said. "But I want to move forward with us, so I want you to know."

She hadn't expected this conversation tonight, but she was prepared to listen.

Luke leaned back against the railing, but continued to hold her hand as he spoke. "My girlfriend, Emma, was murdered in our apartment five years ago in Charlotte. It happened right before we were supposed to move here. Emma was a deputy with Mecklenburg County. In the years leading up to her death, there was a pair of serial killers the law enforcement community dubbed the Sunset Killers. They murdered several women in Charlotte and other parts of Mecklenburg County.

"With her age, physical characteristics, economic standing, and the method with which she was killed," he took a deep breath, "her death was linked to them. There was no tangible evidence, but it seemed to fit. They'd never killed a cop before, and after she died, they stopped killing all together. There were multiple agencies and departments looking for them, but their trail was lost. One of the men has since been found dead in Charlotte, but no one knows where the other one is."

Alexis could feel her face going white as she forced herself to breathe. "She was murdered in your apartment. So, did you—"

His eyes were full of pain and discomfort as they met hers. "Yes, I found her. She was already gone."

Tears welled up in Alexis's eyes, but she refused to let them fall. "I'm so sorry." Her voice was a whisper.

He gave a nod, but was quiet, watching her. Then he looked back out to the water. The sun was setting over Sacramento, which felt significant somehow.

"Her death—there's been no real closure. We don't know for sure if they killed her, and with only one of them left alive, it feels like we're losing the ability to bring anyone to justice." He cleared his throat. "The anniversary is a hard time for me every year, but five years seems more difficult."

He looked like there might be more to say, but he stopped himself.

"The beginning of June—when you first came into the shop. This is what you were dealing with," she said, finally understanding.

He nodded. "I'm sorry about that."

She held his hand tighter and moved closer to him. "Anniversaries *are* hard. There are already so many random triggers in grief—having specific days that bring it to the forefront of our minds is cruel."

He sighed. "Yeah, and my nightmares always get worse around that time."

"Ah yes, our common sleeping issue," she mumbled.

"At least we already know we share some of the same habits," he said with a small smirk.

"Right, that's a real positive," she rolled her eyes in response.

He was quiet again for a minute, but then took a deep breath. "I'm working with one of my previous confidential informants to try to find Will Crawley, the half of the duo who is still alive."

She was sure confusion was written all over her face, so he continued. "My old department, Emma's department, and the FBI are still trying to find him, but everyone's busy with current cases. My informant has more access to the—less savory community in North Carolina and its neighboring states. Obviously, I have no authority there now, but if I can find something that brings them closer to getting Crawley—"

"You might have your answer, plus the possibility of prosecuting him for the murders they know he committed," she finished his thought.

"Yes. I don't expect it to bring peace to me, or Emma's mother, but at least we'll know, and he'll be put where he deserves to be."

"I hope they find him so you can have that closure. Thank you for telling me," she murmured.

"I'm glad you know," he murmured.

She leaned into him again. He put his arms around her as they stood together.

They'd continued walking for a while. He'd been quiet since the conversation ended, but he'd continued to hold her hand. As they parked down the street from her apartment, he spoke.

"Sorry I've been awkward." His discomfort had returned. "Sharing this is already new for me, and I wasn't sure how you felt hearing about Emma."

"It doesn't bother me, Luke. You can talk about her anytime you need to. I want to be here for you," she responded, hoping he heard her honesty.

"Thanks," he nodded, his fingers playing with hers.

He walked her back to her apartment. She wished the next day wasn't Monday. She wanted to prolong their time together. As she walked, her mind wandered into thoughts of how Emma's death and his subsequent move to California must have affected his relationships with his family. She now understood why he'd left out a big part of the story of moving here. He'd said his parents drove him crazy. Had that always been the case, or just after Emma died?

She figured he wouldn't want to get into all that after what he'd just shared with her, so she asked a simpler question. "Do you ever go back to North Carolina to visit?"

"Not a lot, but I'm going at the beginning of August. It's my mom's birthday. I told her I'd be there this year."

"That's nice. I'm sure that'll make her happy. How long will you be there?"

"About a week and a half," he said. It was clear by the tone of his voice that he wasn't excited, but he didn't elaborate.

Alexis wanted to make him smile again, so she said, "Oh, good. Back in plenty of time for Kassie and Brett's wedding. I'm sure Kassie will appreciate that!" She'd confirmed the wedding party with her friend and found out Luke was a groomsman.

"Are you kidding? I wouldn't want to face the kind of wrath she'd unleash on me." Luke laughed. "When I told them about the trip, she glared at me until I showed her the information for my return flight."

She laughed out loud. "Sounds about right! She just wants everything to work out."

"It better, for everyone else's sake." He grinned and pulled her into his arms, kissing her in the soft way he had before.

"I had a good time, Miller," he murmured, a smirk returning to his face as he rubbed his thumb over her flushed cheek.

"Me too, Kruger." She rolled her eyes at his expression, but smiled back at him.

"I'll call you tomorrow," he said. She could feel his hesitation before he let her go.

After she'd let herself into her apartment, she watched from her window as he headed back down the street toward his truck. She'd put herself to the test, and her heart was soaring as a result.

CHAPTER 12

When Luke stepped off the plane in Charlotte Douglas International Airport at eleven-seventeen on the morning of August 4, he already had four text messages from his mother.

Heading to the airport now. An hour ago.

We just parked. Twenty-nine minutes ago.

We're waiting for you outside security. Twenty-one minutes ago.

Do you want to go to eeZ for lunch? Seventeen minutes ago.

Luke was tired and starving, like he always was after flights. He liked to leave in the early morning, which had been just after midnight this time. He'd had one layover and slept on the plane. His parents knew his flying habits. They knew he'd be hungry. They'd made a decision on his behalf.

When it came to sushi, eeZ Fusion & Sushi was his favorite in this area. The restaurant was in Huntersville and about fifteen minutes from his parents' home in Cornelius. It opened around the time he turned twenty and had been a regular haunt of his and Emma's when they started dating years later. His parents knew he couldn't say no.

It wasn't that he and his parents had a bad relationship. There'd never been any big fight pushing them away from each other. But after Em died, they, especially his mother, had treated him like he would never be able to survive on his own. He'd had to leave the apartment he and Emma shared, and his parents had asked him to move in with them, which he had no interest in doing. He was a grown man in his thirties. He didn't need to be living with his parents after he'd been living on his own since college. He'd rented a smaller apartment in a complex near his and Emma's. He'd lived there until he moved to Sacramento.

When he'd turned them down, it seemed they doubled their efforts to be close to him. At that time, he was still roiled in pretty deep grief. He needed his family, but he also needed time on his own to process. They hadn't understood that when he tried to explain. He felt guilt about their relationship on top of everything else, but he still needed his boundaries.

His parents hadn't been thrilled about his cross-country move. They couldn't blame it on Emma's death, because they knew it had been part of the couple's long-term plan. He and Emma had wanted to start a new adventure. The many amenities of California, plus the lower humidity, called to them.

With his parents living in Cornelius and Emma's mother in Davidson, both Charlotte suburbs, they'd grown accustomed to spending time at nearby Lake Norman. There were a plethora of lakes and rivers to enjoy in Sacramento and the surrounding area, not to mention the Pacific Ocean within easy driving distance. They saw themselves exploring and playing in those bodies of water almost every weekend in the spring and summer. He sighed as he reflected on the fact that he'd only been to the ocean twice since moving to the state. The California he and Emma had pictured was much different from the California Luke had been living in without her.

Sounds good. Just got off the plane. See you in a minute, he responded to the texts.

He took a deep breath. He loved his parents, and he knew how much they loved him. This visit would make his mom happy. He had to try to let any frustrations roll off his back.

He stepped aside for a moment, sending another text.

Landed safe and sound, Miller. Try not to agonize too much over my absence. He filled the message with snark. He couldn't wait to see what equally snarky response she'd send.

They'd been talking and texting, and had seen each other several more times since their sushi date. Each time, he kissed her and held her hand as much as possible. There was no doubt in his mind that he was falling for her, but that didn't make his grieving for Emma stop. All of the joy and sadness just existed together. It was the strangest mix of feelings he'd ever experienced.

Sure enough, his parents were waiting for him just where his mother had said. Her face lit up when she saw him. His father grinned.

"Hey, son!" His father, Jacob Kruger, grabbed him into a hug. Jacob always called him "son," as if "Luke" was the actual nickname. He called Luke's brother Jackson "pal." The names had been used for as long as the brothers could remember, so they didn't mind. It was worse when Jacob used to use their real names, because it typically meant they were in trouble.

Jacob Kruger was sixty-three years old, had silver hair, and dark brown eyes. His hair had been a dark blond, but he'd started going gray in his early thirties, so Luke didn't have much memory of the first color. His dad used to be taller than Luke was now, but had lost a couple inches and measured six-foot-four now, just an inch shorter than Luke.

His mother, Linda Kruger, greeted him with, "I've missed you, Lukey," and wrapped her arms around him.

He didn't love the name Lukey, even though it had also belonged to him for as long as he could remember. She also often called him "honey."

Linda Kruger was about to be sixty-two. She was on the taller side at five-foot-nine. Linda had given her wavy, dark brown hair to Luke and Jackson. Her blue eyes went to Jackson, but Luke had his father's eyes.

"Good to see you, Mom." Luke smiled down at his mother and they headed toward baggage claim to get his suitcase.

You will not get annoyed. It's her birthday. It's a special time. No matter what she says, just let it go.

During the car ride to the restaurant, Jacob filled Luke in on the latest news from his hometown. His mother stayed quiet, but when they sat down for lunch she said, "How've you been, honey? We wish you'd come see us more often."

"I'm fine. It's hard to get away from work, Mom." He smiled at her, hoping to distract from her train of thought.

"I just wish you weren't alone." She wasn't falling for the expression.

"I'm not alone. I have colleagues, friends and," he decided to mention his dating life to make her happy, "I'm seeing someone."

Linda's face did indeed light up. "You haven't told us about her! What's her name?"

Jacob looked interested as well, but didn't say anything.

"Her name is Alexis, and it's still new. We met a couple months ago." He wasn't going to go into too many details.

"I'm so glad, honey. You deserve to be happy again. After Emma I thought—"

"Linda," Jacob warned.

"Mom," Luke said at the same time, trying to hide the annoyance already bubbling up inside of him. He hadn't even been in the state for an hour. "Can we talk about my job? Sacramento? How things are here? Anything else?"

"I'm sorry. Yes, of course. But, please, just one more thing." Her mother's eyes looked desperate. "We still run into Susan every now and then. You should go see her while you're here. I'm sure she'd appreciate it. She told me she still calls you sometimes."

He sighed, trying to peruse the menu to give himself a moment to calm down. He met his mother's eyes when he looked up. "Yes, she calls me every year around the anniversary of Emma's death. She pleads with me to do something for the case. She chastises me for running away, abandoning Emma, being too scared to do anything. She usually calls to apologize later, but that hasn't happened this year. Instead, she's called me four times to say the same things. They aren't pleasant calls.

"I know she's grieving, so I keep answering her calls. But I don't think she'd want to see me for a social visit, and I have no desire to face her. I'm not sure I could keep calm."

Linda looked stunned.

"We didn't know. I'm sorry, son." Jacob looked angry.

Linda stuttered, guilt on her face. "I already told her you were going to be here, Luke."

Luke ran his palms down his face, the exhaustion from his flight growing stronger. "It's okay. I'm here to see you, Mom. I'm going to focus on that."

She nodded. He saw tears at the edges of her eyes.

He reached across the table to take his mother's hand. "Don't worry about it. I know you two used to be close and you want to help her."

She gave him a weak smile. They ordered their food and were eating before she spoke to him again, "You look so tired, Luke. We should go home after this so you can rest."

"I'm fine. It's just the time change." He shrugged.

"You don't have to take such an early flight," she said.

"I like leaving in the middle of the night. Not so many people on the plane, and it gives me the possibility of sleep."

"Do you sleep?" His mother's eyes were full of concern.

He knew she wasn't referencing the plane ride. He'd talked to his parents and brother very little about his nightmares. But sometimes it felt like his mother could read his mind. He knew this was another reason he preferred to be away from her.

"I'm fine, Mom."

He got a response from Alexis as they were leaving the restaurant.

Oh, did you go somewhere? I must have forgotten. I'll just have to go to that raging party by myself this weekend.

He grinned. Just the kind of response he'd expected and hoped for.

* * *

"Hey, Lex!"

Alexis turned from the back counter to find Kassidy and Brett at the register. She hadn't seen much of the couple since they'd been back from Southern California. They'd both been slammed with work and last-minute wedding planning. Whereas Alexis and Kassie usually had a few text conversations throughout the week about anything and everything, this week they'd consisted only of Kassie's wedding worries. Alexis tried to be a sounding board for her friend, because Kassie was the type of person who needed to vent to feel better about something.

"Hey, guys! Lunchtime pick-me-up?" Alexis grinned. They both looked spent.

"Yes, please," Brett responded, putting his palms together and making a small bow, as if she were some kind of deity.

She laughed as they ordered; then she saw Zeke out of the corner of her eye. The man still didn't talk to her much, although his overall annoyance seemed to have cooled a bit. She was sure he'd noticed Luke coming into the shop on a frequent basis. Maybe he'd accepted that she and Luke were serious about each other.

"Oh, Zeke, these are my friends, Kassidy and Brett. Guys, this is Zeke."

Her coworker stared at her for a moment, as if trying to remember who she was. The expression stung. *Ouch! Maybe the annoyance has turned into indifference.*

Zeke turned to her friends with a nod. "Hey."

"Nice to meet you," Kassie said with a smile.

But as soon as the words left her mouth, Zeke turned away. Brett was frowning.

"Warm," he muttered. Kassie elbowed him in the ribs.

Alexis blushed with embarrassment and turned to make their drinks.

"What's up with that?" Kassie whispered as Alexis put Brett's coffee on the pickup counter.

"You know how I told you I said no to a date with him? Well, what I told him was that I wasn't ready to date. Then I went out with Luke and he found out."

"Ah," Kassidy nodded. "Some good old-fashioned jealousy then."

Alexis nodded. "Seems that way. He used to be so different. So sunny. He's changed since his accident."

"Maybe he's dealing with lingering pain?" Kassie gave a light shrug and then a smile as Alexis handed over her drink.

"That's all I can think. He can't be that upset about not dating me."

"Oh, I don't know. You're a pretty amazing person, Lex," Kassie said with a grin, but Alexis knew she was being serious.

Kassie checked her watch. "I've gotta get back. Talk to you soon! Don't let him ruin working here. You love it too much," she whispered, giving Alexis's hand a light squeeze. She frowned toward Zeke as she walked toward the door.

Brett gave her a wave as they left the shop. Alexis missed them as soon as they were gone. She looked over at Zeke, but the man was doing his best to ignore her. She sighed. She had to let it go. She had to live for herself and make herself happy. Her rape had thrown a blanket of shame and guilt over the rest of her life. And after all these years, she was not about to be suffocated.

CHAPTER 13

Saturday afternoon Luke was sitting next to Lake Norman. His family and a group of friends were having lunch on the shore to celebrate his mother's birthday. His phone buzzed in his pocket. Checking the screen, he saw Alexis's number calling.

"Hey, Miller," he answered as he stepped away from the party.

"Luke." His name came fast. She was crying.

"What's wrong?" He could already feel his adrenaline rushing.

"Zeke's dead."

"What?" He wasn't sure he heard her right. He walked a little farther away from the celebration.

"He's dead, Luke. On a bike ride with friends in the foothills this morning. There was a blind curve. He was hit by a car. He didn't make it. He was supposed to work the afternoon shift at the shop. His friends called his family. Someone called our owner. Nora found out. She called me." She was crying harder now, her sentences coming in sharp bursts.

"God, Alexis, I'm sorry." He ran the palm of his free hand down his face.

She didn't answer, but he could still hear her crying. He wished he was with her instead of across the country. The sound of her crying was one of the most gut-wrenching things he'd ever heard.

All he could think to ask was, "Do you want me to come home?" He wanted to do *something*.

"W-what? N-no, don't leave your family. My mom is coming over. I just needed to talk to you."

He was pacing. He saw his father and brother looking in his direction with concerned expressions. "I'm here for you, anytime. I wish I could help more."

"You're helping now." He could hear her taking deep breaths. Then there was a noise in the background. "My mom is here now. Can I call you later? I don't want to interrupt."

"You're not. Of course you can call," he responded with what he hoped was a firm but kind tone.

"Thank you. I miss you," Alexis murmured.

"Miss you too, Miller," he sighed, his heart aching as she ended the call.

"Everything okay?" His dad walked over to him.

"One of Alexis's coworkers died in a bicycle accident," Luke answered, turning his phone volume all the way up in case she called again.

"Geez. Is she okay?" His father's eyebrows rose.

"Doesn't sound like it. I wish I could be with her."

"You might wish that even more after you see who's here," Jacob muttered with a frown. Luke looked past him in confusion.

Susan was standing near his mother. Her face lacked expression.

"Why? I told you—" Luke started.

"Apparently your mom had already invited her and didn't think it was right to un-invite her. She didn't tell me until about an hour ago. And that was only because I asked her what was wrong."

"She needs to move past following proper Southern Woman etiquette." Luke felt like screaming, but he grumbled instead.

"That's never gonna happen." Jacob shook his head.

Luke nodded. Talking to Susan was inevitable. He couldn't pretend like she wasn't there.

His mother's best friend placed a cake topped with strawberries on the picnic table. Everyone moved close to sing *Happy Birthday*. Luke and his father strode back to the group. Linda beamed. Luke reminded himself this day was about his mother. He'd try to be polite to Susan, just as he tried to be on the phone.

Luke helped pass out slices of cake and went to stand with Jackson and his wife. Glancing Susan's way, he noted that she seemed deep in conversation with another guest.

"Hello, Luke. Your mother told me you would be in town." He'd taken three bites when he heard Susan at his back. He had to keep himself from jumping in surprise.

Get your shit together, Luke. "Hi, Susan. Glad you could make it." He tried to smile, but knew it must have looked more like a grimace.

"How are things in California?" she asked. There was definite anger in her voice.

He didn't feel like following her emotional roller coaster. He'd made this trip because he knew it would make his mom happy. He hadn't come to deal with drama. "Things are fine."

"I talked to Detective Langley a couple weeks ago," Susan said, ignoring his response. "I told him I'd asked you to help, because I didn't feel like they were doing everything they could. He told me I needed to stop calling you."

"Detective Langley is—" Luke tried to respond.

"They aren't doing shit!" The woman was spitting mad. In all of their many conversations, he'd never heard her talk like that. She'd come ready for this confrontation. "And you're just like Nicholas—leaving me alone in this horrible grief!"

Luke took a deep breath, trying to keep his cool. A few of the guests closest to them were looking over. He could feel Jackson tensed at his side. Luke gave him a small bump with his elbow to tell him to calm down.

"Nicholas was grieving too, but he wanted to find some way to move forward with life. Your all-consuming focus on solving Em's murder was drowning him—making him feel like he was only allowed to grieve the way you wanted him to. That's why he had to leave." As the words flew from Luke's mouth, he wished he could put them back. He could see embarrassment added to the emotions playing across her face. Alexis's phone call and the tension he already felt around Susan had blocked his normal thoughts-to-words filter. He had to try to smooth things over. "Please, this day is for my mom. I came here to celebrate her, and I'd like to do that. Can we talk another time?"

"It's nice that you still have that opportunity—to celebrate your mother. My daughter will never have that again," she growled back and stalked away from the party.

Rage and sadness boiled within him. He wanted to swear, to break something, to tear something apart, to cry. But he couldn't do any of those things. He took another breath and turned to find his mother right behind him. Everyone else was trying to look away, like they'd seen nothing.

Linda put her hand on his arm, tears glistening in her eyes. "Luke, I'm so sorry. This won't happen again."

He nodded with a sigh, pulling his mother into a hug. He couldn't think of anything to say.

* * *

"I could have handled it. I was doing fine!" David protested over the phone.

"That's not what I have been told. You either spent all day glaring at her, or ignored her when she was trying to interact with you. It was obvious you were making her very uncomfortable. This was the best way," Christopher responded.

"Couldn't Zeke have just quit rather than get killed in an accident? Was it even believable?"

"Alexis believed it. She was sobbing at Zeke's memorial service, just like everyone else," Christopher answered as he perused correspondence he'd received earlier in the week. He wanted to line up another job. This one seemed to be stretching on longer than he anticipated. He was starting to wonder if he would lose interest.

"Hello," Thomas greeted as he came on the line.

"Thank you for joining us," Christopher responded. "I would like to explain this new plot twist."

"I was hoping you would. I don't understand how killing off David's Zeke character is going to help us get closer to her," Thomas tried to play up the confusion in his voice, but it was easy for Christopher to catch the underlying anger.

David was silent. He had to be wondering if Christopher would out his feelings for the woman to Thomas.

"Alexis is now wracked with guilt over Zeke's death," Christopher explained. "It was clear she felt bad about dating the cop after turning him down. Zeke will still have a part to play as we turn her guilt into paranoia and fear. Simultaneously, the game shifts toward making Geoff a central character in her life, so that she trusts him.

"I have studied Alexis, both in the past when she came forward about Kurt Leonard, and now," Christopher continued. "She is much stronger than she was, but that doesn't mean she cannot be broken. Now that she and the cop are more serious, she may ask him for help initially, but in the end, Alexis is a person who wants to prove that she can save herself. She kept herself alive for many years. She will want to do the same now. This will drive a wedge between her and her loved ones. We will start small and escalate the plan at a pace that feels natural."

"That sounds perfect. I will do what you tell me to do regarding Geoff. But how are we going to use a dead man?" Thomas asked.

Christopher sat back on his couch, relaxing one arm behind his head. "Tell me, do either of you believe in ghosts?"

* * *

The week of Kassie and Brett's wedding, Alexis ran around in between jobs assisting her friend with last-minute tasks. A calm had come over Kassie, like she could see the light at the end of the tunnel. All of Brett's family had arrived from Southern California, and she was able to enjoy spending time with them. Alexis wanted Kassie to keep that calm, so she helped out as much as she could.

Two days before the wedding, Alexis treated herself to her favorite sandwich at La Bou. She met Luke at what was becoming their normal picnic table at McKinley Park. By the time she got back to Valle Coffee to finish her shift, she felt like she was walking on air. Everything in the foreseeable future looked bright. It was the best she'd felt since Zeke died. As she walked behind the counter, Nora looked up from the drink she was making.

"Kassidy dropped some wedding stuff off for you. I think she said it was the latest schedule for the day. She can be pretty chatty, can't she? Anyway, I put it in the back." Nora frowned and jerked her head in the direction of the back office.

Alexis regarded her coworker for a moment. Nora was a hard-worker and she treated customers well, but her mood with fellow employees wasn't usually positive. Alexis didn't know what Nora's husband did for work, but he had long hours, sometimes night shifts. They had a young son as well. Alexis doubted they had much family time. One could assume this frustrated Nora, but she'd made it clear to Alexis that she didn't want to talk about it.

"Thanks, Nor!" Alexis grinned, not letting the woman's curt response bother her, and headed to put her purse down.

She frowned when she picked up the papers from Kassie and a manila envelope fell to the ground. Her first and last name were written on the front in small print, but there was no return information. She peeked through the door and saw the line was growing with customers needing their afternoon caffeine. She stashed everything under her purse and went back to the registers.

"Nor, do you know where the manila envelope came from? It was under the stuff Kassidy dropped off."

Nora eyed her for a moment and then seemed to remember. "Oh, yeah. A guy came in and dropped that off for you. Maybe a few minutes before Kassidy. We were swamped at the time, so I didn't get his name. He said he was a reporter."

This made some sense. Reporters had always known how to find her. But the story of her rape and Kurt's death were pretty old by now. Maybe it was a follow-up or some new angle? She didn't want to participate in any more news stories.

"Did he say which publication or station?" she asked, but doubted she'd get much more.

"Nope. It's probably in the envelope," Nora answered, waving the question away.

Alexis sighed and smiled at the next customer. She'd check the envelope when she got home.

She rushed into her apartment, holding several grocery bags from the quick trip she'd made to the store. Her purse was slung over a shoulder. She grasped the papers from Kassie, as well as the envelope and mail she'd gathered downstairs. The grocery bag straps were digging into her bare arms—her fault for trying to shove so many things into three bags. She let everything fall onto the counter in her kitchen and heaved a huge sigh.

She went to fish her phone out of her purse to return a call she'd missed from her mom, but the envelope fell to the floor with the weight of a leaf. She eyed it for a few moments, until curiosity got the best of her. She grabbed her letter opener from the counter. The seal came open easily beneath the shiny metal. Her eyes scrunched together in confusion as she saw the contents: a single newspaper article from the *San Francisco Chronicle* dated more than a year ago.

Her heart started pounding as she read the headline: *Videos found in CEO rape case.*

"What the hell?" she muttered to herself.

She shouldn't read it, but her eyes were drawn to the words. It detailed how law enforcement found the stash of evidence against Kurt Leonard in the bottom of a burned-out building in Sacramento. Much of the evidence was video footage of Kurt's many rapes and assaults. He'd set up a camera in his office and recorded every woman he'd trapped there. She was one of those women. Her name wasn't mentioned in this article, but she remembered the day the FBI told her about the video.

As she got to the bottom of the page, she noticed someone had stuck a small adhesive label over the last few lines of text. On it was typed a short message. *Your video is still out there.*

Alexis dropped the article as if it had burned her. Her mind began to spin. She took several deep breaths, holding onto her counter. Who the hell would send her this? What did they mean by it? She had no doubt the video still existed. Was this meant to be some kind of threat? Or a warning? She grabbed the envelope and dug around, searching for any sort of business card or note. Nothing.

She forced herself into her living room and down onto her couch, taking several deep gulps of air. She felt an old familiar urge—the urge to run. Even with all of the amazing therapy she'd had, this urge still lived deep inside her. She'd had to run after Kurt Leonard raped her. Somehow she'd known that rape wasn't the end. She trembled as she thought of all the women he'd had murdered. She wrapped her arms around her legs to keep herself still. She wasn't going to give into that fear again. Kurt was dead. She had a life here now. She had friends and people who wanted to help. She wasn't going to throw it away.

She took another deep breath, stood up, and snatched the envelope from where she'd left it. The article still lay on her kitchen floor. She picked up her phone to call Luke, but another number flashed onto the screen.

"Hello?" she forced as much calm into her voice as she could.

"Lex, I'm really sorry." Kassie sounded distracted and anxious. "They had to fix my veil. I thought it would be done sooner, but they just called me. Brett and I are supposed to make one more run to the venue before the rehearsal tomorrow—"

"No problem, Kassie! I can pick it up. I'll go now." She pinched the article between her thumb and pointer finger, shoving it into the corner of her counter with the envelope.

You're fine. You can tell Luke later, she promised herself as she threw her perishables into her fridge and headed back out the door.

The universe smiled on Kassie and Brett the day of their wedding. It might have been late August, but somehow it was only in the eighties in the foothills. There were a few clouds in the sky, but the humidity wasn't bad. Fire season had already been rearing its ugly head in California, but the air quality was like that of a new spring day. It was shocking to say the least, but no one in the lush vineyard venue was complaining.

The open-air barn reception area was covered in breathtaking batches of flowers, with sunflowers representing the light Kassie and Brett brought to each other's lives. Twinkle lights draped from the rafters, creating a soft ambience as the sun set that night.

"Aren't weddings supposed to be stressful and full of drama?" Luke joked, coming up next to Alexis where she stood on the side of the room, watching the couple dance. He handed her a glass of red wine. She flashed him a smile.

To say Luke looked handsome in his groomsman suit would have been a drastic understatement. She spent much of the time staring at him. Every time he caught her, he'd send his signature smirk her way. Of course, she'd noticed him admiring her more than once—and she liked it.

"Maybe, but not this one." Alexis beamed at Kassie and Brett. "They had to fight too hard to be together again after Kurt broke them apart, so someone is giving them a break."

Luke nodded, but had fallen silent. He looked like he was a thousand miles away. Alexis felt like there was a giant elephant in the room.

"You can talk about her, you know." Her voice came out so quiet, she wondered if he heard her. "I know you loved her. I don't feel threatened by her. I don't want you to ever feel she can't still be a part of your life."

He looked down at her with a small smile and grabbed her free hand with his. "Thank you. I appreciate that. I still find a connection to her in a lot of things. When I moved out here, I thought the sheer distance between me and our home would have brought me some peace."

"Grief really sucks," she said after he'd been quiet again for a few seconds.

"Yeah. It does," he murmured, then took a deep breath. "Do you like to dance?"

She laughed. "Around other people? Like, so they can see me? No, not really."

He chuckled, looking relieved. "Me either. How about a walk outside?"

"Much more my style." She grinned and followed him out of the building into the warm night.

The stars sparkled in the sky as they strolled down a gravel path that led away from the reception and back toward the ceremony spot. The venue staff had been working hard. All the white wooden chairs the guests had used to watch the nuptials had already been folded, stacked, and tied onto carts.

Several of the chairs still had lacey fabric draped along their backs. The light breeze made their soft white tendrils sway like ghostly beings. Alexis shivered as she thought first of the figure she'd seen staring in the window at her paint night, then of the strange manila envelope.

"Are you cold?" Luke's voice was surprised.

"No. I was just thinking. Before I chicken out and don't tell you: someone dropped a manila envelope off at work a few days ago. My coworker said the man identified himself as a reporter, but he didn't include any information about himself. Inside the envelope was a news article about the videos Kurt made—about when they were found in that burned building. You were there, weren't you?"

He nodded, his face dark.

"Whoever left the envelope put a note on the bottom of the article that said my video 'is still out there.' I don't know what they were trying to accomplish, but I doubt it was a reporter. Reporters always make sure you know how to get hold of them."

Her voice was shaking by the time she finished talking, although she tried her best to make it stop. Luke stood as still as a statue next to her.

"Was there anything on the outside of the envelope? Do you still have everything?" He turned to face her. He was in detective mode now. His face looked calm but serious, as she imagined it did when he was working a case.

"It's all on the counter at home," Alexis said.

"I'll come by your place when we leave," he responded.

"I'm sure it's nothing. A prank. Or someone giving me what they think is new information." It was hard to believe the words as she said them, but she was trying to make herself feel better.

"Yeah," Luke said, but he didn't sound convinced. "I'll take it all to the office."

"Thank you." She put her arms around him, pulling him in for a kiss. His lips met hers without hesitation and then became more passionate, but she could feel tension flowing through his body.

CHAPTER 14

Luke's mood soured the week after the wedding. He worked his cases and made basic conversation with his colleagues. Brett was on his honeymoon, so the person who would have bugged him to talk wasn't there to do it.

His work didn't suffer. If anything, he plunged himself deeper into its complicated depths. But when he wasn't working, he felt like he was waiting. Waiting for news from Langley. Any news at all. If the FBI was any closer to finding Crawley in Alabama, he hadn't heard. If Sheridan had made any headway on the killer's whereabouts, he hadn't said. Waiting. He told himself millions of times to leave it to Langley. Langley, his team, and the FBI would find the man. And if they didn't, Sheridan would. He couldn't control the situation. He had no control.

He knew the real catalyst for this current round of anxiety was the envelope Alexis received. He'd brought the envelope and newspaper article in, but they'd led to nothing. No return address information, no discernible marks, no fingerprints. His thoughts were dark, and he hated that. But Emma's death made it too easy to assume he would lose Alexis too.

Another detective interviewed Nora about the man who left the envelope, but Alexis's shift lead had been so busy when it happened, she couldn't remember much. She said she thought he was about six feet tall and had brown hair, but he'd been wearing a plain blue baseball cap, so she wasn't sure. She believed he'd been wearing black slacks and a gray shirt, but her confidence on those details seemed lacking as well.

Calm the hell down. There's no reason to believe she's in danger. It was probably just a sick prank. He wasn't the kind of person to exist in a state of worry. He needed to get out of his head. On Friday after work, he called Alexis.

"Hey, Kruger."

"Hey! Miller, you sound pissed." He could hear her rustling around in the background.

"Ugh, no, sorry. I'm rushing, as usual," she laughed in response. "I can't find some of my supplies. Ouch! Stupid paint brush."

"Want me to call you back?" He found himself grinning. Not that he wanted her to be hurting herself with paint brushes, but the randomness was what he needed.

"No, no, it's okay. Oh, there they are!" she said in a triumphant tone. "Okay, I'm good. What's up?"

"Do you have any of your plethora of jobs this Sunday? Want to get away for a day?"

Alexis was quiet for a moment. "Just a seven o'clock painting class, but the morning and afternoon work! Where do you want to go?"

"Tahoe City? It'll be swamped, I'm sure, but—"

"That sounds great! I haven't been there since last summer. Maybe for lunch?"

"Yeah, that'd be nice," he said, her excitement lifting him from his funk.

"I can't wait! Sorry, I've gotta go. I wish I hadn't been so busy this week. Would you say you've missed me or Brett more?" she teased.

"Miller, that's not even a contest. You know how close Green and I are."

She laughed with delight. "You're right. I don't know what I was thinking. See you Sunday, Kruger!"

Her laugh rang in his ears after the call ended. It was amazing the difference one sound could make.

It was already in the high seventies by the time he picked her up Sunday morning. The high was forecasted for one hundred two degrees, but Tahoe would only be in the mid-seventies.

"It feels amazing to be escaping the heat," Alexis sighed, pushing her sunglasses up over her hair as they drove toward the freeway.

She was wearing a blue sundress, a light gray cardigan folded over one arm. The blue of her dress made her red hair look like fire falling around her shoulders. He had to work to keep his focus on the road. Her eyes shone at him as he took her hand in his.

"How was painting on Friday? It was one of your wine and paint thingies, right?"

She laughed, rolling her eyes. "Yes, I believe that's the technical name for it. I'm going to drag you to one someday. Maybe you'll enjoy it a little bit!"

Not in a million years, he thought to himself. "Nope. I like you, Miller. A lot. But I'm not doing that."

"Oh, come on! It's just supposed to be fun. And it's not complex painting. Doesn't getting a little tipsy and doing some painting with Kassie and Brett sound like a good time?" She turned to face him with a silly grin.

He could play this game. "That sounds like my worst nightmare. Extra therapy kind of nightmare." He laughed, shaking his head to drive home his opinion.

She let out an exaggerated sigh, but her grin didn't fade. "Okay, how about if the world is ever ending and you can't give me details for whatever reason, but you have to get me to understand how dire the situation is, show up at one of my wine and paint thingies. Then I'll know things are serious."

Luke passed her another look. Her face was lit up with the joke of it all, her blue eyes sparkling in anticipation of his response. The joy he felt in that moment was something he wanted to capture and keep forever. He wished they weren't driving down the freeway. He would tuck her fiery hair behind her ears and pull her in for a kiss.

"I'll agree to those terms." He returned her grin.

She settled back into her seat, a satisfied expression on her face.

"You don't think it's kind of sad that I won't go unless the world is ending?" He didn't want their banter to end.

"Nope, it's something! I'm wearing you down, Kruger," she smirked back. He shook his head with a chuckle.

"And Friday was an interesting night." She smiled to herself as she answered his initial question. "There were these three couples there who had to be in their seventies. We were painting this forest scene with an open meadow area to the right," she motioned with her hands as she spoke. He loved watching her talk about painting. "And they were all including clumps of marijuana plants in their meadows. They were snickering like they had this big secret. They were having a great time, and honestly, their paintings were the best ones."

He laughed out loud. "I guess we know their favorite recreational activity."

She nodded with a grin. "They were a fun group."

A Journey song came on the radio. Luke turned it up without thinking.

"You like Journey?" she asked in a tone that told him they had a common interest.

"Is there anyone who doesn't?" He turned it up a little more.

"I hope not!" she responded, squeezing his hand and gazing out the window as she swayed to the tune.

She was silent for a few minutes when the song ended. Then she turned back to him with a curious smile. "Tell me more about your hometown. You said it's called Cornelius, right? What'd you like to do as a kid?"

"Yeah, Cornelius." He felt himself smiling at the thought of it. "It's a lakeside town. Less than thirty-five-thousand people—so different from Sacramento. It had a tight-knit feel. The kind of place where you know the same people your whole life.

"We were always out by the lake, like the water was an extension of our lives. My dad's owned a sail boat for as long as I can remember. And if we weren't at the lake, we were playing baseball at one of the parks, skateboarding, convincing our parents to drive us to Charlotte. It was a pretty idyllic childhood. 'Course I didn't realize that at the time, like all kids. I appreciate it now, even with the pain being back in that area brings."

At this point, he wanted to stop talking about himself. "Ever been to that part of the country?"

"No. I'd love to someday though. I'd like to do a lot more traveling. I guess saying I don't have the time is an excuse. I think with everything that's happened, it's just hard to step out of my comfort zone." She sighed, brushing her long hair off a shoulder, twisting it together with a finger and letting it unravel on the opposite shoulder.

He nodded. "I get that. We'll go somewhere together."

Her eyes were shining again as she turned back to face him. "Where?"

"Anywhere you want. You deserve it," he answered, catching the quick surprise in her eyes before a grin spread across her face.

After parking in an open lot outside the Boatworks Mall, they got a patio table for lunch at Jake's On The Lake, where they could gaze out on the boats docked on Lake Tahoe. California was in its almost-perpetual drought, so the lake's level was low, but it still brought him comfort. Lakes always reminded him of his roots and grounded him with their tranquility.

Afterward, they walked down the road to Commons Beach. The beach was full of families. The smell of barbecue and sounds of a local band drifted through the air. Children screeched and ran as they explored the playground. Despite what Luke was sure must still be a frigid temperature in the mountain lake, a large number of people were swimming and splashing in the water.

They found a spot on the shore and settled down on a blanket Alexis pulled from her tote bag. He watched as she twisted her hair into a low bun and plopped a sun hat on her head. She was applying sunscreen when she looked up at him with a questioning glance. He realized he was grinning again.

"What?" she asked.

"You think of everything." He inched closer to her, resting his hand on her leg.

"Most of this is because I'm Irish," she laughed back. "I can burn in a matter of seconds."

He was about to kiss her when his cell phone buzzed. The number was blocked. His heart rate shot up as he thought of Sheridan.

"Sorry, I need to see who this is." He held up his phone.

"No problem. I thought I might go for a swim." She motioned toward the water, her silly grin returning.

"Good luck with that," he said with a smirk as she settled back on her elbows to relax.

He walked a good distance away from her, trying to remove himself from as much of the noise around them as he could. He tapped the screen to answer the call.

"Hello?"

"Kruger."

He didn't recognize the male voice on the other end of the call, but it held a clear southern accent.

"Who is this?" His heart threatened to burst from his chest.

"Will Crawley. Heard you were looking for me."

Shock hit Luke as if he'd run into a brick wall.

Stay calm. Stay professional. Get what you can in case it's really him.
"Crawley. How'd you get my number?" His tone was casual, almost conversational. Thank God for everything he'd learned in his job.

"Took it off the man you had looking for me. Sheridan? He didn't need it anymore," Crawley murmured.

Luke squeezed his eyes shut for a moment. *Shit. He could be lying. Don't let him get to you.*

"And where was that? Alabama?" Luke questioned.

"Nah, Kruger, I've kinda made my career on avoiding cops. Don't need to give that up now. But I know you live in Sacramento, California. Know you moved there after your woman died. Aren't you a little outside your jurisdiction?"

Luke took a deep breath. Crawley mentioning Emma's death had him seeing red. His gaze moved to Alexis, who was still watching the water. He moved several feet closer to her, as if Crawley could come through the phone and attack her too.

"We're not talking about me right now. Sheridan was only the first. You know they're not going to stop until they find you. The people you know seem more open to talking these days. Wouldn't it be nice to stop running? Stop hiding? On your own terms?"

"Nah. I'm having a good time. I go from state to state as I please. So far it seems to be working for me," Crawley replied with a deep chuckle. "But one other thing, Kruger, before I go. I didn't kill your girlfriend, so your personal vendetta against me is a waste of your time."

Luke was quiet.

"That's what this is about, right? That's why you want them to find me. Otherwise you wouldn't give a shit where I was."

Luke ignored the man's weird attempt at guilt or whatever it was. "Then who killed her? You're well connected to that community, so I have no doubt you know."

"I might. But you're forgetting that I don't want to be caught. Ratting someone out will get me killed," he said in a tone one might use to speak to a child.

"Then you'll continue to be blamed for killing a cop, which won't help you when you *do* get caught. And Freeman? Did you kill him too? I find that hard to believe. Why would you want to take the blame for all those murders all on your own? So, I'm guessing you also know who killed him. When they find you, you'll be charged with the deaths of all of those women, your partner, and a cop. They won't care to listen to any bullshit story you have at that point," Luke pointed out, his voice still calm.

"It's been more than half a decade. No one's found me yet." Crawley didn't sound the least bit worried.

"It's about the long game, Crawley. You have no idea what's going on around you." Luke could feel himself slipping. He was too invested in this. He had to keep his cool.

"Thanks for your concern, but I'm fine. I said what I called to say. This conversation is done now. Stop wasting your life, Kruger. Move on with those you can trust."

Fucking life advice from a murderer? "Crawley," Luke began, but the man had already ended the call.

Luke stared at his phone for a moment, his mind racing. He had to call Langley as soon as possible, but he couldn't give him the details he needed to while he was here. He also didn't want to involve Alexis in any way. He turned to see she was looking over at him, concern written all over her face. He couldn't imagine what his expression must look like.

He jotted quick notes in his phone so he would remember as much of the call as possible. Then he opened his contacts list and clicked Langley's phone number.

"Hey, Krug. What's up?"

"I just had a surprise call from the person we're all looking for. I'm not in Sacramento right now. It'll take me a couple hours to get back there. Can I call you then?" Luke rushed the words.

"Shit," Langley whistled in astonishment. "Yeah. I'll be waiting."

Luke ended the call and strode over to Alexis.

"What's wrong? Who was it?" She tipped her hat back to see him where he stood, towering over her.

He sat down on the blanket, moving close to her. "Crawley," he murmured.

Her eyes were confused, but that was replaced by shock. "That's the guy who—" she trailed off.

Luke nodded. "I have to call Langley, but I need to get home. I have to remember as much of our conversation as I can. I typed some quick notes, but I need to sit down and recall all of it."

"Oh, okay," she responded, already standing up to get ready. He could hear the disappointment in her voice, although it was clear she was trying to hide it.

"I'm sorry," he mumbled, feeling horrible, but also jumping out of his skin from the adrenaline he was now riding. He put a hand on her cheek so she would look at him instead of fussing over the blanket.

"It's okay. I get it. This is important. We can come back another time." She put her hand on his, giving him a reassuring smile. "Do you want me to drive your truck? You can make more notes in your phone if you want—or call Langley. If you're comfortable with me—"

"That's okay. I need—"

"Privacy?" she suggested.

"Yeah." Luke nodded.

"I understand." She motioned with her hand, as if trying to wave away any guilt he might feel.

She was quiet for most of the drive home, but still smiled over at him when he took her hand.

Just before they reached her apartment, she said, "Thank you for today. I needed it."

"Me too. Next time it'll be for an entire day." He still felt like shit for bringing her home early. But what choice did he have?

She motioned for him to stay in his truck once they were parked. "Do what you need to do." She leaned over the center console to give him a kiss. He put his hand in her hair, pulling her a little closer.

"Thank you. I'll call you tonight," he said as they parted.

She nodded and let herself out of the truck. He watched until she got to the stairs leading up to her apartment. Then he made his way home.

CHAPTER 15

Alexis didn't get the chance to paint for pleasure until the Saturday following their Tahoe trip. She woke early, feeling the need to create. She started with the many colors of a sunset. She wanted the sky to look like it was glowing. But then the bottom of the piece became darker and darker, as if it was already shrouded in the coming night. In the foreground, she added two ghostly figures. They reminded her of the billowy lace on the back of Kassie and Brett's wedding chairs. She stepped back to take in the painting as it was so far.

"Kind of cool in a creepy way?" Alexis questioned herself.

She wasn't sure who the two figures were supposed to be. Her and Luke? All of a sudden, she didn't like how impermanent they looked, so she painted over them. Luke was gone for the weekend. He'd called Langley about the conversation with Crawley. Then he'd gotten a call to go to Charlotte to talk to Langley's superiors and the FBI in person.

She'd been disappointed when they left Tahoe, but she'd done her best to hide it. This all felt so new to her. The fact that she hadn't been in a romantic relationship for many years coupled with the trauma of her past and his grief, meant a unique foundation to their story. But it was clear Luke cared for her. He was nothing but kind and always considerate of how safe she felt in any given situation. Their banter brightened her days. And yes, they'd both felt significant pain, but they could relate to each other because of that.

Alexis was sure their relationship would have rough times, but she was just as sure that she was falling in love with him. They could do the work they needed to do to be together.

Her phone dinged to remind her of her dinner plans. Kassie and Brett had taken a cooking class during their honeymoon in Maui, and Kassie was dying to make one of the recipes for Alexis. Looking at the clock on her wall, Alexis realized hours had gone by. Pretty normal when she was wrapped up in painting. She needed to eat and head to the store for the few ingredients Kassie requested she supply.

She left her painting to dry, cleaned her brushes, and was out the door.

When Alexis walked from the cool air of the grocery store, the heat enveloped her, making her sleepy. It felt nice for a moment and then became suffocating. Sacramento Septembers were still warm—she couldn't wait for the cooler temperatures of October.

She clasped her keys in one hand and two grocery bags in the other. She pulled her sunglasses down from the top of her head, giving her eyes relief from the blinding light.

She scanned for her car, finding it after a moment of confusion. A giant SUV had parked next to it, blocking her sedan from view. When she was about fifteen feet away, she saw movement flash in between the vehicles. A man was looking in her passenger window.

"Excuse me," she called in a shaky voice, reaching into her purse for the yard-duty-style whistle she kept within easy reach.

The man turned to look at her. He was wearing a hat, but his expressionless face was unobscured. It was Zeke.

"W-what?" she heard herself say.

A sudden, incessant round of honking came from the row behind her. She spun around to look, but the noise stopped. When she turned back to her car, the man was gone. Equal parts of her wanted to run and approach her vehicle to investigate, but her legs wouldn't seem to move.

"Are you okay? Do you need help?" asked a young grocery store employee, walking past her toward the cart return.

"Um, yeah, I'm fine. Did you see anyone over there, by that SUV and sedan?"

He turned his head to look in the direction her finger was pointing. "No, but I wasn't really looking. You sure you're okay?"

"Yes, thank you," she responded, and he walked away with a small shrug.

She made her way to her car, walking in a full circle around it. She now clutched her whistle and keys in one hand. There were people walking through the parking lot and the noise of cars from the street, but there was no one around her.

"You're losing it, Alexis," she said to herself. Still, she'd been so sure she'd seen Zeke standing right in front of her. But Zeke was dead, so that was impossible. It was obvious she needed to unpack more of the guilt she felt about him in therapy next week.

She checked the inside of her car three times before she got in. Then she threw her bags on the passenger seat and drove through the lot, looking down each aisle. No sign of the dead man anywhere.

* * *

According to David and the man Christopher paid to watch him, Zeke's interaction had gone well. David had followed the plan, letting Alexis see his face and then getting out of there when Thomas laid on his horn in another nearby vehicle.

Alexis was startled and searched for Zeke afterward. It had gone off without a hitch. Christopher didn't trust David and Thomas, mostly David, to complete this project without self-sabotaging, so the parking lot incident was a true surprise.

But Christopher had already thrown his own curve ball into the project. If Thomas didn't kill David when he started fucking everything up, it would be amusing to see if Alexis could figure out what was going on. He enjoyed testing others––seeing how their minds worked. So, he'd had one of the actors he used for his past California projects drop off the envelope at Alexis's coffee shop. It was just a small clue. It might not result in anything for now, or ever. But if she did some digging on the video of her rape, she might figure out that Zeke was David and that her past had come back to haunt her.

She might still end up dead, but either way, it would be thrilling to watch.

* * *

On Tuesday after her Valle Coffee shift, there was a knock at Alexis's door. She'd just sat down to read a book she'd been trying to start for months. She sighed, hoping it was a salesman she could turn away.

When she called out to ask who it was, she was surprised to hear Geoff Morgan respond.

"Oh, Mr. Morgan—" Her voice reflected the confusion she felt as she opened the door.

The man had an awkward expression on his face, but gave her a small smile. "I'm so sorry to bother you. My colleague and I were doing some business next door. Now my car won't start. Neither of us has jumper cables. I was wondering if you might. I hoped me asking you would be okay because we've met before. My colleague can give my car the jump, so you wouldn't need to worry about that."

She felt bad for him, but that didn't make her any more comfortable with the situation. Two guys she didn't know.

"Um, yes, I have some. They're in the trunk of my car." She hesitated for a moment longer and then told herself it would be a quick interaction. "I'll get them for you."

"I really appreciate it." He clasped his hands in front of him in a gesture of gratitude, exuding some of the charm she was sure he needed in his business.

She grabbed her car keys and followed him down the stairs, turning in the direction of her car. Geoff crossed the street and motioned toward her while chatting to a brunette in a well-tailored cream-colored suit. His coworker was a woman! Some of her anxiety dissolved.

After grabbing the cables, she crossed the street, giving his colleague a smile and nod.

"Hi, I'm Anna Marks." The woman, who looked to be in her forties, put out her hand for Alexis to shake. Confident vibes flowed from her. "Sorry about this. We have a meeting back at the office, which we're already late for." She rolled her eyes in Geoff's direction.

Geoff gave a sheepish smile. Alexis had the feeling Anna intimidated him.

"It's no problem," Alexis said with a soft smile, trying not to make things more awkward for these two than they already were.

Geoff went to take the cables, but Anna grabbed them instead, attaching them to both vehicles with ease. Alexis noticed they both drove a Lexus. Anna glided to her driver-side door and started her car. Geoff looked like he wanted to crawl into a hole. Alexis felt like she should try to distract him from the situation.

"You haven't heard any news about the break-ins, have you?" She motioned to the two buildings. She knew Luke was following the case and would have told her if they had any leads on the burglar, but she wasn't sure what else to talk about.

He looked surprised for a fleeting moment, but then responded, "No, nothing yet. Maybe he'll try to hit other places and they'll find him that way. You must be anxious to get him off the street."

Annoyance struck her. Yes, she dealt with anxiety every day, but she didn't like men she didn't know thinking of her as weak in any way. It seemed to erase the possibility of her winning in a physical fight. "I'm sure it will make us all feel safer," she said.

"Of course," he said with an emphatic nod, like he was trying to apologize for what he'd just said.

"Geoff! You have to start your car!" Anna yelled at her coworker, her impatience obvious.

Geoff blushed in embarrassment. He strolled around the back of his car and jumped into the front seat. Alexis saw him heave a sigh of relief as he turned his key and the engine came to life.

Anna removed the cables in a flash, handing them to Alexis with a near-blinding grin. "Thanks again so much!" She slammed both hoods, gave a wave, and jumped back in her car. "See you there," she called to Geoff out her window as she pulled away from the curb.

He waved back in acknowledgement and rolled down his window, his face returning to its usual charming expression. "Thank you. Anna's, understand-ably, very serious about the job. Being late is a big pet peeve of hers. You've saved me from the lecture a car ride back with her would have included," he finished with a laugh.

"I'm glad I could help," Alexis smiled back, but she'd thought Anna was pretty awesome.

"See you around." He flashed another smile and was gone.

The guy seemed harmless enough—a little less perfect than he'd been the first couple times they interacted, which she could appreciate.

She checked the clock as she let herself back into her apartment. She was teaching a beginner's painting class that night, but if she rushed through an early dinner, she could still give herself twenty minutes to read. She flopped down on her couch, wishing there were more time in a day.

* * *

It was almost three in the morning. Christopher had been sleeping for a couple hours, after returning home from an interesting evening with a woman he met in a bar. He awoke to the sound of his phone dinging with an incoming text message. He stared at the ceiling of his apartment for a moment before reaching for it.

It worked, *read the text from Thomas.* I could tell the strong female element put her more at ease.

Christopher nodded to himself and responded, On to the next step.

CHAPTER 16

On Tuesday night, Luke's phone rang as he was climbing into his truck. He smiled down at her name on the screen. "Hey, Miller, what's up? I thought you'd be in class."

"Hey." Her voice sounded frustrated, maybe a little frantic? "I *am* in class right now, and my students have promised not to tattle on me for being on the phone."

He heard some muffled laughter in the background. "What's going on? You okay?"

"Yeah, I'm fine. I just have a favor to ask. My mom got off her shift at the hospital a bit ago. She takes the bus, but I guess there was an accident on the line, so her bus is late."

"Oh, yeah, heard about that," he confirmed.

"She stayed late, so her coworkers are gone. I don't want her to have to figure out how to use a rideshare service for the first time at night. Kassie's working late covering some city meeting, and she thinks Brett might already be asleep. You mentioned some rough cases at work, right?" Her original thought seemed to meander and fade away. He heard more talking in the background. She had to be feeling guilty about her class.

"Yeah, I'm just leaving the office. Want me to take her home?"

"Yes, I would really appreciate that! I mean, if you can."

"Yeah, no problem. Where will she be waiting?" He started his truck.

"In front of the main medical center entrance, not the emergency entrance. I mean, I don't want to take time out of whatever you wanted to do tonight," Alexis backtracked.

He laughed. "You seem to be having some warring thoughts, Miller. Do you want me to pick her up?"

"Yes."

"And don't you need to get back to your class?" Luke tried hard to stop his laughter.

"Yes," she sighed.

"So—Wait, are you nervous about me meeting your mom?"

"You know what? I'm just going to talk her through the Uber app," she responded.

"No, I'm definitely going to pick her up now! I'm assuming she looks like you. I'll figure it out. Bye, Miller!" he said in a peppy tone.

"Okay fine, I'm nervous about it," Alexis said in a whispered growl.

"Why?" He tried to keep his voice from shaking with laughter as his amusement grew.

"You don't think it's a weird way to meet your girlfriend's mom? And I don't know what she'll say to you! I love my mom more than anyone! She's fantastic! But that doesn't mean she won't say embarrassing things about me! What if you two don't like each other? What am I supposed to do then?" Her words were still coming out in a harsh whisper.

He had to put the call on mute so she couldn't hear him breaking down, barely able to breathe through the laughs.

"Luke?"

He composed himself as much as possible and took the phone off mute. "You're overthinking this. You're amazing. Your mom raised you. I don't think I'll have much reason to dislike her. And with my eternal sunshine personality, what's there not to like about me?"

"You're not helping."

He could almost see her eye roll. "I'm going to do my girlfriend a favor by picking her mother up from work. If you could have my girlfriend let her mother know I'm on my way and then have said girlfriend go back to teaching her class, that'd be great. I'll check in with her later." He wasn't even trying to hide his laughter now. Teasing her was too much fun. "Bye, Miller."

He heard her take a deep breath. "Bye, Kruger."

When he pulled up to the loading area outside UC Davis Medical Center, he spotted Eileen right away. She really did look a lot like her daughter, just a little taller with much lighter red hair. She brightened when she saw his truck. Alexis must have described it.

"Mrs. Kelly? I'm Luke Kruger." He parked and went around to the passenger door to shake her hand and let her in.

"Nice to meet you, Luke." Her smile was the same as her daughter's. "You can call me Eileen. Thank you so much for the ride. My daughter sounded a little flustered when she called to tell me you were the one picking me up."

Luke could tell by her voice that she also found humor in the situation, so he said, "Yeah, I was giving her a lot of grief. She was worried we'd hate each other." He started his truck and maneuvered out of the parking lot.

Eileen chuckled. "I doubt I could ever hate you. I actually want to thank you, for taking her to the hospital the day of the break-in. You made sure the most important part of my life was safe. And I can tell how much she cares about you. Her face lights up every time she mentions you."

"I feel the same way about her," he answered.

"I'm glad. She deserves someone who treats her like the most important person in the world. After everything she's been through, she deserves only great joy." Eileen gazed out her window.

"I agree." He cleared his throat. "Did she tell you I was one of the first people to talk to her, after she came forward to the police?" He didn't know why he felt like having this conversation with her mother. Maybe because she had a calming presence, and he was never sure how much Alexis wanted to talk about it.

"Yes. I'll forever be grateful for Kassidy, who gave her the final nudge she needed to come out of hiding. And it was your number Kassidy gave her, right?" Eileen's face turned back toward him.

He nodded. "I've heard a lot of horrible stories and seen a lot of horrible things throughout my career. I think I get numb to it all sometimes. Back then, her story just seemed sad. Now when I think about it, I get angry. Angry that I can't go back and change what happened to her." As he spoke, he realized his feelings about Alexis's trauma must pale in comparison to what Eileen had experienced. "I can't imagine how it felt for you while it was happening."

The words seemed like a lame afterthought, but she gave him a weak smile.

"I think I experienced every emotion known to man many times over during her isolation. I did my best to be strong for her. I did whatever she needed me to do. Kept all of her secrets without question. At first, I tried to convince her to go to the police, but her intuition about Kurt stopped her. She just knew he wouldn't let his victims go free. She was right. So, now I will always do whatever she needs me to do to keep her safe—whatever it takes."

Something about this declaration made Luke uncomfortable. He didn't like the idea of Alexis feeling she had to disappear or keep secrets again. Or that she had a built-in accomplice in her mother. But there was no reason she'd need to do either of those things now. Kurt Leonard was dead. The criminal organization he'd worked with was all but dismantled in California.

"There shouldn't be any need for that again," he responded, feeling like he had to get these words out in the universe. Like he could rid the future of any threat that would make Alexis run.

"I'm sure you're right," Eileen smiled back. He noted relief on her face.

He steered the conversation toward lighter topics. By the time they reached Eileen's small East Sacramento home, they were laughing about the attempt Alexis's father made to put her in soccer when she was six.

"For some reason, he thought she'd be a natural, but she's always been more artistic and tech-savvy. She spent the season tripping over her own feet and the ball. She made one goal, but it was against her own team." Eileen wiped tears from her eyes as she recounted the experience.

Luke found himself grinning. He could picture little Alexis getting so frustrated, because she had probably wanted to be an amazing soccer player. Without a doubt, she'd tried her hardest. He wondered if she'd had nicknames back then, things her friends called her while they played together. He wondered if she'd ever feel comfortable reminding him of her birth name.

"Thank you for the ride, Luke. I'm grateful my daughter has you in her life," Eileen said as she got out of his truck.

"Anytime," he responded and waited until she was in her house before driving away.

"How'd it go?" She must have called him right after her class ended. Her voice was anxious.

"It was o-k-a-y," he said, drawing the word out. "She didn't want to talk much. It felt pretty awkward." He couldn't help himself.

She was silent for a beat. "Wait, really?"

"No, not really. It went fine. She was talkative, told me embarrassing stories about you, and we don't hate each other," he chuckled.

"Kruger, has anyone ever told you that you're infuriating? I'm coming over there," she grumbled back. "I don't believe she told you any stories."

"As the kids say, Miller, 'Don't threaten me with a good time.' And yeah, she did. Soccer when you were six."

She sighed. "I just—so many parts of what you just said were upsetting."

He laughed loudly. "I try. Are you still coming over?"

"Of course, because I have to know exactly what she told you!"

At some point, they fell asleep on his couch after some wine, a movie, and passionate kissing that left him pretty desperate for more. But Alexis seemed like she was trying to gauge her comfort level. He would keep waiting, because above all, he wanted her to feel safe. Still, it wasn't easy when he woke up with her so close to him. He stared up at the ceiling for a while, trying to go back to sleep, not sure of the time. There was no hint of the sun rising outside his windows.

His phone buzzed from the side table. He grabbed for it to turn the volume off. It was just after two in the morning. Who would be texting him now? The preview on the screen showed Langley's name, so he unlocked it to read the full message.

Hey man. Sorry to text. Needed to let you know Crawley is dead. Found in an apartment near his cousin's place in Alabama. Didn't look like he'd been there long. Looks like a fentanyl overdose. Call when you're up.

"Shit," Luke murmured to himself, running his hand through his hair as he reread the message. That didn't make any sense. Crawley sounded like he was living the good life when they'd talked. He'd never been connected to drugs before. Why would he do something so stupid?

He wanted to charge off the couch, punch in Langley's number, and find out more information, but he didn't want to wake or involve Alexis. She didn't need additional stress or darkness in her life. He wouldn't have any idea how to convey his emotions anyway, because he couldn't understand everything he was feeling. His brain was buzzing, his adrenaline was rushing, but he forced himself to stay on the couch.

He set an alarm on his phone to give them both plenty of time to get up for work. She'd have to go back to her place to get ready. He'd call Langley after she left. He tried to relax and ignore the questions slamming through his head, but sleep didn't happen. He spent the next few hours staring at the room around him, watching the first tendrils of light break through the darkness.

Alexis jolted awake when his alarm sounded. She smiled up at him with content, sleepy eyes. He tried to return the gesture, but the way her expression changed told him he was doing a bad job.

"Are you okay?" she asked.

"Yeah," he said as he kissed her and sat up. "Langley texted and said he had some information about Crawley, so I'm going to call him back before

I leave for work."

"Oh! I hope it's good news—or helpful news at least," she grimaced at her words. "I wish it was the weekend so we could have a full morning like this."

"Stay here this weekend, or whenever you want," he responded, wishing he didn't have to let her go, didn't have to call Langley, didn't have to hear once again that Emma's case was going nowhere. With Crawley dead, they had no leads left.

She grinned at him. "I'd like that. I haven't been in a relationship for a long time, and I have to say, I don't miss the games those guys would play. You're very refreshing, Luke." She waggled her eyebrows at him as she stood from the couch, stretching her back.

He chuckled in surprise. "I'm sure I played my fair share of games, but I'm almost thirty-eight. I don't have time or a need for that anymore." He stood, acting like his hip was bothering him.

"Yeah, you don't have much time left." She shook her head with an exaggerated eye roll, then stood on her tiptoes to give him another kiss. "Lunch at the park later?"

"Sounds good. I'll let you know if anything changes." He walked her to her car and made his way back inside.

He took his time getting ready for work. When he finally called Langley, he almost hoped his friend wouldn't answer. He wanted to pretend Crawley's death wasn't real.

"Hey, Krug. You got my text?" Langley asked, testing the water.

"Yeah. They're sure it was him? The guy hid for years without issue. He sounded content when I talked to him. He didn't have a history with drugs. Why would he mess with fentanyl?" Luke's thoughts were coming out in an inarticulate jumble.

"It was him. I saw pictures. I thought the same things, and I don't know. We're working with the feds to get all of his family interviewed. Maybe they'll have some answers," Langley sounded just as frustrated as Luke felt.

"Now none of his victim's families will get the justice they've been waiting years for. And Em's case. I know he said he didn't kill her, but he was the only lead we had."

Langley sighed. "Luke, I don't want you to think we've given up on Emma. I'm sure you'll get a call from her mother when Crawley's death comes out in the media. Just send her to me. Maybe something will come from the family interviews. Things may just—take a while."

"Yeah," Luke mumbled, knowing Langley was doing his best. "Did anyone find Sheridan's body yet?"

"Not yet. Maybe he didn't really kill him. Maybe Sheridan was working with him," Langley suggested.

"I don't think so. I worked with Sheridan for years. He may not have been the best person, but he never steered me wrong," Luke said. "Something's off here, Langley. I can see Crawley killing Sheridan, but Freeman? What threat would his partner have posed to him after so many years?

"Also, Crawley had no remorse for the women he killed. He didn't outright admit he killed them, but he clearly felt no remorse. But he took the time to call me and tell me he didn't kill Emma. And then indicate he knew who did. I don't know, I think I believe him.

"And the overdose is the weirdest thing of all. If Crawley were going to use drugs, you'd think he'd at least be smart about it," Luke muttered.

"These are all things my team has been asking itself," Langley sighed. "And yeah, the overdose is baffling. I trust your intuition. If you believe he didn't kill her, then we'll figure out who did. But let's see where the investigation on Crawley goes. If he left any information behind, the FBI will find it. We're in this for the long haul. We're not giving up."

"You're right, and thanks, man," Luke said, somehow filling his voice with confidence and gratitude. But his list of questions still bounced back and forth in his brain.

CHAPTER 17

As the days of October drifted by, Sacramento started cooling down. The Bay Area girl in Alexis rejoiced. It felt like the weather was ushering in a chance at something new and exciting after a long, anxious summer. The summer had brought her Luke, but so many stressful, random things had also happened. She was eager to move forward.

She hadn't had another Zeke sighting, so she believed her sanity was still intact. Her therapist explained that situation as someone lurking around the parking lot looking to steal things. When Alexis saw him, the guilt she felt about Zeke had manifested itself into seeing his face on that man's face. She and her therapist spent more time working through her issues surrounding Zeke, leaving her feeling like she was finally ready to set his memory free.

"Good morning!" A voice called out on a Friday. Alexis looked up from the drink she was making to see Geoff standing at the register. She gave him a wave as one of their new employees took his order.

They'd discovered his company's new office was a few blocks from Valle Coffee, and they'd chatted several times when he'd come in to get a drink. He was a nice guy, but she did find his persistent, super friendly personality a bit exhausting.

She made his drink and met him at the pickup counter.

"I asked Anna to go to lunch with me today," Geoff explained after giving her a beaming smile. "I'm trying to make things better with her. We're working together a lot more, and it always feels awkward. She agreed, which surprised me."

"That's great. I hope it goes well!" Alexis tried to sound encouraging.

It looked like a thought flashed through his mind. "Will you come with us? We're going pretty early, because she has an appointment this afternoon. She was singing your praises after the jumper cables incident, because you had them at the ready." His face took on a sheepish smile. "I think you being there would help smooth over any tension. Orchid Thai at eleven?"

"Oh, uh," she responded, hoping she didn't sound rude as she thought of how to turn him down. She and Luke ate lunch together a few times a week, but his work on a multiple-homicide case had him more quiet than usual and eating lunch at his desk every day.

She'd mentioned her boyfriend several times to Geoff in different conversations, so unless he just didn't care, she didn't think he was trying to be anything other than friends. She was sure Luke was too confident in their relationship to mind. She'd told him about the jumper cables day and that she'd seen Geoff at the shop a few times since then. They'd laughed over the fact that they'd both checked his real estate license to make sure he was legitimate.

She realized she'd just talked herself into the idea of going. "Sure, I can meet you guys there."

Geoff asked me to go to lunch with him and his coworker, Anna. The one who was with him when he needed jumper cables, she texted Luke after the man left.

Ok. Have fun! Go somewhere with a lot of people. You never know with real estate agents, was the response.

You're funny, she sent back with an emoji rolling its eyes.

Can't wait to see you. This case is insane.

I have The Painting Palate tonight. Come over after? she replied.

Gladly! Call me when you're done.

Alexis was starving by the time she walked into Orchid Thai a few minutes after eleven. She had to make sure she wasn't drooling as she thought about curry sauce, noodles, and stir-fried vegetables.

The restaurant had just opened, so Geoff was one of the only customers. He was sitting at a table by the windows, perusing a menu, but Anna wasn't with him. Alexis frowned, walking over to him. "Hey. At least I'm not the only one running late." She motioned at the empty chairs around him.

Guilt made its way across his face. "She's not coming. I'm sorry. I guess her appointment got moved to an earlier time. It's in Davis, so she had to leave before lunch. I should have stopped by the shop to tell you, but I was meeting with clients right before this. If you'd rather leave, I completely understand." His words were sincere, but his eyes held deep embarrassment.

She felt bad for him once again. It wouldn't hurt to have lunch with him, right? Maybe this could be part of her personal growth. The restaurant had an open feel. Once it started filling up with other patrons, her comfort level would rise.

"Um, no, that's okay. I'll stay. I'm so hungry!"

She took a deep breath as she removed her jacket and placed it and her purse on the empty seat next to her. She chose to sit in the seat up against the window. Geoff was sitting in the seat across from her things, so it gave them more space. As she told herself to relax, she glanced out the window, watching the breeze blow some leaves down the sidewalk. There were a few clouds in the sky, but no chance of rain yet. The scene brought her a moment of pure peace.

"You look so content right now," Geoff said. She turned to see him smiling at her.

"Oh, yeah," she answered with a small laugh. "I love fall and winter. So, seeing all the leaves on the ground makes me happy."

"I like fall too. You know, I grew up in this area, but I've never gotten used to Sacramento summers." He made a face to go along with his comment, then returned his gaze to the menu.

"I spent most of my life in the Bay Area, so it's been an adjustment—a very difficult one." She nodded, needing only seconds to pick her dish. "After all the days over 100 degrees this summer, I actually miss the Bay Area fog."

After they ordered, they chatted about their childhoods. She enjoyed the casual conversation. He didn't say or ask anything that led her to believe he was interested in her in a romantic way, so calm replaced her last hints of anxiety.

They started talking about the upcoming holiday season.

"I've already been to Apple Hill twice since September," she laughed. "Do you obsess over going up there too?"

"Where?" he asked, just as he took a bite of noodles.

She was confused for a moment, so she didn't answer. He was chewing, but at her pause, she thought she saw a strange expression cross his face. It was gone so fast that she didn't have time to analyze it.

"Apple Hill! You've never been to Apple Hill?" She tried to laugh in order to dispel the awkward feeling hanging in the air. How could he have grown up here but not know about the famous foothill farming community that celebrated all-things apple in the fall? It was one of Alexis and Eileen's favorite places to go together.

"Oh, Apple Hill! Sorry, I thought you said something else!" he laughed back, but it didn't sound authentic. "Yeah, I try to get there a couple times. I'm a little too obsessed with my job. I've been trying to force myself to find more time to relax—to meet new people. That's why I'm glad we've become friends!"

Would Alexis describe them as friends? Maybe. Before this, their interactions had been brief. She supposed there wasn't any harm in him using that word. Still, something was off about him. She didn't think he knew what Apple Hill was. But why would he lie? Sure, it was possible he'd never been there, but to be a real estate agent in Sacramento without hearing about it in passing seemed strange. And he had tried to cover up his ignorance. Alarm bells were going off in her head. She tried to ignore them. Maybe her reaction had been a little too judgmental? Maybe it had bruised his ego and he felt the need to recover? People lied sometimes. That didn't mean they were bad.

"I'm glad you're trying to enjoy life a little more," she said. "There are so many fun things to do in Northern California."

"Agreed! We're lucky to live here," he grinned in reply and took another bite.

She steered the conversation in another direction. The rest of the lunch seemed normal. He gave her a smile and simple wave when they parted ways at the door. She returned the gesture, trying to ignore the nudging feeling in the back of her mind.

*   *   *

"I believe I asked you to research the Sacramento area. I sent you the information I compiled as well. Apple Hill is on page fourteen." Christopher sighed as he reviewed the document he'd emailed.

David and Thomas were on the other end of the call. Thomas was seething.

"You sent me a thirty-five-page report on this horrible portion of this god-awful state! How the hell was I supposed to read all of it in time?" Thomas growled.

"I sent it more than a week ago. If you want to have the believable backstory of being a Sacramento-area native, some work is required on your part." Christopher squeezed the bridge of his nose. He could feel the beginning of a headache, which wasn't an ailment he normally suffered from. Thomas had said he was willing to do whatever was needed to secure Alexis, but it was clear he was too lazy.

"This wouldn't have happened if your actress had been there to play her part! She was supposed to show up, participate in conversation with both of us, then get a call that she had to leave early! She didn't do that, so Alexis was suspicious from the beginning." Thomas sounded like he was putting his phone directly on his mouth to speak.

"You just told me things were going great until that little faux pas. You now appear to be trying to place blame elsewhere," Christopher corrected.

"I wouldn't have been thrown off if the actress had been there. And she could have deflected questions like the Apple Hill one if necessary, since she is familiar with this region," Thomas spat the word "region" as if it didn't deserve to have even that much of a distinction.

"Unfortunately, she had other matters to attend to. Ones that paid her more money than what we offered her. I was not able to convince her that this job outranked one that paid her more. She said she'll return in the future if time permits," Christopher said, keeping his voice monotone.

"We paid her upfront for a multiple-month contract! I had no idea she was out looking for other employment. And what are we supposed to do now? If we can't use the character of Anna, will Alexis be willing to spend time with Geoff? What am I paying you for if you make plans that don't work? Maybe you should have stayed in Sacramento where you could pursue low-level jobs." Thomas's voice grew darker as his words progressed.

Is he trying to sound intimidating? Does this scare people? *Christopher wondered.*

He was certain David was scared of Thomas, but that was because he wanted the same woman Thomas wanted. Christopher had no such reason to be concerned.

"You are paying me because I am the best at what I do. I worked in the Sacramento area and throughout California for years. I know it well. I've managed hundreds of successful projects—the details and outcomes of which would make someone like you afraid to sleep for fear of the nightmares you would have.

"I am doing my best to direct both of you through this project. For reasons I don't understand, you want this woman. I'm not sure what it is about this particular one, but if you want to have her, you must put in the work. She is a high-profile person with anxiety bred by trauma. She also now has a cop for a boyfriend. We have to be very careful. If things go downhill, we can still take her by force, but that will require the development of a new plan."

"This is all obvious. Why are you talking to me like I'm a child?" Thomas muttered.

"I'm talking to you like someone who made a very large mistake. You said she noticed. You need to tread lightly the next time you see her, or you will have law enforcement at your back."

"I'm not worried about cops," Thomas replied.

Christopher took a deep breath. "Gentlemen, I believe our time working together has come to an end. I wish you both luck in your endeavors, but I have other projects to pursue."

"You can't fucking quit!" Thomas yelled. "I paid you a huge amount of money!"

"That you did. As for my part, I have delivered you to this point. You now stand on the precipice, unwilling to acknowledge your error. You have proven to me that you are not willing to take my direction. So, why am I necessary? You have a great deal of money. Find someone else to help you."

The silence was deafening. Christopher let it linger, opening his laptop. He assumed the two men were communicating with each other somehow. He sighed. It was eleven-seventeen at night in Berlin. He could be out doing other things.

He was about to end the call when David spoke, "You'll help us because you'd like to maintain your freedom."

"Excuse me?" Christopher frowned.

"The FBI is still looking for you, Christopher. We know exactly where you are. And sure, you could try to flee, but the information we have on you—your contact information, current work habits, pastimes—all of it will be invaluable to them in finding you, I'm sure," David said, his voice quiet.

A threat! They *are* desperate, Christopher thought to himself, but part of him wondered if they would follow through.

"We need your assistance with this project," David continued after a moment, as if giving Christopher time to sit in anxiety. "Thomas recognizes that he made a mistake, both in not reading the material you provided him and in his con-versation with Alexis. From now on, we will both do everything you tell us in order to make this project a success. We realize you are an incomparable asset."

Christopher shook his head. Such idiots.

He couldn't help but ask, "Is that true, Thomas?"

"Yes," came the man's muttered response.

Christopher made sure they heard him sigh. He tried to make it a nervous sound. "Very well. I need some time to plan. Do not do anything in the meantime." He ended the call.

Christopher knew Thomas wouldn't wait to act. He would try to fix the situation on his own. After this conversation, Christopher had a firm grasp on the size of Thomas's ego. He also now understood that David had more power in this scenario than he'd first thought. Christopher would play his part. By some miracle, maybe the two men would still get Alexis. If not, it would be amusing to watch them crash and burn.

* * *

Alexis planned to tell Luke about the weird conversation with Geoff, but he looked so exhausted when he got to her apartment, she decided to wait. The multiple-homicide case was wearing on him. She doubted she wanted to know the details if they were disturbing enough to get Luke down. She also tried to avoid her usual local news sources, for fear the story might trigger her anxiety. She'd go out of her way not to socialize with Geoff and bring the conversation up to Luke when things settled down.

They relaxed in her bed, talking about their favorite movies. She mentioned *Tremors*. He admitted he'd never seen it, or any of Kevin Bacon's films.

"Sorry, Kruger, but that's unacceptable. We can't be together unless you have seen and appreciated Kevin Bacon's entire filmography," she smirked, renting *Tremors* through Amazon.

"Wasn't he in that dancing movie, though? I'm not watching that," he grimaced back.

Her jaw dropped. "You mean *Footloose*? Did you just call it 'that dancing movie'? Wow, I can see there is a lot of work to do here. Tonight, we'll start with *Tremors*. I'm sure you'll like it. Maybe next week we can address how you can call one of the best movies of all time 'that dancing movie.'"

He rolled his eyes and gave a dramatic sigh, but admitted just before he fell asleep that he enjoyed the movie, eliciting an I-told-you-so grin from Alexis.

She was a light sleeper, so her eyes flew open when he tensed a few hours later. When she looked over at him in the dark, he was staring up at the ceiling. Luke was so good at being charming, aggravating, and guarded when he was awake, but he was vulnerable when he slept. She felt such strong empathy for him, it hurt. She knew what it was like to have a mind that betrayed her while she was trying to escape the world for a while.

She reached out and took his hand under the covers. He didn't say anything or look at her, but he held her hand as if he was afraid to let go and closed his eyes again.

It was like a light switched on. In that moment, she knew she was ready for the next step. Luke made her feel safe. She knew he cared about her. She wanted nothing more than to show him that she felt the same.

When she opened her eyes the next morning, it was almost eight-thirty, which felt like an extravagant sleep-in. She could hear him getting coffee in the kitchen as she snuck into her bathroom to brush her teeth. Her heart raced with excitement and nerves. She met him at the door to her bedroom. His hair was mussed, he looked exhausted, and he was already handing her a cup. Her nerves began to threaten her confidence.

But the look in his eyes and that slow smile sealed it for her. She didn't think she'd ever seen anyone look at her with such fierce—what was it? Not lust alone. Love? They hadn't said that word yet, but she was almost positive that was the expression written across his face.

She put the coffee cups down on her dresser. Confusion and something like sadness replaced his previous look as he watched his cup be put aside. She laughed and stood on her toes to wrap her arms around his neck. Her kiss started slow and then deepened. She hoped he would understand, because she didn't know how well she could form coherent words.

"Uh, good morning, Miller," he responded, putting his arms around her waist and pulling her closer.

"Good morning," she said against his lips, running her hands through his hair as he sighed with pleasure. "I'm ready."

He lifted his face from hers to study her eyes. She saw that same look of love and lust in his. "I think you can tell how I feel about the thought of making love to you, but you're sure?"

"Most definitely." Her heart threatened to slam right out of her chest as she removed her pajama top, a blush hitting her cheeks. "That is, if you think your coffee can wait."

He chuckled as he caressed his hands up and down her bare back, bending to kiss her neck. Then he picked her up and moved toward her bed. "Yeah, I think I can deal with that."

CHAPTER 18

God, he loved her.

It was late in the morning now. He watched her drowse, pulled close to his chest. Love was a feeling he never saw himself having again after Emma died. Then Alexis appeared, or reappeared, in his life. He felt guilty for being able to love again when Emma had lost her chance at life and everything that went with it. He'd never wanted to talk with Emma about what would happen if either one of them died—he should have. He'd always love her. She would always be with him. But he was sure she wouldn't want him to wallow alone forever. She wasn't that kind of person.

He'd been staring off into space, but he looked down to see Alexis was looking up at him.

"Serious thoughts, Kruger?" she asked with a smile.

He felt a grin spread across his face. He kissed her and brushed some hair away from her eyes. "How are you?" He ran one hand lazily up and down her back. He'd checked in with her a couple times as they explored each other, encouraging her to communicate with him. Her feeling safe was still his top priority.

She closed her eyes and sighed. "I'm very good. Probably the best I have been in a long time." She checked her bedside clock. "Why do I have to get up?"

"You don't *have* to," Luke teased, putting his arms around her.

"I have a painting class at three, so I think I should eat something," she laughed in response.

"They'll find someone else. I can bring food right to you in bed," he grinned.

Alexis pushed away from him with another laugh. "And support me financially?"

"If you want," he said with a shrug.

She rolled her eyes and got out of bed, pulling her pajamas back on. She reached for him, pulling him from the bed and into another deep kiss.

"I'm getting mixed messages here," he chuckled.

She put her hand in his, each of them collecting a cup of cold coffee from the dresser. They'd made it to the kitchen when there was a knock on her door.

He raised an eyebrow. "Expecting someone?"

"No, not that I know of." She wrinkled her brow as she gazed toward the door, where another knock sounded. She padded over, checking the peephole. As she pulled away, the look on her face was strange. He felt the hairs on his arms rise.

When she opened the door, he heard a familiar voice say, "Hi, Alexis. How are you this morning?"

Why was the real estate agent here?

"Hey, Geoff. I'm good. How are you?" There was a definite awkward tone in her voice.

"I'm great, thanks. Some of my coworkers decided last minute to head up to Apple Hill this morning. Since we were just talking about it yesterday, I wanted to see if you'd like to go with me."

Luke frowned. He had no issue with Alexis having male friends, but it sounded like this guy was asking his girlfriend on a date.

"Sorry, I can't," Alexis said. The kindness in her voice sounded forced. "I have to work today. But maybe Luke and I can join you guys another time."

"Hey, man," Luke said casually, catching the surprise on Geoff's face as he walked up behind her.

"Oh, good morning." The man recovered, flashing Luke a too-bright smile. He turned back to Alexis and said, "No problem, I understand. I'll check in with you next time. Maybe lunch again soon?"

Geoff met only Alexis's eyes as he said this, making it clear Luke was not included in the invitation.

Who the fuck does this guy think he is?

Alexis gave him a small smile, but said, "Oh, maybe. They're changing my shift at work, so I need to see how that goes first."

What? She hasn't mentioned that, Luke thought with a frown.

"Sure thing! Have a good day!" Geoff gave her one more smile, this time including a small nod to Luke, and left.

When the door was closed, her fake expression fell from her face, leaving obvious anxiety. She shuffled past him into her kitchen. He followed close behind.

"Hey, what's going on? You didn't tell me your work shift was changing."

"It's not changing. It's probably nothing—just leftover paranoia," she responded, putting two pieces of toast in the toaster and pulling eggs from the fridge.

"Did he do something to you?" He could feel himself getting angry. His imagination was too vivid.

"No." Alexis turned to face him, but she didn't move toward him for comfort. Was it that she was used to taking care of herself? Or that she wasn't sure how he'd feel about what she had to say? "He said something odd during lunch. Now I feel like he's trying to cover it up. Something feels off about him."

"What'd he say? The guy seems pretty fucking brazen." He took a breath to try to clamp down on his anger. It wasn't useful in this situation.

"It wasn't anything to do with me," she responded, guessing his thoughts. "But I know what he did today was strange. No, it's just that he said he grew up around here, but when I mentioned Apple Hill, he didn't know what I was talking about. Then he tried to act like he hadn't heard me correctly, but

I'm sure that was a lie. Now he shows up asking if I can go to Apple Hill, like he's really trying to double back on his mistake."

"He obviously has a big ego. Maybe you wounded it, and he wants to look better in your eyes," he muttered.

He wanted to say so many other things. *Tell that asshole to stay away from you. Don't hang out with him anymore. Why did you suggest we go with him another time? Why didn't you just say no to lunch in the future if he's giving you a bad feeling?*

But he didn't say anything. He wasn't trying to give her orders or make her feel stupid. Silence grew around them as he tried to keep his face neutral.

"I'm not going to spend time with him anymore," she said, her eyes full of an emotion he couldn't identify. "I don't know what's going on with him, but—"

She trailed off and was quiet for a moment. She seemed to be hesitating to tell him something. She sighed and words tumbled from her as if she knew she had to get them out before she couldn't.

"I know you thought I was crazy back when I made that *Final Destination* comment, but sometimes I wonder—all those women Kurt had murdered—I was supposed to be one of them."

A chill crept up his spine. He thought back to her mother's words. Alexis's intuition was strong. He shook his head. Those thoughts weren't helpful. There was no threat to her now, and anyway, he wouldn't let anything happen to her.

Luke moved to put his arms around her, and she melted into him. *Damn it, she's scared. She needs comfort, and you're angry about the fucking real estate agent.*

"I've never thought you're crazy, Alexis. You've been through unimaginable things. Survivor's guilt is—well, it can mess with your mind. At least it has with me. Don't be afraid to talk to me about things like this. I want to be here for you."

"Thank you." She hesitated again. "But it wouldn't make any sense, right? Kurt doesn't have any known associates left. There'd be no reason for anyone to come after me. But so many random things happened over summer—"

"No, there wouldn't be any reason for someone to come after you. There was no love lost for Kurt when he died. And the FBI is keeping heavy tabs on the organization's activity." He rubbed her back with his hands. "But I get it. You've dealt with a lot in a short period of time. However, I think Geoff Morgan is just an awkward, unrelated asshole."

"Don't hold back, Luke," she sighed and kissed him, a small smile touching her lips.

"I won't." He smirked and couldn't help but add, "Just tell me if he gives you any problems in the future."

"Oh, yeah. That sounds like a great idea." She rolled her eyes. "I'm sure I can take care of it myself."

She started to make the eggs, but he put his arms around her and she turned, giving him a deep kiss. He almost told her he loved her, but it didn't feel right as a follow-up to the conversation they'd just had, so he decided to wait. He could still feel tension running through her body.

"I know you can, but I'm here to help whenever you need me."

"Thank you. I'm so glad I have you," she smiled up at him, then rested her face in his chest. He could feel her relax little by little. "Should we make this more of a late lunch? It doesn't take me long to get ready and get to class."

He pulled her away from him with a giant grin. She batted her eyes in mock innocence. "Miller, you don't have to ask me twice."

He wrapped her in another kiss as he reached behind her to turn off the burner.

"Do you have to work tomorrow?" He kept his arm around her shoulders as they left her apartment that afternoon.

"No, but I'm having lunch with Kassie." She reached to hold his hand with hers, looking up at the clouds building in the sky. Her face was so peaceful, as if those clouds grounded her.

"Stay at my place tonight? I promise I won't make you late." He passed her a grin and she raised one eyebrow.

"Luke, you shouldn't be making promises you know you won't try to keep." She poked him in the ribs.

He laughed out loud, moving to avoid her finger. "Miller, are you saying I'm not a man of my word?"

"In this case, yes. You know Kassie will call both of us if I don't show up, so that'll help," she smirked back. "But yes, I'll be there tonight."

He gave her another long kiss. He learned his lesson years ago about appreciating what he had when he had it. He wished he could stop time for a while to keep her with him.

As she got in her car, his phone rang in his pocket.

Susan. He'd been waiting for the call, hoping it wouldn't come.

His face must have showed his frustration, because she gave him a funny look from inside her sedan. He waved it away. "Don't be late, Miller!"

She rolled her eyes and stuck out her tongue before driving away.

He began the trek down the street to his truck, accepting the call. "Hi, Susan."

CHAPTER 19

Alexis was right on time to meet Kassie for lunch in downtown Sacramento the next day. They paid for their sandwiches and went outside. The air was cold, but they found a table in a sunny spot. Alexis took a moment to enjoy the sounds of life all around her. She'd lounged in Luke's bed that morning, her head on his chest as they talked about everything that came to mind.

He'd grown quiet after a while. When she pushed herself up to look at his face, she'd seen a nervousness in his eyes. It worried her for a moment until he said, "Miller, you came out of nowhere. I never expected to feel something like this again, but I do. It's so easy with you, so comfortable, but somehow exciting at the same time. I'm happiest with you. I love you."

It was a shock to hear the words—the best kind of shock. Her stomach flipped, and she felt like she had to be glowing. "I feel all those things about you. I love you too, Luke."

He'd pulled her into a tender kiss and held her like she might disappear. She'd never felt so needed by someone. It felt like a huge responsibility, but also as simple as taking a breath. She hadn't wanted to leave that moment, but her dates with Kassie were too important to cancel.

"So, things with Luke are good then?" Kassie gave her a knowing look.

"Wow, am I that obvious?" Alexis laughed.

"You said you were spending time with him this weekend, and you look very happy and peaceful. I've seen you happy, but I don't know that I've seen you so at peace."

"I feel that way—I haven't in so long. It feels amazing," she responded, feeling a blush grow on her cheeks. "He told me he loved me this morning, and I said it back. And it was so easy. I didn't hesitate. Never in a million years did I expect to feel love for any man. When he first came into the coffee shop in June, I didn't want to have anything to do with a guy."

Kassie stood up to give her a hug. "That's wonderful, Lex! I'm so happy for you!"

Alexis squeezed her friend, taking a deep breath of the crisp autumn air. As she went to sit back down, she noticed a small black sedan pull up in front of the office building across the street. It parked partially on the red curb. The driver seemed unconcerned as he used his clicker to lock the vehicle and gave his keys a light toss into the air and caught them again.

She could have looked away then, but she caught a glimpse of the man's face as he turned it in the direction of a honking horn. He gave it a second's attention, then made his way into the building. Alexis's heart felt like it stopped. *Zeke.*

He didn't see her, but his face was clear as day.

"I might have been a little nervous about you dating Luke, but I've never seen him happier either. It's clear how he feels," Kassie was saying.

"What the hell?" Alexis heard herself mumble.

"What?" Kassie looked up from her food.

"Sorry, I'll be right back." Alexis stood up so fast, her chair almost tipped over. She sped over to the crosswalk at the corner.

"Lex, where are you going?" She could hear Kassie calling.

The traffic light was in her favor. She was across the street in seconds, charging toward the building. She flashed a look at the car. It held a New York license plate. She tried to memorize the characters, angry with herself for leaving her phone back at the table.

What the hell was going on? There was no doubt in her mind she'd seen Zeke. This was the second time, but this time, she was sure.

Alexis took a deep breath before entering the building, trying to calm herself down. Anger and frustration had replaced her initial shock. The feelings were fueling her bravery. She was going to take that for all it was worth. She heard Kassie call her name again, but she didn't turn around. She was going to find out what was going on. She peered at the names of the building's resident businesses on a directory hung on the right wall. She didn't recognize any of them. The building was nothing special inside. Probably built in the 1950s or 1960s, it was sterile and cold.

She approached the security guard's desk. He greeted her with a confused smile. She was sure the expression on her face must be difficult to decipher.

"Can I help you?" the guard asked.

She heard Kassie's boots come to a stop behind her.

Time to practice whatever acting skills she might have. "Yes, a man just came in a few minutes ago. His black car is parked out front. He's a good friend from college, but I lost his number when I got my new phone. I was riding my bike and happened to see him. I called out to him, but he didn't hear me. Is there any way I could speak with him?"

Not a great story, but it was what her brain came up with on the fly. She doubted her skinny jeans, suede boots and curled hair presented the image of someone who'd just come off a bicycle.

The guard eyed her for a moment. "I'm sorry, ma'am, but the last gentleman who walked in was a visitor. I'm not allowed to give out visitor information."

Of course. "Oh, that's a bummer. Well, okay. I'll leave a note on his car," Alexis sighed, giving the guard a wave and a smile as she turned to walk out. "Come on, Brenda. He said he can't help." She looped her arm through Kassie's and steered her toward the door.

"Brenda?" Kassie muttered as they walked out.

Alexis intended to study the sedan again, but gasped when she saw it was gone.

"What? How did he get out of the building?" Alexis stopped short, not sure what to do next.

"Who? Lex, what's going on?" Kassie's frustration came through in the question. Alexis knew the reporter in Kassie hated not having all available information.

Then she noticed her friend had grabbed both their bags before she left the table.

"Can I have my purse, please?" Alexis tried not to sound impatient.

Kassie raised an eyebrow, but handed it over. Alexis pulled out her phone and made a quick note with what she hoped was the car's license plate number. But she had no idea how to find out who it belonged to.

"You saw a black sedan parked here when we went inside, right?" Alexis hoped Kassie would say yes. She already felt crazy enough seeing a dead man walking through the streets of Sacramento.

"Um, I think so. I saw something parked here, but I was pretty focused on following you," Kassie responded, watching as Alexis recorded the building's address in her phone. She also made note of the business names she remembered, but was sure she could look those up later.

"While we were talking, I saw a man get out of the car and go into that building." She dreaded saying the next sentence, so she forced it out. "It was Zeke, Kassie."

Her friend was silent for several seconds, her eyes scrunched in confusion. "Your coworker who died?"

"Yes, although clearly not dead. I'm not in the habit of seeing ghosts. I swore I saw him one other time before this, but thought I imagined him. But I know this was him."

"But how? Didn't he die in a bike accident? Didn't you go to his memorial service? And his family was there, right?" Kassie questioned.

"Yes, I know, but I swear this was him." Alexis felt sure just moments ago, but now, with some time to reflect, it was so easy to doubt herself. What if she hadn't got a good enough look at the man? That car wasn't Zeke's. Not that she'd known Zeke very well, but that man's mannerisms—just the way he moved—hadn't been like Zeke's.

"I was so sure. Do you think that's crazy?" She sighed. Why would her mind be looking for Zeke? She felt like she'd made leaps and bounds when it came to dealing with the guilt she felt about him.

Kassie gave her a small smile. "You know, after everything we've both been through—after the insane things that happened to so many people because of one man—I have a hard time calling anything crazy anymore. So, I'm not saying it's impossible you saw him, but why would he would fake his own death just to stick around here?" She stopped to think for a moment. "Can you text me his full name and anything else you know about him? I'll see if I can find anything about his past."

"Ever the sleuth." Alexis returned her friend's smile. "Thank you, Kassie."

Kassie's phone buzzed and she checked her screen. "Ugh, sorry, I have to go. Sounds like there's some kind of spontaneous protest going on outside the Capitol. My editor wants me to see what's up."

"No problem. Sorry about lunch." Alexis frowned. They'd made their way back across the street, and she motioned at their food.

Kassie waved the apology away. "Don't forget to send me that info. Talk soon, Lex!" Then she was off, jogging in the direction of her car.

Alexis looked after her for a moment, ever-grateful for her friend. Then she turned her gaze back to the building across the street. She pulled out her phone and stared at the license plate number, hoping some meaning would jump out at her. Nothing came to mind.

As she walked back to her car, she called Luke, wondering whether she should tell him about seeing Zeke.

"Hey, Miller, I was just going to call you. I'm heading to North Carolina." He sounded like he was rushing.

The statement surprised her so much, it took her a moment to process it. "Uh, did you tell me about that?"

His voice was warm as he responded, "No, I'm sorry. My parents need help with something, but I don't want to take much time off work, so I'll be flying back tomorrow night."

"Oh, okay. Are they all right?" She unlocked her car, realizing she was really hungry. She'd only had a couple of bites of her sandwich. After Kassie left, she'd felt anxious sitting there, staring across the street at that building. So, she'd cleaned everything up and left.

"They're fine. They're just having this awkward thing with one of their old friends, so I said I'd come help mediate. My mom called right after you left. Are you on your way to my place?"

Alexis thought it strange that he'd fly all the way across the country to help his parents with a disagreement, but maybe there was more to the story he didn't know yet. "Yeah, I just got to my car."

"I have to head to the airport now, but I'm going to leave my door unlocked for you. You can get your stuff, or stay as long as you want. And I'll leave a key for you on the kitchen counter. You can keep it." He was rushing again. "Sorry, did you guys have a nice lunch?"

It was clear he needed to focus on whatever was going on with his parents. She didn't want to cause concern, so she decided to wait until he got back to tell him about Zeke. "Yes, it's always good to see her." She wasn't lying, because she hadn't said the lunch was nice, and it *was* always good to see Kassie. Especially when she could support Alexis through what was either a mental health crisis or a ghost sighting.

"That's good." The call was quiet for a few seconds. She could hear him closing his apartment door. "I love you, Alexis. I had a great time this weekend."

She smiled to herself. "I love you too. And so did I. Have a safe flight. Will you text when you get there?"

"Yeah, right when I land," he confirmed, such a caring tone in his voice that it was easy to forget about Zeke for a moment.

She heaved a sigh as they ended the call, and headed toward his apartment. They would both have something interesting to talk about when he was back.

"I'm not working tomorrow. Do you want to take a walk on your lunch break?" Eileen asked over the phone as Alexis was walking through the front door of her apartment. She'd spent a little time at Luke's, but it felt strange to be there without him. Although, having his key join the others on her keyring had been an exciting moment, even *if* she'd been celebrating alone.

"Sure, that sounds nice," Alexis answered, cradling her cell phone between her ear and shoulder so she could open her laptop and set it on the table.

"And you said you'll ask Luke about Thanksgiving soon, right? It's less than a month away."

"Mmmhmm." Alexis opened Google and typed in the name of the first company she'd seen on the building's directory. She'd written all the names down on a piece of paper at Luke's place, but wanted the familiarity of her own apartment before she started her research.

"Babe, are you listening? I just want to make sure he's not going to his parents' house so I know how big of a turkey to buy." Her mother chuckled at her clear distraction.

"Oh, sorry! I don't think he usually goes home for holidays, so I'm pretty sure he'll be joining us. But I promise to check when he gets back in town."

"Okay, thank you! I'll let you go, but see you tomorrow at the park?" her mother asked.

"Yes, sounds great!" Alexis confirmed. "Love you, Mom," she added to apologize for her inattention.

"Love you always, hon!" Eileen responded and ended the call.

Alexis loved talking to her mom, but she had to look up the companies before her uncertainty overwhelmed her. She was already full of doubt over what she'd seen. With Kurt, there had been a tangible threat to hide from, but these ghost sightings were something very different. All she knew was if she had really seen Zeke, one of these companies had to hold a clue as to why.

The first business popped up as a financial advisory firm in Sacramento. Its website gave a Sacramento history dating back to the 1970s, with no apparent connections outside the capital city. Nothing obvious there.

The second company was a temp agency, also Sacramento-based, although it had satellite offices in surrounding cities and towns as well. It was started by two college friends in the 1990s and had moved its headquarters to that building seven years ago. She knew Valle Coffee didn't hire from temp agencies, but maybe if Zeke was alive, he needed a new job? But she thought about the way he had parked right in front of the building, somewhat on the red curb. The way he'd tossed his keys in the air with such confidence. He wasn't there to look for a job.

Alexis let out a loud sigh. Maybe this was all a waste of time. She had no idea what she was looking for. Still, she typed in the third company's name. Titan was a pharmaceutical research and manufacturing company. She wanted to slam her laptop closed in frustration, but forced herself to click on its website. She'd only ever heard of the huge international or global pharmaceutical corporations, but this one seemed much smaller.

"Hang on," she muttered to herself.

Titan was headquartered in New York—Manhattan to be exact. This made her take pause. This was a major difference from the company's building companions. It merited a further look, right?

She pulled up a page about the top officers and board members, looking for anything that felt connected to Zeke. When she clicked on the bio page for Titan's chief executive officer, Thomas Loefler, something about the man's face, his wide smile full of whitened teeth, seemed familiar to her. She didn't know why. It wasn't Zeke. She didn't know the man, but there was something there.

Her phone rang next to her, making her jump. Brett's name was on the screen.

"Hey," Alexis answered as she tried to slow her slamming heart.

"Hey, Lex. Kassie's still at the Capitol, but she asked me to get back to you about Zeke."

Alexis laughed. "Can never say she doesn't work fast." She'd texted Kassie

Zeke's information after getting to Luke's apartment. "Are you in the office today?"

"Yeah, I had some other stuff to work on and didn't want to wait for tomorrow. Our case load has been slammed. So, I couldn't find anything abnormal about the guy. Just regular life documentation and his death certificate. No criminal record or known alibis. Everything seems on point."

Alexis sighed with disappointment. Of course this wouldn't be easy. "Did she tell you why I asked?"

"No, just that you had a weird feeling about him. Is something going on? He died in an accident a while back, didn't he?"

Thanks for keeping the theoretical sighting a secret, Kass, she silently acknowledged her friend.

"Yeah, he did. Everything's fine, Brett. Thanks for looking," she replied, then thought for a moment. "He didn't seem familiar to you in any way when you met him in the shop, did he?"

"No, should he? You sure you're okay?" he asked again.

"Yeah, I'm good. Just curious." There was no point in making this a big deal right now, because she had no idea if anything was going on. Zeke had no record. Brett found Zeke's death certificate. Zeke was dead.

"Okay. But please tell Luke or us if something happens." Brett didn't believe her, but he was trying not to be invasive. No doubt he would grill Kassie about it later.

She had no intention of hiding anything from Luke. She just wanted to know if she had a legitimate story to tell him. "I will. Thank you for taking the time to look him up. I appreciate it!"

"Sure, Lex. Talk to you soon." He ended the call. She dove back into Titan's website.

She ate a quick, early dinner in front of her computer screen, learning everything she could about the company's short history. She then did a separate search on Thomas Loefler, but was surprised to find so little information on him. Shouldn't a man in that kind of position, in a company that seemed to be gaining momentum at an exponential rate, have a lot of published and recorded interviews under his belt?

In the entirety of her search, she could only find two pictures of him—the one on his bio page and one on some gossip website's coverage of an event Titan employees attended in New York. She stared at his face. It was unfamiliar, but that smile—something was still nagging her about that smile.

Her alarm sounded on her phone, causing her to jump once again. She'd set it to remind herself to go to bed. She couldn't believe she'd been doing this for hours. She closed her laptop and headed for her room, Thomas Loefler's face still drifting across her mind.

CHAPTER 20

"*How was it possible that she was eating there at that exact time?*" David yelled.

"*Stranger things have happened,*" Christopher responded, leaning back in his chair with his eyes closed.

"*I got a message Thomas wanted me at the office right away! I didn't even see her when I parked! The elevator door was closing on my face when she walked into the building! I had to go out the back and move the car! The guard said she was asking about me!*"

Christopher wished the man would lower his voice. His head was throbbing. Were there any two more inept men in the world? First, Thomas took it upon himself to show up at Alexis's apartment. That hadn't been a surprise. But now this? Unless David was lying, he had accidentally orchestrated another Zeke sighting. Alexis was sure to figure the whole thing out. She was smart. How could she not?

"*But she didn't catch up to you. She didn't talk to you. This will add to her confusion and fear,*" Christopher said. And he was sure it would, but she was getting braver. She'd been brave enough to follow David into the building. She was going to figure it out.

"*This has to work. Thomas will come after both of us if it doesn't. Remember everything we know about you,*" David muttered.

"It will work," Christopher said, but he didn't try to sound convincing. "Stick to the plan."

He ended the call. For once in his life, he wondered if he was tired of drama.

* * *

As Luke's plane neared Sacramento International Airport Monday night, he thought back on the scene at his parents' house early that morning. He'd arrived just after midnight. Susan was there when he pulled in the driveway. She'd been there since late Sunday morning. He'd tried to reason with her over the phone, but she'd refused. His parents were at a loss, so he'd gotten on the first plane out of Sacramento. It felt strange to be flying across the country again so soon. He wished he could be with Alexis instead.

Susan was sitting on his parents' decades-old sofa when he walked in. She was holding a cup of tea. There was a plate of cookies on the coffee table in front of her. At twelve-thirteen in the morning. For a moment, he wanted to grab and shake his parents.

Susan showed up at their house unannounced and demanded that they talk about Em, the case, and how Luke was "giving up" now that Crawley was dead. And they gave her tea and cookies. She'd been there for lunch and dinner too, so he could only guess they'd provided her those meals as well. There was a very awkward air in the room, but his parents were sitting in chairs opposite her, holding their own cups. At first glance, it would appear the three had come together for a pleasant visit. At twelve-thirteen in the morning.

"Hi, Mom, Dad, Susan—" Luke wasn't sure how to handle this situation.

His father turned toward him with a hint of desperation in his eyes. He looked exhausted. His mother flashed him a half-hearted smile. Luke knew his mother's Southern hospitality was requiring her to act like this was a normal experience.

"Luke, I didn't expect you to actually come." Susan's voice was strained.

"Mom, Dad, are there any leftovers? I'm starving."

"Yes, son, we'll get you some." Jacob Kruger jumped out of his chair as if it was on fire. He pulled Linda with him, the words she was starting to say to Luke were cut off as they disappeared.

Luke turned to look at Susan, trying to keep his face calm and polite, as if he was interviewing an innocent witness. "Susan, this is not what Emma would want." He motioned around the room.

"Don't talk about her. I know how much she loved you, and you're not honoring her," she spit out the last three words. He could tell she was tired too, which couldn't be helping her emotions.

"I've had this conversation with you so many times. I don't know what else to say." He struggled to keep his calm.

"What you should say is that you'll help find her killer!" She stood up. "Just like me, I don't think you believe that nonsense about Crawley. His death doesn't make sense. Someone is trying to cover something up. We need to keep looking!"

He ignored her words, because she was missing the point. "You can't show up at my parents' house and refuse to leave, Susan. That's unacceptable. You need to call Langley and—"

"Langley won't talk to me! He never calls me back. When I do reach him, which is very rare, he hangs up on me!" she yelled.

This managed to stun Luke for a moment, and he stood staring back at her. But he recovered enough to reason that Langley wouldn't hang up on her unless she was being hostile or irrational, which wouldn't be a surprise.

"He's busy. And if you're not being cooperative with him—"

The woman held up her hand. "I understand I haven't been kind to you over the years, Luke. It's easy for me to be angry and blame you. I have to hold on to that, because it keeps me connected to you. I know I seem insane, but you are the only one who will listen to me anymore. Langley doesn't help. I've tried to be nothing but kind and understanding when I speak to him, but he never has time. I know he's been telling you to refer me to him. He's giving you lip service. He's never given me the impression that he cares about Emma's case."

A strange feeling passed through Luke—a dark thought blooming in his mind—but it was ridiculous, so he pushed it aside. Another question came to him. He blurted it out without thinking.

"What will knowing bring you?" He paused for a beat at the confused look on her face. "What will it bring us, knowing who killed her? She's gone. She's been gone now for what feels like forever."

"And no time at all." She sighed with a nod. "I don't know. What is knowledge like that supposed to bring? Closure? Some sense of peace? And now with the Sunset Killers dead, maybe we'll never know. But I don't want to assume those men killed Emma. I don't like assumptions; I like facts. And if I have to lose my daughter, my only child, I want to know *without a doubt* who did it. Maybe it won't bring me anything, but I want to know. Don't you?" She folded her arms across her chest and held his gaze.

He didn't know how to answer. For the first time in a long time, she was speaking to him in a rational way, and he agreed with her. Would Susan live the rest of her life in frustration, anger, and disappointment if they didn't find out who killed her daughter? She'd been driving him nuts the last five years, but he didn't want that for her.

"Susan—"

"I should go," she said as if coming out of a fog. She stood and picked up her purse. "You're right, I shouldn't have come here. Please tell your parents I'm sorry." She passed by him on her way out of the house, but stopped a few feet from the door, holding his gaze. "I'm not going to give up, Luke. No matter how long it takes and how few answers there seem to be. And, I'm sorry, but I won't stop calling you, because I need you to keep fighting too." She nodded once and left.

Luke let out a huge breath. He put his head in his hands as he sat down on the sofa. He could hear his parents murmuring to each other in the kitchen.

He was sure they'd heard the entire conversation.

He wasn't sure how to move forward from here. He couldn't give up on Emma, but his past life was overtaking his current one. He wanted to give Alexis everything. She deserved that and more, but Emma's murder would always be there, a dark cloud mixing with his grief.

He came back to the present as the plane descended over the Sacramento Valley. He stared out into the dark sky, letting his eyes lose focus. He loved Alexis. He needed her. He could make all of this work. It'd be worth it to come out the other side with her hand still in his.

* * *

On Wednesday night, Alexis drove to Luke's apartment right after he'd called to say he was heading home from work. It was the first chance they'd had to see each other since he got back. He'd spent the last couple days sounding exhausted on the phone. She wondered if he'd slept during his trip.

Her next few days were busy, so tonight was the best night for them to spend time together. She felt weird letting herself into his place while he was there, so she decided to knock. She'd just laid her knuckles on his door when it swung open and he was standing in front of her. His eyes were tired, but there was that signature smirk on his face.

"Hey, Miller." His voice sounded way too sure of how much she'd missed him. She laughed, giving him a little push back into his apartment. He closed the door and grabbed her into his arms, kissing her like they would never see each other again.

She came away breathless, her cheeks hot, raising an eyebrow in her own teasing response. "It was just a few days, Kruger."

"Mmmhmm," he answered, his lips back on hers.

Alexis took his hand as they walked into the living room and sat down on his couch. "So, you didn't want to talk about your trip over the phone. How was it?"

He looked at her with a weak smile, pushing some hair behind her ear. "I'd rather talk about that later, or not at all."

"Yeah, but I wouldn't be able to deal with that," she laughed back.

She wondered if the trip had something to do with Emma. He never willingly brought Emma or her murder up. It was the deepest, darkest part of him. She knew talking about himself at that level made him very uncomfortable. But sometimes she needed a little window into that darkness. Without it, she felt like she didn't truly know him.

Luke sighed, running his palms over his face and through his hair. "Emma's mother, Susan, showed up at my parents' house unannounced on Sunday, and she wouldn't leave. She's upset about the status of Emma's case. She'd called me Saturday when you left for your painting class, but she didn't say anything about her plan to go over there. My parents called me on Sunday after you went to see Kassidy, but Susan wouldn't talk to me over the phone." He stopped. It was clear he didn't want to continue.

"So, you flew out there," Alexis murmured. "Luke—" She wasn't sure what she was going to say next. On top of the grief and guilt he already dealt with on a daily basis, Emma's mother was adding stress to his life. She couldn't imagine how the woman must feel, losing her child, but it wasn't fair that Luke had to bear the brunt of her grief on top of his.

"She's frustrated. I get it. Things are going nowhere. But I told her she can't just show up at my parents' house because she feels like I'm not doing enough. She ended up agreeing but said she's going to keep calling me—" He cut himself off, cringing. He turned his face toward his wall of windows.

"Oh. Does she call you often?" she asked in a casual tone, knowing this was information he hadn't meant to give.

"Yeah. It used to be once a year, on the anniversary of Emma's death. But it's been several times this year already." He stood and moved toward his kitchen. She waited a few moments before following, trying to give him space.

"She wants to stay in touch?" She knew it wasn't that simple, but she was hoping he'd open up even more.

He looked down at the cup of water he'd just poured for himself. "No, Alexis."

She could tell by his voice that Luke knew she was pressing for more information. So, she waited for him to continue. He searched her eyes, but she stood her ground in silence.

"She calls to remind me, to make sure I remember the case isn't solved. To ask me why I'm not doing more to find her daughter's murderer," he said in slow, tense words.

Alexis wasn't sure what to say at first. "Wait, she calls to blame you for Emma's unsolved case?"

She could tell he was getting more and more uncomfortable. He finished his water in a few gulps. "Miller, I don't want to talk about this anymore. I want to spend tonight with you without thinking about any of that."

"I want you to be more open with me," she blurted.

His eyes met hers with a pained expression. "I know. I'll try. It's not easy," he answered.

"I'm sure, but it's a big part of your life. I'd just like to understand it better. It seems like she's—harassing you."

Luke sighed. "It's not pleasant. She doesn't believe the Sunset Killers murdered Emma. She doesn't like that it was chalked up to them. She believes someone else did it."

"You didn't sound convinced they killed her either. Has someone found new evidence? Your friend—" Alexis couldn't remember the man's name.

"Langley? No, he hasn't found anything new yet. And I didn't want to talk about it before, but Will Crawley is dead. Any leads he could have given us if we caught him are gone too."

She sighed, taking a moment to process that information. "I know you want to solve this case. I can't begin to understand what it would mean to you, but—" She wanted to reach for him here, but maybe she was overstepping. So, she planted her hands in the back pockets of her jeans. "What if you can't? Is she just going to keep calling you? Are you going to be able to forgive yourself?"

"You know how to cut straight to it, don't you, Miller?" He gave her a weak smile. "The answer to those questions is, 'I don't know.'" He ran his hand through his hair. "I hope I won't have to find out."

He stopped and regarded her for a few moments. "This is a big ask of you. I love you. You make me incredibly happy, but I want you to be happy too. Like you said, this is a big part of my life. I'm not sure when it will be resolved. And you know the grief will always be there. Do you still—"

Her heart was aching as she anticipated his question. Just then her phone blared from her purse, and she was yanked out of that moment.

"I'm sorry. Let me turn it off." But when she checked the screen, she noticed it was her mom calling. She didn't hesitate to answer. "Mom, what's up?"

Luke looked curious, then opened his fridge in search of food.

"Did you ask him yet?" Eileen responded.

"What?" Alexis shook her head in an attempt to get past her confusion.

"About Thanksgiving. Did you ask him yet? You said you were seeing him tonight," her mother said in a cheery voice.

"Mom." Alexis closed her eyes in frustration.

"I just need a quick answer!"

Alexis turned back to Luke, hoping her face conveyed how apologetic she felt. "My mom would like to know if you're joining us for Thanksgiving."

Luke's face was shocked for a quick second. Then he started laughing. And his laughter made her grin. Soon she was laughing too. "You can tell her yes; I will be there."

Alexis fought to talk through the laughter as she conveyed the message.

"What's so funny?" Eileen questioned.

"I'll t-talk to you tomorrow, Mom," Alexis said, ending the call. She strode over to Luke, wrapping her arms around him. "I love you. I have no interest in leaving."

He picked her up so fast, she laughed again. As he carried her to his bedroom, everything felt right once more.

CHAPTER 21

"We have to get you a tree. Christmas is only two weeks away," Alexis said, standing in front of the windows that lined Luke's living room wall. "It would look perfect here!"

She'd brought a box of Christmas decorations over. He knew it was her favorite holiday, and she felt bad that he wasn't spending it with his family. So, he smiled at her from his apartment entryway, where he was hanging a wreath on his door. Honestly, he couldn't care less about Christmas. Emma had loved Christmas too. Since she'd died, the holiday only made him think of her. This year, he was trying hard to enjoy it again for Alexis's sake. He had a girlfriend he loved. He should be making new, happy memories.

And if spending Christmas with Alexis and Eileen was anything like spending Thanksgiving with them, it was sure to be memorable. The mother and daughter were a lean, mean cooking machine. They chatted the entire time they were in the kitchen, never missing a beat in any of their recipes. Occasionally they would allow Luke to do something like baste the turkey, but most of the time he just watched in amazement. They'd both been shocked during dinner when he told them he never watched the Macy's Thanksgiving Day Parade, and he'd been pleasantly surprised to find both women preferred apple pie over pumpkin.

He came back to the present still grinning at the memory. Alexis's face held a faraway gaze now, as if she was imagining his potential tree in all its glory in front of her. It was pouring outside—one of the first major storms they'd had this year. He'd rather be staying warm in bed with her instead of talking about trees.

"We can try, but if we can't find one, we can just spend more time at your place," he responded.

She glanced over at him with a raised eyebrow. "I know what you're trying to do, Kruger. You still need a tree. Maybe we can get a fake one. I don't usually condone fake trees, but it seems like something you'd be more willing to put up with."

He laughed out loud at this. "You know me well, Miller."

His phone rang. He was distracted as he watched her turn her attention to something outside the window, so he forgot to check the number on the screen before answering. "Hello?"

"Stop investigating her death," said a muffled male voice he didn't recognize.

"What? Who is this?" Luke pulled his phone away to look at the screen. Caller ID unavailable. He clicked into detective mode.

"You need to stop. You're going to get other people hurt or killed. You've no idea what you're doing." The voice was rushed and anxious, as if worried someone was listening in.

"Can you tell me more? Are you in danger? Who is going to get hurt?" he responded.

"He's been covering this up a long time. He's not going to stop killing until you let it go. He doesn't care who has to die." The words came out in a flurry.

"Who? I want to help, but I need to know—"

The phone beeped in his ear. The call was lost. Confusion filled his mind. The only thing he'd done related to Emma's case in recent days was to request information from a coroner's office in Alabama regarding Crawley's death. He'd also inquired about Sheridan, whose body was finally found in a shallow grave in the William B. Bankhead National Forest, not far from where Crawley was living. Was his request really enough to set off a murderer who'd already been on the run for years? Still, the phone call was the first real lead he'd had in a long time.

His eyes went to Alexis, to see if she had overheard him talking, but she didn't seem to notice he was there. Her face was pale.

"Hey, what's up?" He strode across the space between them and used a gentle grasp to pull her toward the couch.

She sank down onto the cushion, looking anything but comfortable. She shook her head, taking a deep breath. "You'll think I'm crazy. I think I'm crazy. And then you'll probably be pissed."

He sat down next to her, pulling her close. Tension flowed from her, but she seemed relieved to be held. "I've told you I'll never think you're crazy. And I'll try to keep my temper in check."

She nodded against his chest, then moved away so they were face to face. "I saw Zeke, just now, outside. He was wearing his barista apron. Standing across the street on the sidewalk in the rain. He wasn't looking at me, but was definitely looking at your building. He was just standing there, and then—." Her words became a little more frantic as she finished.

"What?" Luke frowned as he registered what she was saying. He charged from the couch and was at the window in seconds. It was still pouring. There was no one standing on the sidewalk down below.

"I watched him walk away," she completed her thought in a soft voice.

"Are you sure? You said he was in his barista apron?" Luke was already thinking she still felt guilty about Zeke. She'd explained all that after the guy died. Maybe she'd seen someone else and thought it was him. Luke lived on the third floor of his building. She'd been standing right at the window, so it'd be possible for her to see someone at street-level, but the beating rain could have aided in obstructing her view.

"I'm pretty sure. Ugh, it's so easy to doubt myself now! But there's something else, Luke. The day you left for North Carolina to talk to Susan, I saw him when I was having lunch with Kassie. He was across the street. He was dressed like a hipster, driving a car that was way too fancy for a barista to be driving. He didn't see me, at least I don't think so. He went into an office building, and I—I followed him."

"Uh, what?" Luke could feel that temper they'd both mentioned rising. He realized he was frowning and had crossed his arms in front of him. He tried to bring his face back to the neutral expression he'd use when interviewing a source. He loosened his arms, letting them hang by his side. He felt ridiculous.

"You don't look okay," she said, motioning at him.

"Sorry, I'm trying. Keep going."

She looked up to the ceiling for a moment, as if appealing for help from some higher power. "I went into the building, Kassie followed me. He was already upstairs by that point, I'm guessing. I went up to the security desk and asked the guard, but he said he couldn't give me any information. By the time I got back outside, the car was gone. I don't know how he left so fast."

"What made you want to follow him into the building? I know you said it was him, but if I saw a dead guy walk into a building—"

She rolled her eyes. "You're not taking this seriously."

"I am!" He raised his hands in front of him, losing some control of his emotions. "I just don't understand why you would do that!"

"Because I think someone is fucking with me, and I want to know why!" she yelled as she stood up.

He stared, waiting for her to go on. If she believed she'd seen Zeke, he had to wrap his head around it. She rubbed her face with her hands, and in the space of that moment, his mind shot back to the phone call. He needed to figure that out, needed to call Langley to see what the hell was going on back there. His past and present were warring for his attention, but he needed to be here for Alexis now, so the past would have to wait.

"Did you see his body at his funeral?" Luke had to start in the most logical place.

"What?" Her face went pale again. "Oh, no. Someone said he'd been too—" And now she looked like she might be sick, so he crossed the space between them again, taking her back into his arms. "Too, you know, by the car, so an open casket hadn't been an option."

He nodded. "Okay. But his family was there, right?"

"Yes. It seemed like a legitimate funeral. His family was there. His mother was devastated. His friends told stories. People laughed and cried. There were pictures of him when he was little, a teenager, an adult," she recounted.

"Were there any moments that felt off to you? Any little pieces of time that made you pause, even for a second?" he questioned.

Alexis sighed against his chest. "I don't think so, but I was in a fog that day, so I might not have noticed even if there had been."

"When you're comfortable doing so, try to think about that day. See if anything comes to mind. Did you happen to get the contact information for any of his friends or family? Could you remember any of their names?"

"Not his friends, but his mother's first name was Amanda. I have to think about her last name. It was different from his, because she'd gotten remarried at some point. But I think I can remember if I try," she said, her face scrunching in thought.

"Okay, that could help. Was there any kind of program? And do you remember the name of the funeral venue?"

"There was a program. I have it somewhere in my apartment. I can find it for you. The funeral was held at East Lawn Memorial in East Sacramento. His mother lives out of state now. She had his body flown there so she could be close to him." Her voice quaked as she finished this sentence.

"Interesting." A tiny alarm went off in Luke's mind.

"What?"

"That just seems convenient," Luke responded. "He was living here. He must have liked it. You told me at some point he was always out doing things. Sounds like he had friends in the area. Maybe other family members? Do you know anything about his father? It just seems like he'd be buried here."

"He told me his parents got divorced when he was a teenager, but he didn't talk about them much. There were other family members there, but I didn't see or hear anything about his dad, so maybe something happened to him or they weren't on good terms. And, I don't know, it makes sense to me that his mom would want to have him close. I don't know that his burial was something he even thought about. He was so young."

"I guess. But there are two parts to this that could support him still being alive—closed casket and he's not buried here. No one can check his grave." Luke found himself believing this could be real. Maybe Zeke was alive.

Alexis pulled away from him, looking anxious. "I don't know. This is nuts, right? Why would anyone fake their own death? Also, he barely knew me. Why would he be targeting me with his con?"

Luke raised an eyebrow. "You seemed sure it was him. It's very possible that, for whatever reason, someone is deceiving you. I can check on him when I'm back at work."

"I don't know what I'm sure of right now. Seeing him walk into a building seemed more real. Seeing him standing on the street in a barista apron in the rain makes me feel like my mind is playing tricks on me. Maybe I'm trying to see him again, to validate the last time. I think I just need some time to think about it. I have a therapy appointment tomorrow. Maybe that will help. And Brett already looked him up. He couldn't find anything."

"Ah, okay." Why was he bristling at the fact that she'd asked someone else for help? He'd been leaving town when she saw Zeke before. At least she'd asked for help at all. "Well, if you want to give me the funeral program and any information you have about his mother or anyone else who was there, I can look into it."

"I will. Thank you." Alexis stood on her toes to kiss him. "Can we go back to talking about your future Christmas tree?"

He sighed. "Let's go out and see what we can find. It looks like the rain is letting up."

She grinned and went to grab her coat and purse. Luke didn't like how unsettled he felt. Why did she backpedal on seeing Zeke? It was obvious whoever she saw scared her. Luke had tried to be supportive, but it was like his ideas made her talk herself out of her belief. He didn't know why someone would be conning Alexis, but he wanted to put a stop to it.

Damn it! He remembered the phone call as they were walking out the door. He'd have to get in touch with Langley when they got back.

* * *

A few nights later she was reflecting on her talk with Luke as she readied her supplies for class. The rest of their day together had felt awkward, even though he had in fact found a Christmas tree. Her wishy-washy reaction to the Zeke sighting must have frustrated him. She knew he'd been trying to help. But she also knew why she'd backed off the idea by the end of the conversation.

For years, she'd hidden from Kurt Leonard. She'd kept herself in a mental state of fear that she'd hardly survived. For so long there was no proof that she needed to hide. No one had any idea he was involved in the murders of so many of his former employees.

She'd felt crazy. Crazy and alone. She didn't want to feel those things again. She trusted that Luke believed her, but she no longer wanted to believe herself. She didn't want to have another reason to run. She wouldn't acknowledge a new threat—especially one that made zero sense.

She was teaching an intermediate class on the post-World War I modern art movement of Precisionism. It was a combination history/hands-on lesson. She'd studied the movement while in hiding and all but skipped into the classroom she was using that night. Painting lush landscapes was her go-to for bringing herself peace. The sharper lines and industrial look of Precisionism art felt like the kick of darkness and drama she needed to switch things up. *I'm a painting nerd, and I love it!* she sang to herself as she finished setting up.

"Hi, Alexis!" A familiar voice stopped her in her tracks.

"Oh, hi, Geoff," she said in an attempt at sounding pleasantly surprised instead of startled. She hadn't seen him around, which she'd been grateful for. How was she going to tell him she didn't want to continue their friendship?

He was sitting in the second row, but he came up to talk to her as other students began filing in, immersed in different conversations.

"I've been wanting to take one of your classes. This one sounded interesting!"

What is going on with him? Has he ever painted before? He's never mentioned that when I bring it up.

He must have seen the question in her eyes, because he said, "I know it's an intermediate class, but I'm just going to do my best!"

"Oh, okay," she laughed in response. She offered a lot of beginner classes. Why did he want to take this one?

"I'll let you get to it." He gave her a little wave and smile and made his way back to his seat.

She watched him with a covert eye throughout the class, trying at the same time not to let his presence distract her. He stared at the canvas as if lost in thought, every now and then adding a new line or two to his creation. She watched his eyes. They seemed genuine.

All of a sudden, a grin filled his face, as if he had experienced some kind of Precisionism breakthrough. It was a quiet moment in the class. Everyone was busy trying to create their own masterpieces. His smile was so confident and gleaming, it almost hurt to watch. *He must spend a lot on teeth whitening.*

The image of Thomas Loefler flashed through her mind, making her chuckle to herself. Did a man have to have blinding teeth in order to be a powerful professional?

Wait a second. It couldn't be. She added a little more to her painting, then took a slow walk around the room, offering some advice and answering a few questions. She passed Geoff, who grinned up at *her* this time. She nodded toward his painting with a small smile, although she wasn't paying attention to what she saw.

She took the seconds of him looking at her to study his face. She tried to memorize every feature. Her stomach began feeling queasy as she made her way back to the front of the room. She reached into her purse to pull out her phone.

She brought up Titan's website and clicked through to the bio page, finding Thomas Loefler's picture. Was that the same grin as Geoff's? It was a different face, different colored eyes, different hair color and texture. But why did she think that was the same smile?

Was this why Thomas Loefler's face had tugged at something in her brain? That grin? They were both younger-looking white men, but there weren't many similarities after that.

This is crazy. You're looking for things that aren't there. Zeke and Geoff weren't connected. There's no reason why Geoff would be using multiple identities. They just happen to have similar smiles.

Alexis stashed her phone away. She had to get back to work. She threw a glance at the class. Most of the students were still lost in their painting progress, a few were chatting. Geoff was staring at her. She caught a quick moment of an inquisitive frown on his face, but then he sent her another smile. She did her best to return the expression before turning back to her easel.

Her mind buzzed the rest of the night. A class she should have enjoyed was now a blur as she went through the motions. *Forget about the smile. It's not him. First Zeke coming back from the dead. Now Geoff having multiple identities. Ridiculous. It's not your intuition. It's just fear.*

She must have done a halfway decent job for the rest of the class, because almost everyone gave her positive comments as they were leaving, some asking for feedback or clarification on specific parts of their paintings.

Geoff was one of the last ones in the room, still adding to his canvas. There were three more classes in this series. Would he be attending all of them? He strolled up to her with a confident look on his face. She tried to look busy packing up, but he stood waiting.

"This was great! What do you think?" he asked, holding his painting in front of him.

Alexis was surprised at how far he'd gotten—and how good it was. His artwork was full of dark, hard lines, with near-perfect shadowing on skyscraper buildings bathed in moonlight, stylized to look like a true Precisionism piece. She almost felt like she could reach through the paint and feel the stone, steel, and glass with her own fingertips. For a moment, she forgot her reservations against him.

"Wow! You made it sound like this class would be difficult for you. That's impressive." But something about those skyscrapers once again caused that nagging voice in her brain. She'd seen them in pictures, videos and paintings millions of times before. "Manhattan?"

"Thanks! And yes. I love it there. Have you ever been?" he asked, beaming at the buildings.

"No, I've never had the chance." She shook her head. *Titan's office is headquartered in Manhattan. Thomas Loefler's office. No! Stop that! It's just a coincidence.*

"You should go! It's the best place to be." For a second, he had a faraway look in his eye.

So why does he live here then?

He must have seen something in her face, because he gave her the same inquisitive look as when he saw her checking her phone. Then he motioned toward her painting, which she'd forgotten about.

"You made it clear in our conversations how important painting was to you. I never wanted to sound like I was trying to compete. That's why I never mentioned it myself. Anyway, it's obvious I still have a long way to go before I could match your talent."

She glanced back at her artwork. The happiness she should have felt painting that night had been dimmed by her distracted mind, which annoyed her. She'd chosen the Sacramento Delta King riverboat as her subject. Its bright-red paddlewheel and hotel sign were displayed in the foreground. Two shadowy figures leaned against the railing of the deck just beyond.

Alexis didn't like that his presence had taken away the joyful experience painting usually brought her. Her appreciation of his work began to turn to jealousy. Why was he here? He hadn't come to the coffee shop since he showed up at her apartment door asking about Apple Hill. She figured he'd moved on from whatever he wanted out of their relationship.

"I don't know about that," she responded, trying to smile—trying to keep her eyes away from his mouth.

Geoff didn't acknowledge this response, but said, "I wanted to ask you something. Seeing as Christmas is in a couple days, I was wondering if you'd like to go see the Fab Forties lights with me tonight." There was that whitened grin again. How had she never noticed it before? It was so blinding.

She didn't want to deal with rejecting him now. She was tired. It'd been a two-and-a-half-hour class. Two and a half hours of teaching, advising, and painting. She wanted to head to Luke's place, start a Christmas movie, and fall asleep in his arms in his bed. She sighed. She wished she could be there now instead of having a very uncomfortable conversation.

No way around it. He needs to know. But I'm not going to blame myself. I've mentioned Luke so many times. He even saw him in my apartment!

"Geoff, I think you may have the wrong impression of our relationship. I've enjoyed being friends, but I'm dating Luke exclusively. And I have a feeling you want to be more than friends, so I don't think we should spend time together anymore." After the words were out, she wished she could become invisible and sneak out of the room.

She was sure he would deny it—say she was wrong and try to make her feel like an idiot. Kind of like Zeke had before he died.

"That doesn't make sense," he said in a confident tone. "Why would *you* date *him* exclusively?"

"What?" She wasn't sure she'd heard him right.

"Alexis, you probably don't realize this based on how you carry yourself, but you're gorgeous." Geoff motioned with his hands, as if he was an attorney outlining compelling evidence for a jury.

To Alexis, this seemed like a dig covered up by a shallow compliment. She had no idea how to respond.

"You could be with anyone. You deserve a man who will take care of you, treat you how you should be treated, provide everything you could ever want. And someone closer to your age. God, how old is that guy? He looks weathered and angry, like life has trampled him. That's who you want to spend your time with?"

She realized her jaw had dropped. She was floored. Her thoughts ricocheted around in her head. She took a breath, ready to give a scathing speech. But how did she start it? *Okay, words come out of mouth.*

"This will be the last conversation we have. After this, I want you to stay away from me." She felt her adrenaline rush. Now she was ready. "How dare you? I barely know you. You have no right, absolutely *no right*, to comment on who I spend my life with. Also, I don't need anyone to take care of me. I take care of myself. That will always be the case. Luke respects that; he supports and empowers me. And he's been through more shit than you could ever imagine, so if you think that makes him seem weathered, then I feel sorry for you, because you are clearly out of touch with reality. Now, I would like you to leave."

It was his turn for some moments of silence, but instead of surprise, he stared back at her with an all-knowing gaze. "I've talked to him enough times to know exactly what he is. Guys like that crave chaos. They like problems, because they always want to be fixing something, conquering some sort of evil. Whatever life crisis he's having at the moment will get solved. He'll get bored. Or, the drama will wreck him. Either way, he'll start treating you like shit. He'll get angrier and angrier at the situation he's in. He'll move on from you because he won't be able to take it anymore. You'll see."

With that, Geoff turned and was gone. She shivered and finished packing her supplies. She was relieved to see there were other groups of people in the parking lot as she left, with no sign of the real estate agent.

What the actual hell, was all she could think to herself as she headed toward Luke's apartment. She had to tell him about the encounter, but she felt like she would burst apart if she tried to do that now. She watched the sprinkles on her windshield become pelting drops. Soon it would be winter. Time was flowing by, still sending Alexis tests along the way. And if she were being honest, it was starting to feel like she was failing.

CHAPTER 22

"*I'm done playing games with the bitch. I tried doing it the nice way, but I don't have time for this. I don't care how high-profile she is. She's not falling for any of it. We'll have to move forward,*" *Thomas said, meaning he was ready for the abduction.*

"*Of course. I will draw up the plan,*" *Christopher responded.*

"*Which means no more playing Zeke's ghost, right?*" *David asked with an annoyed growl.* "*Standing in the pouring rain was a nice touch.*"

"*The plan will take time to put together, David,*" *Christopher said.* "*It has to be perfect, because there will only be one chance. In the meantime, we will need to use Zeke. Alexis still doubts herself, even though she is becoming stronger every day. She may or may not believe her visions of Zeke, but either way, they are providing a distraction. If she becomes too preoccupied by this distraction, by trying to discover the truth of Zeke, it could still put the wedge we need between her and her loved ones. As we already know, Alexis feels the need to save herself. She won't rely on anyone else to help her.*

"*We know she told Kassidy about the sightings, because Kassidy was with Alexis when she saw David at Titan. It is very likely she also told her boyfriend. This could work in our favor. When she disappears, they will think she ran away again, to hide herself from some new threat. They will look for her, but by then you will all be safely out of California.*"

Truthfully, Christopher put David in the pouring rain to piss him off, but he believed in the importance of Zeke's ghost to this project.

"But what if the Zeke sightings make her run before we can take her?" David muttered.

"Then you will follow her out of town and take her that way." Christopher answered without missing a beat. "We can plan for multiple scenarios."

David gave a quiet sigh of acceptance.

"How will we take her in a way that's peaceful enough not to be noticed? She's sure to raise alarm if Zeke approaches her, and she no longer trusts Geoff," Thomas said.

Which is your fault, because you are unable to control yourself, *Christopher thought to himself, but responded,* "We have to create a shocking situation. Something to completely remove her from her comfort zone. Something to put her in a panic. She won't be thinking clearly enough to analyze who she should take help from. I'll come up with several ideas and get back in touch with you. Please be patient and give me time. As I said, this plan must be airtight."

*   *   *

The holidays went by in a blur. Alexis filled them with such joy, Luke tried to hold onto every moment. He'd let her cover his apartment in decorations, and it was surprising how many ornaments they'd fit on his faux tree. She spent so much time at his place, she'd even added some from her own tree. He'd watched more Christmas movies than he'd seen since Emma died. He felt like Christmas songs were playing from the time he woke up to the time he went to bed—and he didn't hate it.

They had Christmas dinner at her mom's house. On Christmas morning, he had called his parents, who had his brother and sister-in-law over. He'd talked to them for over an hour. It was the longest conversation he could recall in recent memory. Alexis looked proud when he ended the call. He couldn't help but grin back at her. Her support was changing his life for the better.

Even with the continuous celebration, he'd still catch Alexis in moments of contemplative silence. In those brief periods of time, she looked anxious. But when she would break from her thoughts and catch him watching her, she would give him an easy smile and move on to something else.

She never talked about her Zeke sightings. He'd tried to find out anything he could about the man and his family with the information she'd given him. But there'd been no holes in Zeke's story, before or after death. His family seemed legitimate. Luke had a friend who lived an hour's drive from Zeke's mother. He drove to the cemetery Zeke was buried in and even checked the man's headstone. The grave was adorned with fresh flowers. He sent Luke pictures for proof. Luke also checked with the coroner's office and the funeral home. Everything checked out.

A few days after New Year's, Alexis told him about her confrontation with Geoff. He didn't like that she'd waited so long, but he kept that thought to himself.

"I can't believe that piece of—"

"Please don't do anything, Luke. I took care of it." She'd held him tightly and kissed him with such conviction that he'd let it go.

It was hard to focus on an idiotic real estate agent when the holiday hangover left him trying to ignore an idea that had been bugging him since before Thanksgiving. It was absurd, so he tried to shove it to the farthest corners of his mind. But it sat in the forefront, festering like a wound.

He wasn't ready to confront it when his phone rang on a Thursday in late January. Langley's name was on the screen. Luke was on his way to work, but he was running early, so he pushed the button on his steering wheel to answer the call.

"Hey, man! How you been?"

"Busy as always, Krug, but good. Haven't heard from you much. That new girlfriend taking up a lot of your time?" Langley laughed.

"Yeah, and I'm the happiest I've been in years."

This seemed to give Langley pause. "That's great, Luke. You deserve it. Hey, I saw your dad last week. He said Susan camped out at their house for most of a day in the fall? And you flew out just to talk to her? Man, that lady's crazier than I thought!"

His friend's words made him bristle. Yes, Susan annoyed the hell out of him, but he'd never be okay calling her crazy.

"Yeah, it was interesting. She's pretty desperate to hear anything new about Emma's murder since Crawley's death. She said she's had a hard time reaching you on the phone, and when she does, you hang up on her? But I'm sure that's not true."

"Kruger, come on, you know how she is. I can't spend all day fielding calls from her, and I won't tolerate belligerence. I need to ask you about something else. Gray said she talked to you a couple weeks before Christmas? You got some kind of threatening phone call about Emma's case? Why am I just hearing about this? Why didn't you call me first?"

Luke steeled himself. He'd expected this conversation. "I did call you first, but couldn't reach you. I wanted someone there to know, so I called Gray. I didn't feel threatened. It was more a plea for me to stop looking for Emma's murderer."

"Why didn't you tell me later?" Langley's frustration was obvious.

"I didn't want to put another thing on your plate. I know you have a lot going on. I figured Gray would fill you in anyway."

That was true. But it was also true that the nagging idea kept him from calling Langley back.

His friend was silent for a moment. "Luke, you gotta tell me about anything related to Emma's case. I need to know."

"You're right. I'm sorry. Did anyone else get a call similar to mine? Since I'm not the only one trying to figure this out, I was hoping the person might have also called at least one of the detectives." Luke felt like he already knew the answer to this question, but he had to ask anyway.

"No. You were the only one they called." Langley's tone was casual, but Luke thought he heard a tinge of annoyance just below the surface.

"Interesting. Had to be someone with some kind of an in though, right? How else did they get my number?" Luke questioned.

"I don't know, Luke. I think it was a prank. Maybe they knew Sheridan. Maybe he gave it to them before he died," Langley suggested.

"Naw, Sheridan wouldn't share my number without asking. And what reason would they have to pull such a fucked-up prank? I think this could be a real lead."

"A lead to what, Kruger?" Langley snapped, and Luke fell silent. "We have no way to track that call. Gray had nothing to go on! Luke—" His voice calmed. "You've been killing yourself over this for too long. But *now* you'll finally get the chance to live your life—to enjoy that girlfriend who makes you so happy."

"Alexis," Luke said. Langley met her, so why was he acting like she didn't have a name. "And what are you talking about? What's changed that will give me a chance to live my life?" Luke pulled into the parking lot, putting his truck in park but leaving the engine on.

"The FBI found a confession letter two days ago. Crawley admitted to killing Emma. He acted alone. He said Freeman was already in Alabama by that time."

Luke's world felt like it was closing in around him. He took several deep breaths and gripped the steering wheel of his truck to keep himself grounded.

"Why didn't you start this conversation with that?" he managed to ask, although his voice choked on the last word.

"I'm sorry. I should have. I haven't been looking forward to telling you— since I know you didn't believe Crawley killed her," Langley answered with a compassionate tone.

"Are they sure the letter's real? Where did they find it? Crawley's been dead for months." The words flew from Luke as he was still trying to process Langley's response.

"They got a warrant to search his brother's house based on some deleted texts they found on Crawley's phone. They discovered a strong box buried in his brother's attic. Inside were some of Crawley's fake IDs, a stack of hundred-dollar bills, a couple knives we believe he used on some of the victims, a gun we think he also used in some of the murders, and the letter about Emma. He mentioned the other murders, but called her out by name. It sounds like he watched her for a while. He knew who she was, how much she wanted to bust him and Freeman. He must have thought she knew how to find him, so he killed her before she could bring him in," Langley's voice was low and pained as his words ended. "I'm so sorry, Luke. I asked to be the one to tell you, but our new captain wants to call you too, if that's okay."

Luke sat very still in his truck, his head against the rest behind it, his eyes closed. "Emma never said anything about knowing where Crawley was. Yeah, she was just as desperate to find him as the rest of us, but she didn't have any specifics."

"As far as we know," Langley responded.

"She would have told me!" Luke growled.

"Maybe she was trying to involve as few people as possible so as not to bring attention to herself—so she had time to build evidence." Langley sighed. "I don't know."

"That doesn't make sense, Alan," Luke said in one of the rare circumstances he felt the need to use Langley's first name. "Emma wasn't assigned to any case regarding the Sunset Killers. She was one of the deputies to respond to the scenes of a couple of the murders, but she wasn't investigating. And what about that phone call? That person indicated there was still someone trying to cover up Emma's murder. Crawley was already dead by then."

"These are things I can't answer," Langley said. "All I know is that we have a confession letter. I'm hoping this brings you and Susan the closure you've been looking for."

Luke shook his head. This wasn't right. It wasn't true. It couldn't be this simple—not when he'd been so sure there was something else going on.

"Are you okay if Captain Edmonds calls you? He just started a few months ago, but finding Crawley has been a big priority of his. He's a good guy."

"Sure," Luke mumbled.

"I'll let him know. I have to go, but I'll call you again soon." Langley sounded as if he didn't know what else to say.

"Yeah, okay," Luke responded and ended the call.

He managed to get out of his truck, taking a minute to collect himself before turning to walk into the office.

"Morning," Brett said, catching up to Luke's quick stride as he took a long sip of coffee from his travel mug.

"Hey," Luke muttered.

"You okay?" Brett turned and blocked Luke's path, analyzing him with a frown. "You look like you just saw a ghost."

"No, Green. I'm not okay." Luke ran a hand through his hair. He heaved a sigh and fought back the emotion rising in his chest. He was finally ready to tell Brett everything.

He wasn't sure how he got through work that day. After he told Brett the whole story, his friend said he should go home. But he wasn't in the mood to face all his emotions, so he stayed. He didn't have to go into the field, which helped. When his coworkers talked to him, he did his best to pay attention and give them appropriate responses. Captain Edmonds called him at lunchtime, which he was sure Langley had orchestrated. His cases kept him busy, but the day dragged.

Luke left the office the moment his shift was up, feeling Brett's eyes on his back after they said goodbye in the parking lot. He needed to see Alexis. She had a class that night, but she almost always came over afterward. He made himself some dinner and zoned out in front of a mindless television show.

Sometime later, he heard her unlock his front door. She bounded into his apartment, unloading her painting supplies just inside his living room, and came over to the couch to give him a quick kiss. He held onto her as she made to stand back up. She moved her face to look at his.

"Are you okay?" Alexis's eyes changed from joyful to worried in a second, and he felt emotion crashing through him.

The words flowed from him, along with his anger and sadness. He was unable to hold anything back. He felt himself shaking as he related everything. She listened, keeping one hand on his.

"And did Captain Edmonds call you?" she asked when he forced himself to take a breath.

Luke nodded, then ran his hands through his hair. "He did, and he was a nice guy. He was proud of the joint effort by his division and the FBI that tied up all the 'loose ends' of the Sunset Killers case."

"He didn't say 'loose ends,'" she shook her head with a cringe.

"He did. I'm sure he didn't mean to refer to Emma's death as a loose end. He's a police captain doing his job, celebrating a win for his team. I can understand that. He was empathetic enough. I'm just not usually on this side of it." He stood up and started pacing. "I just don't believe it. I have no reason to believe Crawley didn't kill her—certainly no reason to believe any of the words that came out of his mouth. There is no evidence—of anything, except that goddamn confession letter. But that phone call telling me to stop investigating her death—something's still going on. Someone's out there still trying to cover something up."

Luke turned around to look at Alexis. She was still on the couch looking up at him. Her eyes were troubled. It was hard to get a read on what he saw in them.

"Am I crazy?" he asked with sincerity.

She stood with a small smile and walked toward him. "If you've never thought I was crazy, how could I possibly think you are?"

He nodded, once again grateful for her. "If Crawley didn't kill her, someone else created that confession letter. But the FBI analyzed the writing and determined it to be Crawley's."

"So, someone forced Crawley to write it before he died?" Alexis suggested.

"That's what I'm thinking. Then they kept it for a convenient time and planted it in his brother's attic. The other things in the box were Crawley's, but they could have taken those from him when they killed him. I doubt he would have had them on him, so the person might have known him well enough to know where he stored them."

"Do you know of anyone who would want to frame him and have such easy access to his life?" she asked.

"I doubt Crawley had many friends. I'm guessing most people would have wanted him in prison or dead. And I'm sure he never let anyone get that close to him. I don't know what his relationships with his family were like." He put his face in his hands. "What am I supposed to do? Everyone else considers this case as good as done. Accepting that Crawley killed her would make life easier. But I can't do that."

"I don't know, but I'm here for you," she whispered with a sigh. He kissed the top of her head and allowed himself to just breathe.

CHAPTER 23

It was painful to watch Luke over the next few weeks. It was warm for February, and Alexis found herself getting annoyed easier because of it. She knew it was probably just fool's spring. Sacramento would cool down again and get some more rain, but in the moment, winter already seemed to be out the door. She felt robbed. Luke's inner turmoil spiked, as if his anger and frustration were also tied to the temperature. She suggested he see his therapist. He went once, but seemed too flustered to go back. This made Alexis nervous, because therapy had always helped him in the past.

Then there was the pain caused by an outside source. Susan had called him at least six times since the police announced the confession letter and closed the case for good. From what Luke understood, Susan didn't believe the confession because she didn't believe Crawley overdosed—much like Luke's own opinion.

"But she probably wouldn't feel content with any outcome," Alexis said with a sigh.

"Yeah. She just wants her daughter back," Luke responded, exhaustion flowing from him.

Alexis understood. She still wanted her dad back.

All of Luke's energy went to his work. Alexis knew him well enough to know he would never let that slip. But when they were together, he would stare into space or fall asleep on the couch or bed next to her. His depression was obvious. She didn't know what to do other than try to get him to talk.

They went to dinner at Kassie and Brett's house. Both friends now knew the entire story of Emma's murder and everything that happened since. Luke was quiet and barely touched his food. Alexis felt awkward. The evening dragged.

"Hey," Kassie said as she pulled Alexis aside when she and Luke were getting ready to leave. "I know you love Luke. We love him too, but it's not right for you to shoulder his grief alone. You're dealing with your own stuff. He needs to talk to someone."

"I tried to encourage that, but he won't. I don't know what else to do. I can't let him be alone in this," her voice cracked as she responded.

"Maybe we can call his parents or his brother? They could fly out. Someone has to get through to him," Kassie suggested.

"That's a good idea." Alexis finally felt a small glimmer of hope. "I'll call his parents tomorrow."

Kassie nodded, hugging Alexis like she might never see her again. "Good luck, Lex. Please let me know how we can help. We're here for anything you guys need."

Brett gave her a sad smile as she hugged him and walked out the door. Luke was already waiting by the car, a shadow in the darkness. For a moment, she felt a random spike of fear, a picture of another figure floating through her mind.

"Calm down," she ordered herself and went around to the driver side of her sedan.

The next morning, she called Luke's parents. The worry in his mother's voice was obvious. His father booked their flight while they were on the phone. They'd be flying in on Tuesday—just a couple days away. Alexis heaved a sigh of relief. She knew his relationship with his parents wasn't always the best, but she hoped his family could provide him a comfort no one else could. A small part of her began to doubt her decision to call them, so she decided to wait to tell him.

Her mother called her later that day. Eileen knew everything as well. "Babe, you've been distant. You know I like Luke. He's a wonderful man, but he seems like he needs more help than just you can give him right now. You need to take care of yourself too. Your healing journey is ongoing, just like his."

"Mom, what are you telling me to do? Break up with him because he's going through a dark time?" she snapped, well aware that she was overreacting, but it felt good to let a little anger out.

"No, sweetheart. But maybe he just needs—some time—to get some help." Her mother's voice was caring, but firm.

"I've gotta go. This is too much right now." She tried to hide her shaking voice, because she was sure she'd break down.

"Okay, honey. I love you."

Alexis was sitting in her car, ready to drive to the Painting Palate. She felt like hurling her phone out the window.

"You need to tell her to stop calling you." The words spilled from Alexis when she got back to Luke's apartment late that afternoon. She'd walked in to see him holding his head in his hands. He'd just gotten off the phone with Susan. Right away, she felt bad about the demand. She'd been trying not to nag about the phone calls. But why shouldn't she say something? She loved him, and this was tearing him apart. She was allowed to express her opinion.

"What?" he responded, as is he hadn't heard her. He'd only slept a few hours the night before. She knew exhaustion was overruling most of his senses right now.

"You need to tell her to stop calling you. And if she won't, you need to stop answering her calls. Maybe block her number if you have to." She tried to make her voice firm, but still empathetic. How the hell did she do that?

"I can't do that, Alexis," he mumbled back.

"Why? This whole thing is killing you, Luke! And she's the worst part of that!"

"You're being dramatic. I'm fine. I'm dealing with grief. This is how grief is. And Susan has no one else to talk to. I have to be there for her." His eyes were dark. His tall frame was hunched in on itself where he sat on his couch.

A sinking feeling filled her. He never talked to her like that. She didn't want to be talked to like that. She paused for a moment. Her feelings were pieces of the trauma Kurt Leonard gave her. She had to step back and see beyond that for a moment.

Luke had no idea what he was doing to himself—what Susan was doing to him. Before she could stop herself, she said, "I don't think this is what Emma would want—you torturing yourself and allowing her mother to do the same. I didn't know her, but I'm sure she wouldn't be okay with this. I know you don't want to accept that Crawley killed her, but—"

"No, you didn't know her. Please don't talk about her. It's great to know you're just another person who thinks I should accept Crawley as her murderer and get on with life." His voice was full of sarcasm and hurt.

His response stopped her for a moment, but she needed to push forward. She took several deep breaths. "I love you, Luke. It hurts to see you like this. I know what you believe, and that's fine. I support you. But you aren't doing anything about it now. It feels like you're giving up." She moved toward him as she finished saying this.

"Why aren't I allowed to process this?" He stood up and crossed his arms in front of his chest, as if he needed to protect himself.

This wasn't Luke at all. She wanted Luke back. That's what gave her the courage to keep talking. "That's the thing. I don't think you're processing it. I think you're wallowing and beating yourself up, and you're letting Susan do the same. Talk to me, to your friends, to your therapist. Do whatever you need to do to process. Come up with a plan of attack to find Emma's real killer, like you used to do. Stop blaming yourself for everything, because I know that's what you're doing."

He stared at her for a few moments. She forced herself with every fiber of her being to stand there, holding her ground.

"I'm doing the best I can. I can't just drop someone who needs my support. I wish you could understand that. And what fucking plan am I supposed to come up with? Any leads I had are long dead." He ran his hand through his hair and looked away from her. "I think I need a little space." He made to go past her to his front door.

"It's your apartment, Luke, I'll go." Her heart was slamming in her chest. If she were being honest, it would be a relief to get out of there. He wasn't getting it. She didn't know how else to help.

She walked to his couch, where she'd left her purse, casting a quick glance out the window. It felt like someone poured ice-cold water over her. Zeke was standing outside again. He was across the street, and he was staring straight up at Luke's apartment.

Alexis turned, trying to find the words to tell Luke to look out the window, but he was already retreating into his bedroom. He said nothing as he went. A fresh bout of anger replaced her anxiety. She grabbed her purse and slammed his front door closed, punching the elevator button with her pointer finger.

Once outside, she sprinted to the nearest crosswalk, which was in the opposite direction of where she'd parked her car. She tapped her right foot until she was able to cross. It was ridiculous, but she was running after Zeke again. When the crosswalk light changed, her feet started walking.

She reached the building he'd been standing in front of. People were milling about. Several cars honked as another cut them off to take a last-minute right turn. There was so much noise. She took a deep breath, closing her eyes for just a moment. She opened them again, scanning the surrounding area. She started walking. He could be long gone for all she knew, but since this person seemed hell bent on torturing her, maybe he'd linger.

She patted the small pocket on the front of her purse. Her pocket knife and whistle sat just inside. She used each step to mentally play back some of the self-defense refresher videos she'd been watching. This was a crazy thing to do. Insane. But here she was.

Luke lived on the border of the downtown and Midtown districts of Sacramento. Alexis walked several blocks down J Street, Midtown unfolding on her right. She stopped short when she saw Zeke again on the corner of 22nd Street. He must have known she was following him, but he ignored her as he turned the corner. She hesitated, but the streets were full of cars and some pedestrians. What was he going to do to her out here?

You're an idiot, she said to herself. Still, she picked up her pace to try to catch up with him.

When she saw him turn down an alley, her nerves picked up again. She might be an idiot, but she still cared about self-preservation. She stopped at the corner and peered down the pavement. Zeke was nowhere in sight. She fought with herself for a minute, but then turned around and went back the way she had come.

She should run. A man who pretended to die was stalking her. Right? Was she losing it? No, she'd definitely seen him this time. And if so, she should run. Her mind raced and she couldn't get a strong hold on any one thought. She knew deep down that she didn't want to waste more years of her life hiding from a threat—this time one that she couldn't explain. But she had to keep herself safe, keep herself alive.

She walked past Luke's building in a fog. She thought about going back up to tell him what was going on. But he was angry. He needed space. So, she kept walking.

How was this going to work out? How was Luke going to get back to himself? And if he couldn't, and she couldn't talk to him about what was happening to her because she didn't want to add more stress to his life, was that a viable relationship? She didn't think so. Her heart ached as she wondered if they both just needed a break.

* * *

Luke woke up on Monday feeling hung over, but he hadn't had anything to drink. Instead, after Alexis left, he raged around his apartment, trying to ignore the immediate feelings of guilt about the way he'd talked to her.

You're such an asshole, he thought to himself now.

He couldn't keep doing this to her. Not having Alexis in his life sounded like another darkness he didn't want to explore, but was their relationship good for her with his trauma tearing them apart? She deserved much more. He remembered the days before they were together when he told himself that same thing, but he'd pursued her anyway. He hadn't expected to love her like this though. His relationship with her was the only thing bringing him a shred of happiness right now. He didn't want to let her go.

So, a selfish asshole, he corrected himself.

If he started trying harder to move forward, maybe he could save things. He would force himself to accept that Crawley killed Emma. He could do that.

He grabbed his phone and clicked her name in his recent calls. He knew she wouldn't be at work yet. But the phone rang several times. He started to wonder if she'd answer.

"Hey," her voice was light when she picked up.

"Hi, Miller." Somehow his habit of calling her by her last name seemed insincere now. "I'm sorry about yesterday. I was a jerk. I know you were trying to help. This has been rough." That felt like a lame description.

She was silent. Was she still there?

"I know it has," she said, her words slow. "But yesterday you seemed like a different person. I couldn't get through to that person."

The confession stung, even though it made sense. He hung his head, trying to think of what to say. He should end this. He didn't want to. He loved her. He was dragging her through his mess. He fought with himself. She waited without a word.

"Alexis—"

"Luke, I love you—" The tone of her voice was unsure. She must have been having the same fight with herself. Like him, she didn't know how to resolve it.

"I love you too—so much." He took a deep breath, making a choice. "I'm going to start getting help. I'm going to make an appointment with my therapist for this week. She said she has openings. I'm not gonna keep going like this."

"That's good. And your parents are flying in tomorrow." The transition was random, and her voice was rushed.

"What?"

"I called them yesterday. I didn't know how else to help you. I figured you'd get comfort from your parents if from no one else." Now she sounded remorseful.

"I—God, my mom must be losing her mind. I wish you hadn't done that. I know I haven't been easy to deal with—"

"No, the way you've been acting can't be described as only 'not easy.'" He heard a flash of anger in her words.

Luke sighed. "I know, but my parents didn't handle their visit from Susan well. They have a lot of guilt about what I've been dealing with, because they don't understand it all. And now they probably think I'm on the edge."

"Then maybe you need to have some frank conversations with them, so they *do* understand what you've been going through. They're your parents, Luke. They want to be there for you."

"That's not something I'm good at doing with them." He was working hard to keep his calm. She was trying to help again. But he felt like seeing his parents and trying to put them at ease would make things worse.

"Maybe this is the right time to get better at it," she said, her voice a mix of firm confidence and empathy.

He covered his eyes with his free hand as he thought. He didn't want to lose her. He said he was going to do the work.

"Okay. When do they get here?"

CHAPTER 24

On Wednesday, Alexis helped Luke cook dinner for his parents at his apartment. She was nervous about meeting them under awkward circumstances, but they welcomed her as soon as she shook their hands. She wondered if maybe they were just thrilled Luke had found someone new, but they seemed interested as she told them about her jobs, her relationship with her mother, and a bit about her childhood.

"Did you get a chance to talk to them yesterday?" she asked Luke as they prepped the ingredients for her mother's green curry chicken recipe. His parents were chatting on his couch with glasses of wine. There wasn't much separation between his kitchen and living room, and no actual walls dividing the two, so she tried to keep her voice low.

"They were pretty tired yesterday. My mom just seemed relieved to see me alive," Luke tried to laugh in response, but the noise was hollow.

Shame ran through her, but it turned into a mixture of guilt and light anger. "Luke, I'm sorry. I—"

"It's okay, Alexis." He gave her a small smile. "I'll talk to them tomorrow morning." Then he turned to get the chicken from the refrigerator.

She hated this feeling. They were so off. She couldn't grasp all the thoughts and feelings running through her head. It bothered her that he hadn't called her "Miller" since their conversation Monday morning. It felt like the universe was chipping away at their relationship. The lack of her nickname was one of the little pieces falling away.

The dinner was comfortable enough. Luke was quiet, but he seemed to laugh for real at a couple things she said. His parents were happy to keep talking to her, although Luke's mother gave him what Alexis was sure were questioning looks a few times throughout the meal. Alexis reached for Luke's hand at one point, and he took it without hesitation. In that moment, it felt like everything was fine. She needed to talk to him again, but she wasn't sure how to do that with his parents there.

Luke didn't have a guestroom in his apartment, so his parents were staying at a nearby hotel. She wondered if she'd have time with him after they left for the night. But as the clock neared eleven, she found herself falling asleep where she sat on his couch. She decided it was time to go. She hadn't planned on staying the night. And it felt weird to go into his bedroom to sleep with his parents sitting in the other room.

"It was so nice to meet both of you. I hope I can see you again while you're here," she said as she stood up and slung her purse over her shoulder. She tried to give them her biggest smile.

"We'll insist on that," his mother responded, giving her a hug. She liked his parents. It'd be nice to think of them as future in-laws, but right now that was hard to picture.

"I told them where Valle Coffee is, so you might be seeing them tomorrow," he said in a low voice when he'd walked her to the door.

"That would be nice. Their order will be on the house." She smiled up at him, reaching her hand to his cheek. He closed his eyes for a moment. When he opened them, she saw so much there: exhaustion, anguish, but still love.

"Do you work tomorrow night?" he asked.

"Yeah, a class." She could feel herself frowning. She loved teaching, but this time she wished she could pass it off to someone else.

"Okay, call me when you're done," he nodded, kissing her.

Why did it feel like they were going to be apart for a long time? Like she should already be missing him?

"Luke, I think we need to take some time to talk, just work through things," she said in little more than a whisper.

He studied her eyes for several seconds. "Yes, we should. After my parents leave?"

"Okay. Night." She kissed him again.

As she walked down the hall to the elevator, she heard him murmur, "I love you, Miller."

Some of the weight came off her shoulders at hearing her last name. She turned with a smile. "Love you too, Kruger."

She felt her face light up when his parents walked through the shop's doors the next morning.

After they'd greeted her and placed their orders, Jacob said, "We're flying home tomorrow morning, but thank you for this, Alexis. We needed this time with Luke. We're going to sit down tonight and have a conversation about what he's been going through. I think it will help."

"I'm so glad," Alexis answered, feeling elated.

"And we're glad he has you. We were hoping he would find someone when his heart was ready. He made an exceptional choice," Linda added.

Alexis felt her face burn with a blush. She also felt the knot in her stomach tighten. Her relationship with Luke was shaky. She wasn't sure it was the best time to accept this praise.

She managed to thank his mother with a small smile.

As she looked away from the woman, her eyes were drawn to a figure across the street. Zeke was dressed in casual clothes and was staring into the coffee shop. She whipped her head from one side to the other to see if any of her coworkers saw him, but they were busy with their own tasks. She wanted to scream for them to look. He'd never been so bold before. She felt the color drain from her face as he nodded twice, then turned and walked away.

"Are you okay?" Jacob's face was full of concern, reminding her very much of his son in that moment.

She took a deep breath, willing her heart to slow down. "Y-yes, sorry! I just thought I saw someone."

Both Krugers gave her a hug before picking up their drinks. *I hope I'll see you again someday*, she silently said as they left.

The rush of customers kept her from going outside to see if she could find Zeke. She felt like she was pushing some kind of limit. Someone wanted something from her. She had to tell Luke. With their already fragile relationship, she wanted to tell him before going to Kassie and Brett. No excuses. She needed to talk to him as soon as possible.

Alexis took a sick day from Valle Coffee on Friday and called Luke in the morning, hoping he would have already dropped his parents off at the airport. Whether they went into their personal issues or not, she would tell him about Zeke.

"Hey, Miller," he said, and she found herself smiling. But something wasn't right. There was a lot of background noise, and he sounded like he was walking right through it.

"Hey. Where are you?"

"The airport," he responded, something like excitement in his voice.

"Oh, sorry. I thought your parents would have left already."

"They did. I'm flying out in a bit," he said in a rush.

"What? Where are you going?" She frowned to herself.

"Shit. My brain isn't working well right now. Susan called me again last night after my parents went to their hotel—"

Alexis cringed. He hadn't told Susan to stop calling.

"—and she said she found something I need to see, so I'm heading there now."

"What is it?" Alexis sighed. After the constant hell Susan put him through, he would still jump on a plane at her first request.

"She didn't want to elaborate over the phone," he said. When she didn't respond, he continued, "I was skeptical too, but it sounds urgent. It has something to do with Emma or the case."

"But she couldn't give you any information about it?"

"No." Luke's voice carried the smallest note of annoyance. "But I'm doing what you suggested. I'm trying to do something to find her real killer. I'm hoping to only be there through the weekend." He seemed to be offering the last part up as some sort of compromise, but it didn't minimize the frustration building inside her.

"That's not what I meant. I meant coming up with some kind of plan. I'm sorry, but I don't get how you can drop everything for some random thing she has for you, after how she's treated you. She hasn't earned that."

He was quiet for a few moments before saying, "It's not about her or what she's earned. It's about this being the last lead I have left. She wouldn't ask me to come if she didn't think it was important. I know you don't understand—"

"I think you're the one who's not understanding, Luke. She's done so much damage to you. Why couldn't you have asked her for more information before flying across the country?"

"I don't want to do this right now. I know how you feel about her. I get it, but this is something I need to do. I'm sorry you're pissed I didn't tell you I was leaving." His words were somewhat drowned by the noise around him.

"You know what? I am pissed. You're flying across the country *again* because of her. And it doesn't seem like you were going to tell me, which also pisses me off, but I'd rather deal with that than deal with how you'll be after you see her," Alexis seethed.

"Sorry you don't want to deal with me," he spit the words into the phone in a harsh whisper. "This is my life, and if you can't *deal* with it—"

"I meant I don't want to deal with the pain you'll be in when you get back. You just said you were going to start doing the work. This is going to set you back!" She was yelling now, trying to force him to hear her.

"I don't need you to be my therapist," he said with a growl.

"Someone needs to be! You won't talk to yours!"

"Wow, I'm going now," he said. "I'll call you later."

"No, wait!" She was fuming, and she made a choice. "We need to take some time apart. This is your focus right now. I can't keep nagging you. And it's been so tense and exhausting. I can't keep doing this. You need to be able to do what you want. I have my life. I need to be living it. I love you, but this isn't working right now."

Her anger subsided. She wanted to take the words back right after they flew from her mouth, but she stopped herself. This was the best thing for both of them. It felt horrible, but it felt right.

He was quiet for so long, she only knew he was still there because of the sounds of the airport behind him. "Alexis, I love you. I didn't want to give up on us, but—" His voice sounded the way she felt. Her eyes welled up with tears.

"I know."

She heard a voice over a microphone behind him. He must be at his gate.

"I have to go." His voice shook with the words. "I'm sorry."

"Me too," she whispered, and the call ended.

Tears ran down her face as she slumped back on her couch. This was what she needed. She could move on and deal with her own problems—once she could get past the feeling that someone was ripping out her heart.

* * *

This better be something. It better be what we need, Luke said to himself, threatening the universe as he trudged onto the plane.

He tossed his suitcase into the carry-on compartment over his seat, earning a scowl from a nearby flight attendant. He put his hand up as an act of apology. He had to compartmentalize the pain for now. He had plenty of time to come back to it in the future.

You fucked up. You just let go of one of the best things you've ever had. You were supposed to do the work so you could fight for her. Is that what this is?

It had to be. And what if Susan somehow had the answer to Emma's case? Then what? Who would he share that victory with when he got back home?

CHAPTER 25

On Saturday, Alexis's mood was foul. She had a mid-morning painting class to get to, but her up-and-down emotions were wreaking havoc on her motivation to do anything. She was pissed at Luke, then she missed him so much it hurt, then she felt at peace with her decision, then something would happen to set her anger off again. She was exhausted. She hadn't slept much. She hadn't told Kassie or her mom about the breakup. She had a therapy appointment the next day, and felt like she needed that interaction before she could tell anyone else.

When she finally left her apartment, lugging her bag of supplies, she was of the mentality that she just needed to get through the day. She could be professional at work. She would fall apart again when she was back home.

She walked down the street toward her car, her eyes cast down, her bag slamming into her thigh with every step. She cursed when she tripped over an exposed tree root as she moved toward the curb. She righted herself and gasped as she looked up at where her car was parked on the corner across the street.

"What the fuck?" She felt the color drain from her face. Her heart picked up speed. Her car was angled in an unnatural way. There was glass all over the ground. She could see bent metal and at least one flat tire in the back.

Her legs seemed to move of their own accord. She jogged across the street, her bag almost sending her to the ground with its weight. She stopped just behind her sedan, her hands flying to her face. Smashed. Windows, doors, mirrors, the roof. It looked like someone had driven straight into the left side of her car. But there was no one around, no other damaged vehicle. She flung her gaze all around her, finding it hard to breathe. She saw no one.

"I—" she started to say to herself, feeling like she needed to sit down. Who was she supposed to call first? Her brain had shut off.

She rummaged through her purse, trying to find her phone. It wasn't in its usual spot. Alexis cursed again as she unzipped the front pocket and shoved her hand in. Now she remembered putting it there when she'd grabbed it off her kitchen counter before heading out the door. She yanked it free. She heard the clunk of several objects hitting the pavement. Her pocket knife, whistle, and a couple old receipts had fallen out of the same pocket. As she bent to pick them up, her purse slipped off her shoulder and fell to the ground.

"Shit!" She wanted to cry as she shoved the loose items into the pocket of her jacket and slung her purse back over her shoulder. She brought up her phone menu to look for her insurance company's number. She was having trouble remembering its name as her mind raced.

"Alexis?" a familiar voice called out. She looked up to see Geoff sitting in his idling car in the street. "I was just going to meet with a building owner when I saw you. What happened?" His eyes were wide, his voice quiet.

"I—I don't know. I walked up and it was like this." She made a weak motion toward her totaled car.

"Where were you going? Can I give you a ride? I'll help you get in touch with your insurance company when we get there." His voice was concerned.

"I have a painting class, but I—" She should stay with the car, right? Would the insurance come right out? She needed to have it towed, right? Did she need to call the police?

"Alexis, I know I was an asshole to you before. I said horrible things about your boyfriend. I was incredibly jealous. I'm sorry. You don't have to have anything to do with me after this, but please let me help you." He got out of his car. She stood there, her phone still in her hand as she watched him take pictures of the damage with his own phone.

"We can send these to your claims department. I can help you call whoever you need," Geoff said, watching her as if he wasn't sure what he should do next. His car still sat running in the street.

"My class starts in a few minutes," was all she could seem to make herself say as anxiety threatened to make her spiral. She didn't feel safe.

"Okay, let me take you there. You can make your excuses, and I'll help you with this. Or you can call someone else to help you. I just don't want to leave you here." His words were desperate.

Yes, that sounds like the right thing to do. "Um—sure." She nodded, forcing her feet to start moving toward his car, casting one last defeated look toward hers.

He opened the door for her, putting her bag of supplies and her purse in the back as she buckled herself in. She looked around. How was he so clean? There were no random items laying around, the opposite of how her sedan always looked.

My car, she thought to herself and closed her eyes for a moment in an attempt not to cry. How was she going to afford another one? She'd paid this one off long ago. She was sure her insurance company wouldn't give her much for it.

She heard him get in the car beside her. She opened her eyes with a sigh.

"It's going to be okay. Everything will work out," she heard him say as he started driving.

Through his mirror, she watched her destroyed vehicle disappear behind them. She told him where to go, and she saw him pass her a pitiful glance.

She was starting to calm down a little as they approached the community center. She could see her students entering the building, canvases in hand. Then she saw another person leaning against the stucco, ignoring those around him. Her heart started racing again.

"Wait, could you—" she managed to get out. Geoff made no sign of slowing to find a place to park. Zeke gave one short wave at the car.

"Geoff, what—" she said, turning to look at his face, which had changed to a look of stone. As they drove by the building, she swiveled in her seat and saw Zeke getting in a black car behind them—the same black car she'd seen the day she followed him into the office building.

She grabbed for the door handle, but she couldn't get it to open. He'd locked all the doors when they got in. She frantically searched for the manual locking lever where it should be by the door handle, but it wasn't there. She went to hit the unlock button by her window, but it had been removed. He had altered his car to keep her from getting out. Her breaths became more rapid as her mind buzzed. She couldn't have a panic attack now. She had to get out.

"Sorry, Alexis. You'll be missing your class today. I called and let them know you've got the flu and you're hoping to be back next week."

"What are you doing?!" She yanked on the handle again, but nothing happened.

"Drop your phone," Geoff muttered.

"What?" she answered, but then realized she was still clutching her phone.

"Drop it!" he yelled and moved something on his leg. She looked down to see a gun resting there.

"What the hell are you doing?" she jumped, her phone clattering to the ground without her even meaning to let it go. "Did you destroy my car?"

"I'm abducting you," he shrugged back. "And there are certain risks to parking your car on a city street."

She undid her seatbelt, throwing a glance in the rearview mirror. Zeke was still right behind them.

"Put that back on." He slammed on the breaks and her chest flew into the dashboard. "You will not draw attention to yourself."

She let out a gasp of pain, but put the belt back on. She sat for a moment, her adrenaline rushing. It was strange how clear her mind felt now that she understood her situation. Yes, she was terrified, but she'd be able to make a plan. She'd trained herself for possibilities like this. She wasn't going without a fight.

You can try to disable him somehow, but you have to do that without getting yourself seriously hurt or killed.

Alexis looked to his dashboard and noticed it indicated the passenger-side airbag was on. She might need that.

Geoff, or whoever the hell he was, turned onto 19ᵀᴴ Street.

"Where are we going?" Her voice shook.

"A place much more civilized than this one," he said back, a notable tone of disgust in his voice.

Her mind was running through her options. She needed to get out of the car. Could she disable him enough to get into the driver seat to take control of it? As they approached the freeway overpass, he made no move to go in a different direction. A thought popped into her head. Nineteenth Street would soon become Freeport Boulevard. Sacramento Executive Airport, the smaller of Sacramento County's two airports, was on Freeport Boulevard. Was he taking her to the airport? Should she wait until they got there? She had no way of knowing if that was their destination, although it would make sense if he wanted to get far away fast. His painting popped into her mind. Manhattan. Was he taking her to New York?

Once he was out of the car and able to fight back with his entire body, it might be harder for her to get away. Zeke was still behind them. It would be easier for her to defend herself against just one person.

She put her hands in her jacket pockets and slumped into the seat, trying to look more pathetic. Geoff cast her a short glance before looking back at the road. To her surprise, she felt metal on her skin. Her pocketknife and whistle still sat in her pocket, crammed in with the old receipts from her purse. She wanted to cheer. The universe had done something right amidst all the insanity. Trying not to let on to her elation, she kept up her slouch as they crossed through the intersection and started under the overpass.

Without letting herself think too much about it, she whipped the whistle out, undid her seatbelt, and leaned as close to his ear as she could, blowing hard into the mouthpiece.

"What the fuck!" he screamed, as the high-pitched sound reverberated around them both. He gripped his ear with his hand. The car swerved to the right. As he tried to right it, she plunged the pocketknife into his leg, wanting to throw up as soon as she felt it going through his skin and into his muscle.

He yelled in pain. The car swerved again. There were several vehicles going in the opposite direction, but he managed to miss them. She kept the knife in his leg, but bent over and snatched her phone from the ground. She shoved it in her back pocket, hoping it would stay there.

"You bitch!" he yelled. She made the mistake of looking down at his leg, where blood was starting to ooze.

Alexis slammed her seatbelt back into place, grabbing the steering wheel from him as he tried to fix their course again. Whether on purpose or not, he put his foot down on the gas. She felt her stomach drop as they picked up speed. She pulled the wheel as hard as she could to their right. As the car sailed toward the sidewalk, she tried to loosen her body as much as possible, hoping the airbag would help her.

Time seemed to slow as they flew over the sidewalk, crashed through a chain link fence, and smashed into one of the overpass's support pillars. The airbag exploded to life in front of her. She tried to keep her breathing regulated to avoid an anxiety attack. She shook her head, trying to focus, but she was seeing life through some kind of filter. There was loud ringing in her ears.

She tried her door handle again, but it was still locked. She found her seatbelt and unbuckled, blood on her hand making the process difficult. Geoff was muttering in confusion and pain next to her. She didn't stop to see the extent of his injuries. She raised herself up as much as possible, leaning over and putting her full weight onto his hunched back.

He growled in surprise. Alexis reached toward his door, trying to hold herself on him as he began to fight back. Her hand moved blindly as she searched, her anxiety beginning to catch up with her now.

"Bitch! Get off!" he yelled, using his body to slam back on hers. She stretched her arm a little farther and found what she was looking for. She pushed all the buttons she could, willing the right one to work. She heard the distinct click of the car doors unlocking. Her breath came out in a whoosh.

She threw herself off of him and at the passenger door. He was grabbing at her clothes, trying to dig his nails into her flesh. She didn't know where the gun had gone. Her fingers found her door handle just as he yanked on her hair. She cried out in pain, but pulled the handle hard, pushing at the door as it opened slowly, the damage from the accident impeding it. She reached around, punching him on the nose.

He cursed again, but let go, giving her enough time to throw her shoulder at her door. It flew open. She fell onto the ground. She scrambled to stand up, but stumbled back down to her knees, dodging the twisted fence wrapped around the front of the car. She could see people not far away. They were yelling and running toward her.

Before she could move, Zeke's car drove up alongside Geoff's. He jumped out and yanked Geoff's door open, grunting as he began dragging the man out of the smashed vehicle and toward his own.

"You stupid bitch," Zeke growled at Alexis as he did this. "This isn't over. The end is coming for you."

"Who the hell are you? Why have you been following me? What do you want with me?" she yelled, her voice cracking.

He didn't respond, busy with Geoff. She stayed in a ready position in case he approached her, but as soon as he had stuffed Geoff into his car and slammed the door, he rounded the hood toward the driver side.

"Hey!" A man screamed from just behind her. She wanted to turn and look, but she didn't dare take her eyes off Zeke. The moment he was inside, he sped away, leaving her more confused than when this nightmare began.

She remembered her phone and punched in 911 just as the yelling stranger and several others reached her.

"Are you okay?" the man asked. "What happened?" He surveyed the crunched car.

"I have no idea," she answered both questions, her whole body beginning to shake as the operator came on the line.

"911, what is your emergency?" The voice was female and calm. She tried to hold onto these observations as she felt herself slipping.

"Two men just tried to kidnap me," she managed to say. Then it was as if her brain and body stopped working. She sat down hard on the ground, her phone dropping from her hand.

A woman who had just arrived at the scene knelt down and was talking to her, but she couldn't hear the words through the rushing in her ears.

The man who had spoken to her first picked up her phone. She could see him talking to the operator, concern etched on his face.

"They're on their way," he said, the words finding root in her ears. "What's your name? Can we call anyone else for you?"

"I need to call my friend. I need my phone!" She knew her voice sounded desperate and strange. He handed the device to her.

"Kassie," she choked out the name when Kassidy answered on the second ring.

"Lex, what's wrong?"

"Geoff and Zeke. They just tried to kidnap me."

"What? Where are you?" Kassie's tone was frantic. Alexis could hear her moving through a room, Brett's voice in the background.

"Under an overpass on 19TH Street, just before it becomes Freeport," she stammered, realizing how insane that sounded.

"I'm on my way. Are you safe? Is anyone with you?"

"I'm safe. There are some people here. Kassie—my mom."

"I'll call her. Should I call Luke?" Kassie responded quickly.

"No," she said and started to cry, feeling like an idiot in front of the growing group of people she didn't know. "Luke is gone. Please hurry."

CHAPTER 26

Luke's excitement over whatever Susan had to show him had waned by the time he landed in North Carolina. After all these years, after all her pleas for him to solve the case or beg others to, he had all but convinced himself she couldn't hold the key. They'd made a plan for him to go straight to her house on Saturday morning, because she refused to see him anywhere else. He spent Friday night at his parents' house, which brought him a small amount of comfort.

His relationship with them was a little easier since their talk in Sacramento, in which he'd unloaded everything he'd been dealing with in the five and a half years since Emma's death. It'd been a long conversation, with him doing the majority of the talking. He'd been exhausted by the end, his mother had been a mess of tears and anger, and his father's face was as dark as a deep-winter storm. Still, just like Alexis had said, it made things better.

Alexis. He saw her red hair and the flash of her eyes. His heart wrenched at the thought of her. Between the time he landed and when he climbed into his dad's truck on Saturday morning, he picked up his phone half a dozen times to call or text her. But what had changed? What improved version of himself could he offer to her? Maybe they'd have a better conversation someday, really hash things out, but for now he would let her go.

As soon as his shoes hit Susan's old wooden porch, her front door flew open. She gave him a small smile and ushered him inside, but her eyes were frantic. He hesitated a moment.

"It's okay. Come on." She waved faster and held the door wide open. He swore he saw her scanning her front yard after he walked through.

As he stepped inside, memories flooded back. This was Emma's child-hood home. She'd lived here until she moved out to go to college, but she'd visited her parents frequently. He'd been in this house hundreds of times, but not since Em died. It looked the same. The grandfather clock, passed down from Susan's maternal grandfather, still stood next to the staircase, ticking time away.

"It's upstairs." She pointed, then took her stairs two at a time, which Luke was sure she had never done before in her life.

Luke followed her into Emma's old room. It looked like teenage Emma was still living in it. He didn't believe in ghosts, but he swore he could feel her here.

The first time he'd been in this room, he'd teased Em about the NSYNC poster on the wall. Right away, she'd put on one of their CDs. He missed the defiant look she used to give him. She'd never cared what others thought of her. He had always admired that.

A sound like the dragging of a full wooden box caused him to look to his left. Susan had pushed Emma's bed away from her and pulled up the corner of the fluorescent-colored area rug that sat beneath.

"What are you—"

"I've searched Emma's boxes a thousand times—the ones you brought back from your apartment," Susan said. "I've taken her room apart piece by piece. I know she hadn't lived here in years, but she came to see us so often I thought maybe there would be something here. I know it sounds crazy, because she was murdered, and no one makes a plan before they're murdered. But Emma was smart, one of the smartest, most prepared people I've ever met. I tried to raise her that way, but I think most of it she came by naturally. So, I thought if there was any chance she suspected something might happen to her, she might leave me something. I haven't found anything in all these years.

"So, I gave up on this room for a while. But the other day I walked by, and it was covered in dust. I was ashamed. I know Emma isn't coming back, but what would she think about me letting her room fall into disrepair? I threw back the rug and moved her bed to clean the floor. That's when I found it again—Emma's secret hiding spot. I don't know if she ever even told *you* about this. One day when she was a teenager, I walked in when her bed was pushed aside. I could see there was a small hole in the floor that could hold papers, maybe a small jewelry box. We never really talked about it. I didn't mind that she had her own place to keep secrets—once I confirmed there was nothing elicit."

With the rug pushed away, Luke watched in surprise as she flipped up a piece of one of the floorboards. It looked like it had broken at some point based on how the board came up. Luke wondered how Emma had discovered it in the first place. Or had she broken it?

"It turns out she didn't leave anything for me, but she did leave something for you." Susan had knelt down and was handing him a plain white envelope, which felt very thin. His name was written on the front in all caps, the way Emma wrote everything.

His heart picked up its pace. He turned the envelope over. It had been sealed, but the flap was ripped open.

"Did you look at this?" He heard the accusatory tone in his voice.

"I did." She shrugged. "At first, I was just angry that she would leave you something and not me. But when I read it, well, it makes no sense. That's when I called you."

"What were you going to do if it was just a normal letter?" His eyes narrowed.

"I don't know. Luke—" she paused, maintaining eye contact with him. "Someday maybe you'll be a parent. Then you might possibly start to understand the pain, anger, despair, and deep confusion that have lived in my heart since the death of my only child. Until you have a child, you cannot begin to know what it would be like to lose one."

He wanted to yell back that she'd sure brought him close enough to understanding that pain and despair while he was also living through his own debilitating grief. But he kept his mouth closed.

He pulled a crinkled sheet of folded printer paper out of the envelope, his hands shaking at the thought of what it might contain.

Luke, I love you. Remember, when times get tough, you can always go for the best fried cheese. She's leaving, but she'd love for you to help clean up the mess. She said there are treasures there. Love, Em

For a moment, all he could think was, *What the hell?*

His confusion must have shown on his face, because Susan said, "See, it doesn't make sense! What is she talking about?"

Luke sat down in the over-stuffed chair in the corner of the room and put his face in his hands, running them through his hair to think.

Fried cheese?

Memories blasted into his mind. They used to call the mozzarella sticks at Taylor's, a sports bar in Cornelius, fried cheese. Emma said they were the best she'd ever had. They used to go there all the time, but after the owner— *What was her name?* After she sold it and moved away, the atmosphere hadn't been quite the same.

They'd become friends with the owner— *Marla, that was it!* She'd chat with them all the time, making her rounds through customer tables. He'd felt like she'd known all about them.

Was this note that old? Emma must have been alive for close to a year after Marla left. Did time matter with this reference? What did she mean about the mess? He tried to think back on Marla's last days at the bar.

"Mess. Love for you to help clean up the mess," he mumbled to himself. He could feel Susan's eyes on him, but he tried to ignore her.

Luke remembered Marla hadn't been happy to sell Taylor's, but her daughter was away at college and her son had moved away with his new wife, so Marla was following them. She'd tried to be her normal happy, joking self, but they'd seen through her.

Emma felt bad for her about something. What was it? She'd wanted Luke to help with something there, which Luke had been too busy to do. *Her office!* Marla had been joking that her office in the back of the bar was a mess, and she was dreading cleaning it up—said it was full of accumulated junk. Emma had helped her. She'd teased Luke about not helping, but his caseload had been intense at the time, so he'd bowed out. Was the note referencing the office? Had Marla left something behind that Emma labeled as treasure rather than junk?

What happened to Marla? He'd lost touch with her after she moved, although he thought Emma might have talked to her on the phone every now and then. Marla had come back to visit a couple times, because she knew the bar's new owners. Emma had tried to see her when she was in town. He didn't have any way to reach her now, but maybe someone at the bar would.

"I have an idea," he said, standing up. "I have to visit this sports bar Emma and I used to go to. I'll call you if I find anything."

"I'll go with you," Susan said eagerly, looking ready to run down the stairs.

"No, I have to do this by myself. I have no idea what I'll find there," he answered. "I'll call you. Don't talk to anyone else about this."

She didn't look happy, but for once, she kept her thoughts to herself and nodded.

The drive to Taylor's took forever in his agitated state. On the way, he told himself a thousand times not to get his hopes up. *Remember, when times get tough...*

She'd been predicting her own death. She'd meant him to find that letter after she died.

You don't know that. She never told you about that hiding spot. How would you know to look there? Did she expect Susan would look there at some point? It seems like a long shot. And it took almost six years. Maybe you're reading too much into this.

His adrenaline couldn't care less about reading too much into it. It propelled him forward as he found a parking spot and made his way inside. Taylor's had just opened for the early lunch crowd. The middle-aged man behind the bar nodded to him as he approached. He was in nicer clothes than Luke expected a bartender or server to be wearing, so he hoped this was the guy he needed to talk to.

"Good morning. My name's Luke Kruger." He showed the man his license in case that would be necessary. "My girlfriend and I were friends were the former owner, Marla Khumalo, before she moved away. I have reason to believe my girlfriend may have left something here with Marla. I know that probably sounds crazy—"

The man held up his hand and Luke stopped. "Mr. Kruger, I'm Julian Walker, the current owner. Marla hasn't been back here in years. Her kids all moved to Oregon, maybe three years ago, and she went with 'em. She told me my one condition of buying the place was to let you or your girlfriend into the back office if you ever showed up. She didn't know why or if that would happen, but she insisted. I didn't love the idea when she first told me, but I've honestly forgotten over the years. Can't believe you're here now."

Luke was stunned. "Yeah, it's taken a while," was all he could manage to say.

Julian waved him behind the bar and down a brightly lit hallway. They passed the kitchen on the left and kept going a few more steps. Julian stopped at a simple wooden door on the right. Luke was surprised to see not only a handle with a lock, but also a deadbolt lock.

"Marla had the deadbolt installed before she left. I know she kept both locked when she was still here, but sometimes I get a little lazy about the deadbolt. My staff hardly ever comes in here."

Was the deadbolt to protect whatever Emma left behind? Luke questioned.

The office was small and much darker than the hallway outside it. There was a small window on one wall, but the blinds on it were drawn. Unlike how Marla had described it, Julian seemed to keep it pretty organized.

Julian stood to one side while Luke gazed around.

"I hope you know what you're looking for. Marla wouldn't tell me what it was or where it was. She said she didn't even have details about it, just that your girlfriend told her it was important. After I bought the place, Marla would visit every now and then. She and your girl would come back here each time. I asked Marla if whatever they were doing could get me or my business in trouble, but she said not to worry about it. I had to take her at her word. We'd known each other a long time, and she'd never lied to me."

Luke nodded. "It's just something Emma needed me to have." He had no idea where to start and no clue what he was looking for.

"Your girl—she was one of the last ones killed by that pair of guys all those years ago, wasn't she? I remember from the news."

"Yeah," was all Luke wanted to say.

"Crushed Marla when it happened. She wasn't sure what to do with whatever's in here, so she left it, assuming you'd be in for it."

I wish I'd known sooner. Luke's heart ached.

Julian cleared his throat and said, "Well, I'll leave you to it. I gotta get back out front. Let me know if you need anything. I'm trusting you like I trusted Marla."

Luke made eye contact with the man and held it. "Thank you, Mr. Walker. I promise your trust is well placed."

Julian nodded and left, shutting the door behind him.

Luke heaved a frustrated sigh, running his hands through his hair. *What the fuck do I do now, Em?*

He half-heartedly searched Julian's desk, but he doubted Emma would have left anything in such an obvious place that was so often used. He searched the walls for any kind of concealed safe, but there was nothing. As he walked by a large metal filing cabinet, his shoe caught on the corner of a ratty mat sitting underneath. As the corner came up, he noticed the wooden floor underneath looked different.

"No way," he whispered to himself.

The filing cabinet felt like it was full of bricks and glued to the floor, but after a lot of low-volume cursing, he was able to push and pull it closer to the desk. He pulled the mat up and let out the breath he'd been holding. The floor was newer and there was a square cut into it, like a trap door. There was a small hole on one side, just big enough to fit a finger into.

"You moved that goddamn filing cabinet every time? What's with hiding shit in floors, Em?" He shook his head, realizing she'd been trying to use the hiding spot in her bedroom floor as its own clue. It made sense. She wasn't going to make whatever it was easy to find.

He pulled up the piece of wood and placed it carefully to the side. The hole underneath was deeper than he expected. The building's cement foundation lay at the bottom. Inside was a metal box held closed by a combination lock. A miniscule laminated piece of paper was attached to the top of the box.

It read, "cop date."

"Cop date," he repeated.

A date they went on? A significant day having to do with them being cops? The day one of them started the job? He could barely remember the month and year he started with the Charlotte-Mecklenburg Police. He couldn't remember when she started with the sheriff's office or when she graduated the academy. He took a shot, trying his graduation date. At least that one stuck out in his mind. Sure enough, the lock came open. Then he felt like a real ass for not knowing hers when she had known his.

She's probably somewhere laughing, wishing she could tell me she had to look it up, he decided. That felt like something she would do.

He opened the box, which was covered in dust and some dead bugs. He dug through it, lifting its contents up with hesitation. An eight-by-ten photograph in a protective cover lay upside down on top of documents, more photographs, and flash drives. In Emma's handwriting, the eight-by-ten was dated about one month before she was killed. He turned it over, his heart threatening to break out of his chest.

The picture was taken from a distance. Luke didn't recognize the area the three men were standing in, only noting that it appeared to be on the edge of some woods. There was space between the figures, two of whom were Crawley and Freeman. Based on his body language, the third man looked very at ease talking with the Sunset Killers.

"Shit. No, no, no," Luke said in a strangled voice. That nagging voice in the back of his mind jumped to the forefront as he sat down on the floor, trying to breathe.

The third man was Alan Langley.

CHAPTER 27

"*How did she get a knife?*" Christopher wanted to laugh. He didn't spend much time indulging in uproarious laughter, but he wanted to in that moment. This was simply insane.

"*I don't fucking know! Thomas put her purse in the back, and she didn't get out of her seat. All he saw was her phone!*" David growled.

"*Maybe she keeps one taped to her body,*" Christopher muttered.

"*You idiot! Do you not understand that Thomas is going to kill us? He'll kill us both without thinking twice! This should have been easy! You were so sure of this plan! And now she's gone! He has no way to find her. He's going to come after you because of that!*"

Christopher leaned forward in his chair, his humorous mood gone. "*If Thomas were smart enough to ruin or kill me, he would have been able to subdue that woman. He would have followed my advice from the beginning. He would not have destroyed this project at every turn. He would not have put his trust in you, a man obsessed with the same woman he was. No, neither you nor Thomas is a threat to me. And if either of you attempts to come after me, I will kill you.*"

Christopher ended the call and turned off his phone with a sigh. He only worked on referrals from now on.

* * *

Alexis was alone again. It felt like the universe was telling her this was how it had to be. She'd moved closer to her mom, made friends who cared about her, found jobs she liked, fell in love. She'd gotten comfortable. And bam— her life was turned upside down again. She had no idea why.

"Who the hell are they?" she asked the four walls around her.

She tried to research Zeke and Geoff, although she understood those were fabricated identities. Then she Googled Thomas Loefler again, but her searches gave her nothing new.

What made her so special to them? They'd created entire lives for themselves in order to weasel their way into hers. She thought back to the first day she'd met Zeke. His voice had caused a negative reaction in her body, like the memory of it was being kept deep within her. It was another small piece of her trauma she hadn't yet been able to grasp.

She tried to play his voice back in her head, but it didn't help. She groaned in frustration and put her head down on the desk in front of her. Guilt coursed through her. What would Kassie and Brett think when they went to her apartment to look for her? Her mother knew she was safe, but no more than that this time. And Luke. Her heart ached at the thought of him. They weren't a couple anymore, but, like grief, love didn't just go away. Would he be angry? Sad? She shook her head and stood up. If she wanted to keep her sanity, she couldn't think about Luke.

* * *

On Monday afternoon, Luke's phone rang from where it sat on the table next to him. He was so tired that the ringing brought him out of a light doze. He was in yet another interview room, this time waiting to speak to representatives from the FBI. He'd spoken to detectives from his prior department that morning. There was still Emma's department to speak to. Langley had been taken into custody Sunday morning, after all evidence was removed from Taylor's. Luke was sure Julian was happy to see them go.

They were interviewing Susan too. She was pretty animated and very confident. There was part of him that was proud of her. It didn't erase the way she had treated him, but she'd kept fighting. He felt like she deserved to rub it in everyone's faces a little.

He didn't expect to be able to go home for a couple days, so he'd had to call in to work. He knew he'd been asking a lot of his department, but his lieutenant was more than understanding when he explained why he wasn't there.

He eyed his phone. He shouldn't answer it. The agents would probably come in any minute now. But it was Kassidy's name on the screen. Brett would know why he wasn't there, and Kassidy should be at work.

"Hey, Kassidy," he said, suppressing a yawn. "I'm just about to—"

"Luke, you need to come home," she interrupted, her voice frantic. He snapped to attention.

"What's wrong?" He stood up so fast, his chair clattered backward.

"She's gone, Luke! She just disappeared!" The words came out in a strangled cry.

"What? Kassie—" He shoved his free hand into his hair, a rush of adrenaline flooding through him.

He heard voices in the background and then Brett came on the line. "Hey, it's me. We were going to wait to tell you this until you got home, but on Saturday Geoff and Zeke tried to kidnap Alexis. She believes they were trying to get her to the Executive Airport and were then going to New York. Geoff was driving the car she was in. She caused him to crash it after stabbing him in the leg with her pocket knife. She got out of the vehicle with only minor injuries. Zeke pulled up next to them, dragged Geoff into his car and they got away.

"Alexis told us Zeke threatened her before he left. She went back to her apartment yesterday. We wanted her to be under protection, to at least stay with Kassie and me, but she insisted on going home. Kassie wanted to stay with her, but she wanted to be alone. We tried to argue, but she was getting pretty angry by that point. Kassie didn't want to stress her out more. We went over there first thing this morning. She was gone. There are no signs of struggle. It looks like she packed up a bunch of her stuff and left.

"She sent Kassie a video message this morning letting her know she's okay, but we have no idea where she was at the time. Kassie can't reach her now. Alexis's mom called Kassie this morning to let her know Alexis left her a message as well. It looks like Alexis took her dad's old truck, the one her mom keeps in the driveway. She must have taken the bus to her mom's part of town since her car was totaled—we think by Geoff and Zeke."

"What the fuck?" Luke yelled, his hand flying up in the air as if someone could see him.

Brett sighed. Luke could hear Kassidy murmuring in the background.

"I know it's a lot, man, I'm sorry. That's why we were going to wait to tell you about the attempted kidnapping. Then we found out she was gone. We've already put in a missing person's report, but if you could come home, maybe she'll try to contact you," Brett's voice seemed to fade away, and Luke knew his friend didn't believe the words coming out of his own mouth. Luke could hear what he thought was Kassidy crying.

"Of course I will." He stared around the tiny room. He didn't know how to process what he'd just heard. "Susan found something that led me to Emma's murderer. I'm waiting to talk to the FBI, and—" He ran his hand through his hair as his words simply stopped coming.

"My God. Okay. Shit, Luke, I don't—" Brett started and then seemed to be filling Kassidy in. "Take the time you need. Let us know if Alexis contacts you. We'll do the same. I'm sorry."

"Yeah," Luke mumbled, feeling numb.

The call ended just as the door opened. Luke focused on breathing. "Detective Kruger, I'm Special Agent Hopkins." The first of the two agents stuck out her hand. Luke managed to shake it.

He sat down as he shook the other agent's hand. He just had to get through this. Alexis's face flashed through his mind. He had to find her, but first he had to get through this.

Luke went to her apartment Thursday night after work, using his spare key to get in. Brett and Kassidy met him there.

"It looks like she's just gone out somewhere—like she's going to come right back," Kassidy murmured next to him.

"She left too quickly to plan for everything else," Luke sighed. He pulled his jacket tighter around him. The February air was cold, but without Alexis's bright spirit, her apartment seemed even colder. "Did her landlord say anything?"

"I finally got through to him this morning. He said she sent him a check for four months' rent and a note saying she'd be gone for a while because of a family emergency. She didn't say anything about wanting to terminate her lease, so maybe she is planning to come back." The hope in Kassidy's voice was forced.

"So that means she's paid up through June? How'd she pay four months' rent ahead of time?" Luke asked. He knew Alexis was always careful with her money, but she still lived in Midtown. Her rent wasn't cheap.

Kassidy shrugged. "I think she sells her paintings, on top of all her other jobs."

"Have you talked to her mom since she called on Monday?" Brett asked his wife as he walked carefully around the apartment, looking for new clues.

"No. I left her a message yesterday to ask how she's doing, but she hasn't called me back," Kassidy responded with a shake of her head. "I'm assuming she's working her normal shifts at the hospital."

Luke's gaze went to a framed picture of Alexis and Eileen, which sat in a prominent place on the coffee table.

"This has to be tearing her apart," he said. "I think I'm going to see if she needs a ride home tonight."

Luke pulled up in front of the hospital just after seven that night. Eileen came out a few minutes later, heading toward her bus stop. He jumped out of his truck and walked part of the way toward her. She saw him and stopped, giving him a small wave, but hesitated with her next step.

"Eileen, can I give you a ride home?"

She thought about it for a moment, looking back at him. Groups of people walked past her, going in and out of the hospital.

"Sure," she finally said.

He opened the door of his truck and she climbed in. As soon as he shut his door and started the engine, she said, "You know I can't tell you where she is. I don't even know this time, but if I did—"

"I know," he replied, surprised by how quiet his own voice was. "Did she tell you we broke up?"

"No, I'm sorry," her words sounded sincere, but her tone suggested she wasn't shocked by the news.

"I know how close you two are. She must've told you something about what I've been dealing with."

"Well, a little." Her words carried a tinge of guilt.

"It's okay. None of it's a secret; I'm just not good at talking about it. I respect Alexis, I know I wasn't treating her well. I didn't want to keep putting her through it, but I also didn't want to let her go. So, she made the decision, and it was the right thing to do. But I miss her. And now she's gone." His voice cracked as he said this. "I don't know if she would have called me if I were in town, but I feel horrible that I couldn't be here for her. I wish she hadn't felt the need to run again." He took a deep breath before continuing, "I love your daughter, Eileen. I'm sorry, and I'm here if you need anything."

He cast a glance in her direction after she was quiet for a few seconds. Eileen gave him a weak smile, her eyes shining with unfallen tears.

"Thank you. I wish—I wish things could have been different. I wish my daughter could just have a normal, safe life. I wish you weren't dealing with so much pain in yours."

He nodded, slowing down as they got closer to her house. They sat in silence for a few minutes. When he pulled into her driveway, she motioned that she would let herself out.

"Luke," she said before she closed the truck door. "I appreciate how honest you were with me. I hope you find the happiness you deserve. I hope one day, if you want to, you have a child of your own. It really is the most wonderful journey, even though parts of it can be very difficult." She stared off into the distance with a wistful look before turning back to him. "If I have any more communication with her, I'll let you know."

"Thank you." He nodded again, watching to make sure she got safely into her house before he drove away.

CHAPTER 28

It had been months. Months of being alone. Alexis bought groceries online. She paid with her credit card, but she always put a fake name on the order, just in case anyone looked at the bags on the front step before she managed to bring them inside. Her savings was almost bone dry because of how many months she'd paid ahead on her lease. Soon that four months would be coming to a close. It was almost July. She'd have to let the place go.

What was she going to do with all her stuff in her Sacramento apartment? Could she send something to Kassie asking if she and Brett would be willing to move it out? That seemed like a pretty messed up thing to do, since she hadn't talked to Kassie and Brett in months.

She was staying at her friends' place—a couple she hadn't talked to much in years who were traveling abroad. They didn't ask anything of her except to keep everything clean. She knew she was insanely lucky, but most of the time, she wanted to crawl up the walls. She'd gotten so used to a normal life. She hated the feeling of isolation even more than the first time.

She'd sent her mom a few emails from a new account she'd created with fake information, just to let her know she was okay. Eileen gave brief responses, but she knew Alexis liked to keep all written communication sparse. She didn't believe her mother was in any danger. She'd never told Zeke or Geoff Eileen's name or where exactly she lived.

Alexis had cut and colored her hair, just like the first time she isolated herself. It was now short and brown. She missed her natural red and the longer length she'd managed to grow since moving to Sacramento. She couldn't wear colored contacts this time, because she couldn't part with the money she would need to use for them.

She painted every day, selling what pieces she could online. Thank God the post office picked up packages. She'd never painted so much, but she was getting tired of it. She didn't like feeling forced to paint. It was supposed to help her relax, to enter a more creative space in her mind. But now it just felt stressful, like everything else. And she missed going out, seeing people. How had she done this for so many years? For starters, she'd had a lot more income back then, and a much healthier savings.

She'd bought a prepaid phone plan and turned her regular cell phone off, even though she still paid for it. She was afraid to lose control of the only phone number her friends and family had for her. She had her laptop, but she didn't like using it to access the internet. She didn't want anything traced back to her friends' Wi-Fi. She used the data on her prepaid phone as her window to the outside world.

She needed what she had left of that month's data to sell her paintings, but she couldn't stop thinking about Luke. What had Emma's mother given him? Had he found her killer? One morning, as she sat in bed dreading another monotonous day, she looked up the news for Charlotte, North Carolina. If Luke found anything big, it would have to be in the news.

"Trial date set in case of serial killer cop" was a headline from just a few days ago.

The words "serial killer" caught her attention and she read on. When she reached the name Alan Langley, her heart dropped. He'd been charged with aiding the Sunset Killers during their murdering spree, charged with murdering both of those men, as well as several others in connection to the cover-up, and finally, charged with murdering a Mecklenburg County deputy six years ago. Emma.

Alexis felt the blood drain from her face. "Oh, Luke."

She had to go back to Sacramento.

*　*　*

Luke unlocked his apartment door and pushed it open. He ran his hand through his hair with a sigh. He really needed a haircut. His hair had never been this long. He'd been back in Sacramento for a couple days since meeting with the attorneys prosecuting Langley's case, which was set to begin in a month. Luke was a witness.

He needed this jet lag to go away. In the logical part of his mind, he understood it wasn't just the time change and travel fatigue; it was mental and emotional pain. He had yet another therapy appointment in a couple days. He was doing the work now, like he should have before. It did seem to be helping.

He'd gotten no sleep the night before his latest round of talks with the attorneys, obsessing over the fact that the nagging suspicion he'd had about Langley was correct. He'd tried to assume his former colleague was just getting lazy and sloppy with Emma's case because it'd been so long and he could get away with it. Luke hadn't allowed himself to imagine that Langley was getting money from the Sunset Killers for helping them cover up their murders. That he'd been hiding his crimes all these years, killing people off as he needed to.

Now that Luke was back in Sacramento, he felt like a giant weight had been lifted from his shoulders, but also that the world was smashing him into the ground with the fact that he'd soon be testifying against one of his best friends. He missed Alexis so much it hurt. Theoretically, he knew she was okay. Eileen let him know when she received her daughter's short emails, but there was no communication to anyone else. He watched Kassidy go through periods of anger, sadness, and guilt—watched Brett try to be there for her. Would any of them see her again?

Luke had worked late to distract himself and catch up on his cases, even though his coworkers had been covering for him as much as possible when he was in North Carolina. The sun was already down, but a six-day streak of temperatures over one-hundred degrees had him sweating through his clothes. He went to throw his keys in the dish on the small table between his entryway and living room but stopped short. As his eyes adjusted to the dark of his apartment, he saw a figure across the room from him. His heart picked up speed as he switched on the light.

Alexis sat on his couch, blinking as light filled the room, her eyes dark as they met his. Her legs weren't pulled up beneath her in the casual way she used to sit there. She still had her shoes on. Her body language conveyed her nerves. Her face made it clear she was tired. Her long red hair had been cut short and dyed brown.

"Hey, Miller," he breathed out. The sadness in his voice echoed through his ears.

He wasn't sure what he should be feeling in this moment. He didn't think he could describe what it was to see her sitting in front of him.

"Hey, Kruger," she answered, her voice so quiet.

"Still have my spare key, I guess." He tried to smile as he put his keys in the dish. They made a loud *clunk* as they hit the ceramic, and he saw her twitch.

She nodded, looking like she wanted to say something. He stayed by the table, not sure what to do. He wanted to hold her, kiss her, but his confusion and anger kept him from moving.

"I'm sorry," she finally said as he stayed quiet. "I know I should explain, but I also feel like you already understand."

He ran his hand through his hair again, sitting down on the opposite end of the sectional. "Where'd you go?"

"Just outside San Francisco. I figured it would be the last place anyone would look for me, because they wouldn't think I'd go back there. I'm staying at a friend's place. Everything was too much. With the threat Zeke made—I had to keep myself safe." Her voice broke. "But I read about Langley. Luke, I'm so sorry."

For a moment, he held her gaze. There were tears in her eyes. He had to fight not to pull her into his arms.

"Thanks. Yeah, it's been—" He shrugged, not even sure what word to use to finish that sentence.

"How did you find out? Was it because of what Susan found?" she asked, but then cringed. "If you want to talk about it."

He nodded. He told her about Emma's note, then the box of evidence at Taylor's. "I don't know what tipped her off, but she started investigating him on her own. She had a lot of access to him, because we saw him all the time outside of work. She knew better than to take that on by herself, so I have to think she didn't imagine it would turn out to be as big as it was. Maybe she planned to gather enough evidence and then turn it all in, but he got to her first." Luke paused here, feeling like he might break down. He didn't know if this would ever get easier to think about. He took several deep breaths. Out of the corner of his eye, he saw Alexis stretch her hand toward him in an almost undetectable way.

He folded his fingers together and looked down at them as he continued, "There were pictures, emails, evidence of altered reports. He made close to a million dollars helping Crawley and Freeman. Langley must have caught on to Emma's investigation a couple days before he killed her. He left her a desperate voicemail. It didn't say what exactly he had done or that he would do anything to her. She managed to download it to a flash drive and put it with everything else before she died. He had plenty of motive to murder her, but when he was arrested for helping the Sunset Killers, two of his coworkers came forward with proof.

"They'd been hanging out at Langley's place one night. When Langley left to get beer, they decided to download some—uh, unsavory—videos to his computer as a prank. In the process, they stumbled upon an old email from Crawley. The message specifically mentioned Langley killing Emma and that he'd gotten advice from Crawley and Freeman beforehand. Thank God Crawley didn't give a shit if Langley was caught. Langley responded, acknowledging their help, but telling Crawley not to email him again.

"The FBI pulled Crawley and Langley's phone records. They've made multiple calls to each other over the years since Emma died. Langley called Crawley right after authorities believe Freeman was murdered. It's looking like Freeman was blackmailing Langley. He and Crawley had gone their separate ways, and he was running out of money. We believe Freeman threatened to tell authorities about Langley's involvement in the murders. This freaked Langley out, so he killed him. Langley also called Crawley the morning before Crawley died. Crawley just wanted to be left alone. He called me so I'd stop looking for him. Langley was pissed that he called me, thinking he was going the same route as Freeman, so he killed him. Langley's lieutenant reported that Langley was out sick for three days right around the time Crawley was murdered.

"Langley's coworkers found the email from Crawley to Langley late last year, but they've been too scared to say anything—thinking they'd end up like Langley's other victims. They were the ones who called me in December to tell me to stop looking into Em's death. I guess they thought Langley wouldn't kill anyone else if we all stayed quiet and let him do his thing. The FBI accessed Crawley's email. He'd created a folder of his correspondence with Langley for anyone to find. I'm sure he did that on purpose in case he was killed. It's still not clear if he wrote the confession letter, or if Langley did it himself somehow." Luke took a deep breath and let it go, feeling like he'd been talking for hours.

"After all these years, Susan and I finally know who killed her. We have our closure." He gave Alexis a weak smile. "Susan looked numb the last two times I saw her, but she knows it's the real answer this time. She also knows how lucky she is that Langley never took her seriously or considered her a real threat—probably kept her from being one of his victims. I don't know what my relationship with her will be now, or if we'll even have one. I think for now, we both just need some distance."

Alexis sighed, not taking her eyes from him. "Luke—"

He interrupted her as if compelled to continue. "There's something I thought of after Langley was arrested. When Crawley called me, he said I should stop wasting my life; that I should move on with people I could trust. I thought it was a weird comment before, but now I think he was trying to tell me there was someone from my past I couldn't trust. There're probably a lot of reasons Langley didn't try to kill me, but I guess I'm lucky too." He hesitated for a moment, then asked the question he'd been wanting to ask since he turned on the light and saw her there, "Are you staying?"

She looked away from him and shook her head. "I can't. Not with them still out there."

"The FBI is searching for them. They believe Geoff is actually a man named Thomas Loefler, the CEO of—"

"A pharmaceutical company," she said, something like triumph ringing through her voice.

"Yeah. How'd you know?" He raised an eyebrow.

"When I was at lunch with Kassie and followed Zeke into that building, Titan was one of the company names on the directory. I looked it up later. There was a bio page on Thomas Loefler. Something about his smile seemed familiar. I even started wondering if Geoff was Thomas Loefler when I saw him smile during the class he attended, but I thought I was imagining things."

"He probably had surgery so his face wouldn't be recognized," Luke responded. "You never told me about looking up Titan and Loefler."

"I know." A guilty look crossed her face. "I wasn't sure if it was anything, and you had so much going on. I saw Zeke a couple more times too, before they tried to take me."

He wasn't sure what to say. He was still wondering why she'd bothered to come back if she wasn't going to stay.

"Have they found anything on Zeke?" she asked with hesitation.

"Not yet. Investigators found a Cessna Turbo Skylane housed at the Executive Airport. It was registered to Thomas Loefler out of New York. Airport employees said the man who owned it fit Geoff's description, but they knew him as Tom Loefler. They'd often seen Zeke with him, but they had no information on who he was. The FBI got a warrant for Loefler's Sacramento office, but it had already been cleared out. Now they're working with their New York field office to find any trace of him, his company, or Zeke. The FBI is also looking into the woman who claimed to be Zeke's mother and any of the friends or family who attended his memorial service, but everyone seems to have disappeared."

"That's why I can't stay, Luke. I had to make sure you were okay after Langley, but—"

"Alexis, you would have protection here. This isn't like before." He could hear the light pleading tone in his voice.

"Then they'll wait until time has gone by and I've let my guard down. I don't know why they're after me, but Zeke's threat was very real. I have to figure this out and know they're in custody before I can come back. I just need to find out who Zeke is." She stood up, and he was terrified to lose her again.

He grabbed her hand as she moved past him. She didn't pull away. He stood up, pulling her into a slow kiss. There were tears in her eyes when she opened them.

"Stay with me, just for now," he murmured.

After a moment, she nodded and reached up to bring his mouth back to hers, putting her fingers in his hair. His heart raced as desire jolted through him. He would try to talk her into staying again later, but for now, he had to show her how much he missed her.

CHAPTER 29

Luke's arm was thrown around her, but he was fast asleep. Alexis knew if she were there in the morning, he would ask her to stay again. She didn't want to keep telling him no. She had to leave before the sun came up, which wasn't many hours away.

She watched him as he slept, afraid she might not be able to move without waking him up. She went slow, inching out from under his arm and onto her back. He continued his steady breathing as if nothing had changed. She was sure he hadn't been sleeping well and was glad her presence inspired him to rest.

She thought back on the insanity of the past year—the break-in, almost getting hit by a car, the Zeke sightings, the failed abduction. The article with the cryptic note popped back in her mind. She hadn't thought about that for a long time. It said her video was still out there.

Obviously, in the digital age they lived in, nothing ever really went away. She assumed the note was referencing a copy other than the one law enforcement found. Who else was accessing that video and why? As a longshot, she wondered if Geoff and Zeke had a connection to her video. Had someone been trying to warn her about their random entry into her life?

She allowed herself to think back to that horrible night with Kurt, her adrenaline reacting quickly, but Luke was next to her; she was safe. She wouldn't let herself go too deep, but she searched her mind for anything related to the video. After the rape, she'd blocked out the fact that there had been a camera in the room. It was only because the FBI found the footage and asked her about it years later that she remembered at all. Now, as she searched her memory, trying to focus on the camera, she could see someone in the shadows by the far wall of the office. Right? The figure from her nightmares. Standing by the camera? This was the other person the FBI had always suspected was in the room.

As that thought passed through her head, she remembered a voice. She had heard a male voice, just a few times. A voice doing what? Giving quiet orders.

She felt like she was going to throw up and rushed to Luke's bathroom. Once there, she managed to quell the nausea. She sank to the cool tile floor, taking several deep breaths. She closed her eyes, leaning her head against the wall. She had blocked the voice from her mind—the shadowy figure would often come up in her remembrances of that night, but not the voice. It was a voice she knew, she understood that now. A familiar sound of someone she'd worked with.

Alexis stood with hesitation, making sure to find her balance before taking any steps. She padded back through Luke's bedroom. She was amazed to see he was still sleeping in the same position she'd left him. She wanted to climb back into bed with him, put her body up against his and just stay. But she was so close now. She had to figure this out.

She made her way to Luke's living room, where her temporary phone sat on his coffee table. Thank God for his Wi-Fi. Pulling up her email, she hoped her memory served her correctly. When Kurt's company, Reliant, sent out a digital employee directory during her second year, she'd forwarded it to her personal email in case she needed to reach anyone outside of work. She searched her inbox for her Reliant email address. Sure enough, there was the email she needed. She opened the file and read the names of people she used to work with. She landed on Kurt's extensive public relations department. Many of them were women; she knew he had murdered two of them. Her eyes settled on the name David Crighton. He'd been a lower-level PR associate, but the couple times she'd seen him in the office, she remembered him having a big energy. She needed to hear his voice.

She searched David's name and breathed a victorious sigh when she found a couple videos he'd created on YouTube. As she hit play on the first one, she closed her eyes so nothing on the screen would distract her. His tone was so smooth, so confident. Memories of the past slammed into her. Yes, she remembered that voice from Kurt's office. But Zeke's face flashed through her mind too. He'd managed the slightest change in accent, but without a doubt, that was his voice. Zeke was David Crighton. Her mind had buried David's voice somewhere deep after she'd heard it that night. No wonder she recognized it but didn't understand why on "Zeke's" first day at Valle Coffee.

What did he want with her? What was his connection to Thomas Loefler? Was he trying to finish the job Kurt started? These answers were unclear to her, but one thing she was sure of: the FBI would love to know about David Crighton. And maybe she could do one better—maybe she could find him.

She gathered the minimal number of things she had with her, and gave Luke one last look. Her heart ached at the thought of how he'd feel seeing she was gone when he woke up, but she had to get her life back, so this was necessary.

It was still dark when she locked his door and went downstairs to the car she'd borrowed from her friends. She hadn't wanted to drive her dad's truck back into Sacramento. She looked all around her and scanned the inside of the car before she got in. With a deep breath of hope, she started the engine and headed back out of town.

* * *

Luke had done this to himself by asking her to stay, by holding her body in his arms. He should have just let her go. He knew Alexis felt this isolation was the best way to keep herself safe, but he wished thousands of times that she would just let him help her. They'd find Zeke and Thomas Loefler eventually.

Living the rest of her life like this seemed insane. He thought about trying to find her, but if he managed to do that, would she just run somewhere else?

He went to work, went to therapy, and tried to get over her. He saw Brett and Kassidy often, but their visits always ended up feeling awkward. None of them knew if they should talk about Alexis or just leave her out of conversations altogether.

He talked to his parents a couple times a week. His relationship with them was getting stronger. He promised his mother he would come home for Christmas this year. Life was moving forward, albeit sometimes in slow motion.

On a Friday in mid-July, Kassidy called him just as he was getting home from work.

"Hey, Kass," he answered, putting his workbag down on the couch and heading toward the kitchen.

"Has Alexis contacted you?" Her voice was shaky.

He stopped short just as he was about to open his refrigerator. "Uh, no, why?"

"Yeah, she hasn't called or emailed her mom or me either, but—I saw her today." The last words were rushed.

"What? Where?" Luke suddenly felt like the world was spinning.

"Going into a consignment shop in Midtown, not far from her apartment," Kassidy answered. "I was running late to an interview I've been trying to get for weeks. I should have followed her inside, but it felt weird. She looked fine. Based on her body language, she wasn't in a rush or worried about someone seeing her."

"When was this?" He was already walking toward his keys, but where was he going? Her apartment?

"A few hours ago. I was waiting to hear back from her mom before I called you."

"Have you tried her apartment?" Now he was heading out the door. So much for getting over her.

"Not yet. I just got off work. I couldn't reach Brett."

"He was out at a scene. He should probably be done soon." Luke was already downstairs, heading toward his truck.

"You're going there now, aren't you?" Kassidy asked in a knowing tone.

"Yep," he answered, climbing in his truck and starting the engine.

"I'll meet you there," she responded and ended the call.

He didn't live far from Alexis's place, but he seemed to get there in record time. He parked and met Kassidy outside the apartment building. Then he took the stairs two at a time, Kassidy hot on his heels.

He knocked and waited. No answer. He checked the street for her dad's truck, but didn't see it. Kassidy seemed to be bouncing next to him. He knocked again. Nothing. He pulled her spare key from his pocket.

"Uh, should you do that knowing she could be back?" Kassidy raised an eyebrow at him.

"Yeah, she wouldn't mind," he brushed off the question.

Kassidy rolled her eyes with a sigh as he tried to put the key in the lock. It didn't work.

"What the hell?" he muttered.

"Ohhh," Kassidy whispered.

"Did she change the lock?" he frowned

"Or the landlord did. Maybe she's not living here now. It's been more than the four months she paid for." Kassidy put her ear against the door to listen.

"What the hell are you two doing?" Brett had come up the stairs behind them.

"Trying to get into my ex-girlfriend's apartment, naturally," Luke frowned back at his friend.

"Well, that's creepy," Brett muttered.

"Please, like you weren't involved last time we were all here!" Kassidy spat back at her husband.

"You two need to stop hanging out together. Although, maybe the Bee would enjoy covering this story about one of its very own reporters, Kass?

What's going on?" Brett asked, pulling his wife, who was mid-way through another eye roll, back toward the stairs. Luke reluctantly followed.

"You didn't listen to my whole message?" Kassidy's annoyance was clear.

"Sorry, Kassie. I was out of the office. When I got a quick chance to listen to the second one, I just heard you say you were coming here. Now it seems you're trying to commit a crime, so—"

Kassidy gave Brett a glare to end all glares, and even Luke shrank back from her.

"I saw Alexis today in Midtown. From what I could see, she looked totally fine. But she hasn't contacted any of us or her mom. I tried calling her phone, but it went straight to a generic voicemail. We came here to see if we could find her."

"But the lock's changed," Luke mentioned, scanning the street again.

"You're sure it was her? I'd assume the landlord had the lock changed." Brett gazed up at the apartment from the street.

"I'm sure. I know I've been hoping to see her every day, hoping she'd come back. But this really was her. Her hair was cut and colored brown like Luke said it was when she visited him, but otherwise she looked like herself. But why hasn't she called any of us? Why would she all of a sudden feel safe enough to come back?"

"I don't know, but she's not required to call any of us. Maybe she doesn't want to," Brett offered.

"Brett!" Kassie gave her husband's arm a light smack, passing a concerned glance at Luke.

"He's right," Luke said, trying to keep the frustration and hurt out of his voice.

"But if she's in danger—" Kassidy started to protest, a note of defeat coming through as she let her words wander away.

Luke didn't know what to say. He wanted to search the entire city of Sacramento to find her, but maybe she didn't want that. That didn't seem right after her late-night visit, but he had no idea how she was feeling now.

"We'll keep trying to reach her. We can check in with her landlord. But I think we have to trust her. I don't think she'd come back here if she wasn't comfortable," Brett said.

"I guess." Kassidy shrugged, not sounding remotely convinced. "I hope she'll at least call her mom."

Brett sent a look to Luke, who forced himself to nod.

Alexis's landlord wouldn't confirm if she was still renting the apartment, but the nervous tone hidden in his all-too-casual voice told Luke she was. He and Brett checked at Valle Coffee, The Painting Palate, and called the city coordinator for her painting classes, but no one had talked to or seen her. As the week went by with no calls or emails from Alexis to any of them, he started to wonder if Kassidy had really seen her. Why wouldn't she even contact her mother?

The next Tuesday, he was walking back to his place after grabbing sushi for dinner. Screeching tires in the intersection closest to him led him to look over his shoulder. Two sedans had come within inches of hitting each other. Some choice words were exchanged out their windows, one driver flipping the other off. Then they moved and traffic flowed back to normal. He shook his head as he watched them drive away, thinking the anger they were both feeling would likely result in at least one accident that night.

When he turned his gaze back toward his apartment, he caught a glimpse of Alexis leaving through the building's front door.

"What the hell?" he murmured to himself.

She looked relaxed. She was wearing one of the summer dresses he loved, heading away from him toward the other side of the block. She pulled her phone from her purse and brought it up to her ear. He realized he had stopped walking, a few other pedestrians already maneuvering around him.

His brain kicked back into gear as he called, "Alexis!"

She didn't seem to hear him, but if she were on the phone, combined with the noise of traffic, crosswalk sounds, and the chatter of passersby, his words could have been buried.

His feet picked up speed, but she was already rounding the corner. Where was she going? He called to her again, but she was out of sight. When he reached the corner, she was gone. He felt like he was losing it, but she'd been right there in front of him. If Luke felt like this now, how disturbing must it have been for her to see Zeke again and again when he was supposed to be dead?

For the millionth time, he wished he could have done more for her—found Zeke and figured out Thomas Loefler so she wouldn't have run. He was glad he'd been part of bringing Emma's case to a close, but he should have been more present for Alexis. And now she was alone again, and he had no idea what she was doing. He could keep beating himself up for what he'd failed to do, or he could keep trying now. He turned back toward his apartment, pulling out his phone to call a friend at the Sacramento FBI office.

CHAPTER 30

Alexis was living in a play. She'd never participated in any theater productions in high school or college. She'd never been a fan of memorizing words. Unless she was painting, she had no interest in being in front of a crowd of people. But right now, she considered herself an actor, even if she was an awkward one.

Her goal was to look like she was living a normal life in order to lure David out from wherever he was hiding. She was trusting her intuition again. His threat was very real. She knew he would come for her.

Parts of her days felt like the past prisons she'd created for herself. She didn't contact her friends, her mother, or Luke. But she had to pretend she was interacting with them every day. She moved back into her old apartment and asked her landlord to change the lock. He seemed hesitant at first, but she lied and said she was having problems with a family member and just wanted the extra security, so he acquiesced. She didn't need any surprise visits from people who had a key to the old lock. Her landlord was happy she was back paying rent and utilities. He didn't ask any questions.

She'd gotten a new job at a coffee shop in the Arden Arcade area on the edge of the city limits, but none of her loved ones knew that. She couldn't teach, because that would draw too much attention. She had to find that perfect balance of appearing to live life while avoiding her loved ones who would try to be too helpful.

When Alexis wasn't working, she went grocery shopping, window shopping. She even took the risk of going into Luke's apartment building, although she never went to his door. David had already seen her there in the past, so she didn't consider this a new risk to Luke. She stayed away from Eileen's part of town, as well as Kassie and Brett's. She had no idea if David knew where they lived. She didn't want to lead him to them.

Before she'd packed up her few belongings and left her friends' house in the Bay, she'd sent the Sacramento FBI office several anonymous tips about David. She didn't want them contacting or watching her, but she still wanted them to be looking for him. She needed help, but she still needed her space if this was going to work.

She amped up her self-defense skills and always carried her whistle, pocket knife, and newly acquired pepper spray. She wasn't trained with a gun and didn't feel comfortable having one. She didn't know if Thomas Loefler still wanted her after she stabbed him, so she couldn't count on David keeping her alive for that reason. She tried to stay in populated places. Nighttime was her biggest concern. She always had her TV on and never got more than a few hours of sleep.

She'd almost blown it the other day leaving Luke's building. She'd seen him down the street out of the corner of her eye. She'd tried to keep her casual appearance, pretending to talk on her phone, but her heart had been slamming. She'd heard him calling her name, but she'd gotten around the corner and slipped into a random office building. She'd walked back out only when she was sure he'd be gone. Alexis could only hope David hadn't seen that.

She felt horrible. She was sure Luke would have told her mother, or at least Kassie and Brett, that he'd seen her. The information would get back to Eileen somehow. She hated to think of how her mother might be feeling. She had to keep telling herself this would all be over soon. Then she could try to go back to some semblance of her past life. She wasn't sure Luke, Kassie, or Brett would forgive her, but she hoped her mother would.

She turned her original phone back on, but kept it muted. She wanted to avoid seeing or hearing any calls from her loved ones, because she knew it would be a fight not to pick up.

Alexis visited McKinley Park often. She avoided Luke's regular lunch hour and never sat near the table they'd shared, but with the uncertainty that was her life, she needed that park. Even with the blistering July heat, being there among the life thriving around her brought a sense of peace.

The sun had only been up in the Saturday sky for a few hours as she settled on a bench next to Lake Kiesel and sipped her coffee. She put her prepaid phone next to her. Her permanent phone was just within reach in her open purse. The sun was already warm. She frowned as several construction vehicles parked at the perimeter of the park, unloaded equipment, and began working on the road. The noise sliced through her peaceful morning. But it wasn't loud enough to miss the single word spoken behind her.

"Laoise," the familiar voice said her birth name. Instant adrenaline hit her, but she forced herself not to spin around to see him. She tried to focus on the surprise she felt that he'd said her name correctly. It was pronounced Leesha, but most people wouldn't know that because of the traditional Irish spelling. She'd spent her childhood and adolescent years pronouncing it properly each time it was said. She'd always felt like an imperfect echo.

Her name meant "radiant girl" and was a reference to light. Her parents had tried to have a baby for years before she came along. When they tried for a second child afterward, it resulted in one first-trimester miscarriage and no further pregnancies. Her mother had commented many times how perfect her name was. She'd brought her parents the light they needed—the only light they received from a child. This history was why she could never be mad at her mother for gently refusing to call her Alexis.

"David," she breathed, forcing herself to sound calm.

He rounded the bench, snatching her phone and putting it in his back pocket in one fluid movement. It was so strange to see Zeke standing in front of her, now using David's true voice.

"I assumed you'd figure that out. I always knew you were smart, even though Kurt took you for another one of his bimbos."

"That's a disgusting thing to say about the dead," she hissed back at him.

"I'm not interested in your opinions." He looked around for a few moments, as if making sure no one was watching them. "There's no one around. A miracle for this place. Of course, the barricade I set up will also help with any unwanted federal company," he said with a quick sneer toward the construction.

She frowned in confusion, but before she could say anything, he continued, "I know the games you've been playing since you've come back to Sacramento. I'm surprised you haven't taken more precautions."

"What do you want, David? Who is Thomas Loefler? What does he want with me?" she questioned, ignoring his comment.

"Oh, he doesn't give a shit about you, actually. This was never about Thomas Loefler wanting you. He was here as a distraction. If you had fallen for him, he would have handed you over to me. He was using this whole thing as a test for one of his old employees," David responded, looking out at the water.

"A test? Who was he testing? Who is he really?" she asked, shifting her hand toward her purse.

"His identity isn't important. He was doing me a favor, and I was doing him one. He and I will both get what we want." David clasped his hands behind his head, stretching his back. He rocked from his heels to the balls of his feet. From a distance, she was sure he appeared to be having a relaxing conversation with a friend.

"And what do you want?" She already knew the answer, although she still had no idea why.

"You," he responded, a smooth smile spreading across his face. At that moment she saw something in his hand sparkle with reflected sunshine. Her diamond earrings! That confirmed David broke into her apartment or paid someone else to do it. After another second, he put the treasured items in his pocket.

Alexis knew her rage was immediately visible on her face. She tried to calm herself, sure he was using the earrings as a distraction. She moved her fingers just enough to feel the zipper on her purse. Her phone was inches away. It was locked. She could swipe the screen to call 911. Would she have enough time? She wasn't sure if he had any weapons, but would he be brazen enough to use them in broad daylight? Three people jogged past them on the walk path. She could hear other voices in the distance. She could do this. She'd been waiting for this moment; she would make it happen. She would get her life back.

"Why? We never worked together. I only saw you a few times at Reliant. You don't know me." She tried to sound as concerned as possible, now feeling the hard plastic of her phone case.

"Shut up!" he growled, keeping his voice low. "I know much more than you think, bitch! I helped Kurt with his videography, so he told me I could have my choice of all of you. Then he started killing everyone off, and the organization used *my* footage to learn more about all those women in order to do so! And did I get any compensation for that? I had to get fucking *surgery* to change my appearance because he fucked everything up! I had to create multiple identities for myself! Do you understand how Kurt Leonard ruined my life?"

"Your footage?" she breathed, choosing to ignore his angry pity party. "Those videos were each from one—situation." She cringed as she tried to think of how to describe what Kurt did in the videos. "How would they have helped the organization?"

"I was following all of you for months beforehand!" David sneered back at her. "That's what Kurt was paying me for. You never saw me at work because I hardly needed to be in the building. Kurt wanted to know everything he could about all of them, including you. And after he got what he needed from them, I continued to follow everyone. Except for you, because you ran away. There is so much footage the FBI will never know about—it's laughable! I decided I liked you. You were brave and strong. You fought for yourself. You survived. I am owed you, and I want you.

"I tried to do this the nice way, Laoise. I tried to develop a relationship with you—to make the separation from your family and friends easier. Zeke was perfect for you: young, athletic, exuberant, but you didn't give him a chance—you fell for the cop instead. The cop who treated you like crap the first time he came into that coffee shop. How desperate were you to start something with him?"

"How desperate was *I*?" She was surprised to hear the growl in her voice. "You were using a fake identity to try to abduct me from my home and loved ones, because a man who's now dead promised you a woman as some sort of payment? And because you've decided you like me, that makes this all okay? Am *I* the desperate one?"

For a moment, he looked like he might lunge at her, but he regained his composure. "I'm done talking now. Get up, let's go."

"Good luck with that," she hissed, grabbing her phone, pushing down the top buttons on either side, and swiping the Emergency SOS option on the screen. A blaring sound followed; a countdown on her screen showing the seconds until she was connected to the police.

A switchblade snapped to life in David's hand. He swiped toward her, knocking her phone from her grasp and slicing through the skin of her hand. She cried out in pain, then screamed for help. He grabbed for her hair as she stood up, but she kneed him in the groin. He let out a string of expletives. Alexis turned to run, but he kicked a leg out from under her. She hit the ground hard. She lay there for a moment, dazed. Then she saw her phone under the bench, screen still lit up. The call was active! She thought she could hear someone on the other end trying to talk to her. She reached for it, but he pulled her up again, dragging her with him.

"Hey! Let her go!" She heard a female voice scream not far from them. "Call 911!" She instructed someone else.

"Stay the fuck away!" David yelled back, brandishing his knife. Alexis noticed he was fumbling with something on his leg. God, did he have a gun? She couldn't let anyone else get hurt because of her.

"The cops are on their way! Let go of her!" A male voice screamed this time. Her attention had been focused on David, but she managed a glance around them. A crowd was gathering at a close distance. One man looked as if he was about to charge forward.

"Don't!" Alexis screamed.

"Good idea," David sneered in her ear, moving the knife to her throat. She heard sirens in the distance.

Alexis shoved an elbow into his ribs. He stumbled back, scratching her neck with the knife. She knew he had nothing to lose now, so he came for her again, the knife raised in one hand. She punched his arm away, sending the knife flying. She heard several members of the crowd charging their way. She moved her hip into David's body and grabbed just under his chin. Gripping as hard as she could with her bleeding hand, she used all her force to turn her body and flip him to the ground. She was surprised by the thud that filled the air and the groan of surprise he made.

The sound of running feet and new, urgent voices were behind her now, directing everyone to move back and get out of the way. Blurs of uniforms descended on David, keeping him on the ground. Hands on her upper arms moved her to the side. Words surrounded her, flowed through her ears, but she didn't understand them. *They're arresting him!* a small, victorious part of her brain said.

She sank down, trying to focus on her breathing, trying to make her adrenaline slow and the world stop tilting. She glanced down at her hand. There was someone putting pressure on it now. She heard an ambulance's siren nearby. She closed her eyes and continued to breathe, trying to separate herself from the noise threatening to drown her. She could hear David's voice yelling, but after a while, it faded into the distance.

"What's your name, ma'am?" asked a female voice.

"Alexis. Alexis Miller." She was pretty sure the words came out. In her mind, she could still hear David calling her Laoise.

"Ms. Miller, they're going to take a look at your hand and any other injuries. Just stay here for me." The voice was calm. She was happy to do as she was asked.

The siren stopped. She heaved a sigh as she saw the paramedics come toward her, a renewed sense of the pain in her hand flowing through her, along with a growing sense of clarity.

I did it, she thought, as they helped her to the ambulance. *My life is mine, and I'm never running again.*

CHAPTER 31

Luke took several deep breaths as he parked his truck in Eileen's driveway and shut off the engine. He'd waited five days after the attack to see Alexis, plenty of time for his shock, anger, and fear to die down. At least he hoped so. He didn't want to be an asshole—that was going to be a challenge.

Alexis had been staying with her mom since she'd gotten out of the hospital. Today, Eileen had gone back to work. She'd called Luke two days ago, proposing this as a good opportunity for him to have a private discussion with her daughter. The media had been swarming Alexis again. Eileen was, understandably, being very protective.

Keep your cool, Luke. You're not going to be an asshole. He repeated this mantra in his head as he climbed from his truck and made his way to the front door, his heart picking up its pace. He hadn't seen her since the day she strolled from his apartment building. He hadn't talked to her since she was in his bed. Everything was so different now.

He rang the doorbell and took more deep breaths. Alexis opened the door after a few moments. Her face held no sign of the smile she used to give him. It still felt weird to see her with short brown hair, but those same blue eyes flashed at him, daring him to challenge her.

"Hi," she said, moving to the side so he could walk past.

He trudged into Eileen's living room with heavy feet. Her bandaged hand caught his eye when he turned to face her. He knew from Kassidy that when

David Crighton cut Alexis's hand, he'd caused tendon and nerve damage. The day after the attack, Alexis had surgery, which went well. Physical therapy would help her recover the full use of her hand.

As Luke stared at her injury, he thought about how much worse the situation could have been. Sac PD and the FBI found a gun strapped to David's leg. As he thought about the danger she put herself in, his anger grew.

He opened his mouth before giving himself more time to think. "What you did was incredibly stupid."

She stared back at him, silence pushing down on them. So much for not being an asshole.

"You don't need to understand why I did it," she finally said with a face that looked numb. Her right hand floated to her right ear, briefly touching one of the diamond earrings authorities had retrieved from David when he was arrested.

Kassidy had told Luke that Alexis wouldn't take the earrings off now that she had them back.

Luke sighed. "There's nothing to understand. He could have killed you. If you told me what you had planned when you came to my place—"

"I didn't have the plan then. I discovered who David was after we—" she cut herself off. "I prepared the best I could. I let the FBI know he was going to be in town. I knew if there were too many people swarming around me, he never would have approached me. And I needed this to be over, Luke. I didn't want to hide anymore, so I knew I needed to confront him."

"You were ill-equipped to confront someone who's been obsessed with you for years," he muttered.

"He's not obsessed with me!" Alexis scoffed. "I was originally meant to be part of his payment from Kurt. Then, because Kurt killed the other women he could have had, he developed an interest in me."

"It was more than just an interest, Alexis. The FBI found the place where he was staying in West Sacramento. There were pictures of you everywhere, letters he'd written to you, lists of your favorite things. The guy's insane. He's wanted you since your days in San Francisco. You weren't just some consolation prize. If he couldn't have you, he was going to kill you."

She looked shocked for a moment. It was obvious this was new information. But she didn't allow herself to stay vulnerable for long. She waved his words away, putting a blank expression back on her face. He noticed, however, that her voice was a little weaker when she spoke again, "It's over now, Luke. It worked. The FBI has someone I'm sure they've wanted since Kurt's case broke open."

"It's crazy that you would just shrug it off like that," Luke muttered, then wished he could pull his foot out of his mouth. This conversation was not going the way he'd wanted it to.

"Okay, I'm crazy. I'm stupid." She threw up her arms. "It's good to know where I stand with you. Now, I'd like you to leave." She began walking toward the door, then turned to face him. "Not sure how you could've ever loved someone so crazy and stupid."

He sighed in frustration. "This has nothing to do with our relationship. I'm sorry, Alexis, but you have to understand how I'm seeing this. You put your life in danger when you could have just handed the information you had over to law enforcement."

"I won't keep going around and around about this." She turned back toward the door, but whirled again. "And how can you talk about me understanding your point of view when you never tried to see how much Susan was beating you down? How you nearly killed yourself trying to solve that case! *You* couldn't leave *that* to law enforcement!" Her voice rose.

"Good thing, since Langley was one of the main people on the case! And I *am* law enforcement!" *Wow, maybe I should stomp my foot for good measure*, he berated himself. This argument was becoming more childish by the second.

"You're *not* law enforcement in North Carolina anymore. And I'm trying to talk about how much you let all of that break you, but dismissed me when I was worried about you! Your depression was scary, Luke, and you wouldn't do anything about it."

"I didn't come here to talk about me. I do that enough in therapy," he responded, his voice low.

"Good. I'm glad you're finally getting help." She crossed her arms, her face still dark.

He had no idea what to say next. What did he think he would accomplish here? Part of his original plan for the conversation had been to mention the call to his friend Anthony in the Sacramento FBI office. When he told Anthony about Alexis reappearing in Sacramento, Anthony shared the anonymous David Crighton tips. The tips explained that David had been pretending to be a man named Zeke, until he also pretended to die. It hadn't been difficult to figure out that Alexis had supplied the tips. Although Alexis hadn't contacted the FBI for help when she moved back to the city, the bureau was able to locate David and keep tabs on him because of Alexis's information.

Luke wanted to plead with Alexis—to make her understand how serious her situation had been. "Did you know the FBI was watching David because of the tips you left? They were watching you too. But the night before David followed you to McKinley Park, he switched places with an actor. The actor stayed in David's apartment, and David stayed in a hotel. This actor—he was David's doppelganger. The FBI agents believed he was David until they got a tip that the real David was at McKinley Park.

"Did you know the fake roadwork David arranged had all the streets around the perimeter of the park closed? The agents assigned to you were already dealing with that mess when the agents assigned to David arrived. They all had to leave their cars and run to the park. Sac PD experienced the same thing when it arrived, but because the FBI had already told my department what was going on, officers forced their cars through the barricades. David set up this elaborate plot to take you, Alexis. He tried to stop everyone from getting to you. He knew the FBI was watching him, and he was still that bold. He would have done anything."

She stared at him for several moments without saying a word. Then she lifted her chin and asked, "Do you have anything else you want to say? I have my life again, and I've adopted a very take-no-shit kind of attitude."

He still wanted to kiss her mouth, even when it held a defiant frown directed at him. What the hell was wrong with him?

"I'm glad you have your life back," Luke said. "But it's not like the old days. It's not *Alexis Against the World* anymore. You have a group of people here who care about you and would be devastated to lose you. That came very close to being reality."

There were tears shining in her eyes now, but she was working to keep up her angry front. "Enough with the guilt, Luke. I did what I needed to do. I'm fine. I hurt you, I know—"

He shook his head, cutting her off, realizing nothing he said was going to make a difference. "And I hurt you. It's the way things worked out. I guess now we both move forward."

She kept his gaze, standing her ground. He wanted to pull her into his arms. They'd both been through a lot of shit and needed time to recover. Maybe they just weren't meant to be.

He forced himself to walk to the door, moving past her without so much as brushing against her arm, but he turned before he went outside. Emotion caught in his throat. "Bye, Miller."

Each step toward his truck felt like walking through cement. From behind him, he heard her say, "Bye, Kruger." When he turned to look again, she'd already closed the door.

* * *

Christopher read all about David. He couldn't believe the man had been foolish enough to attack Alexis in broad daylight. He shrugged it off. One less annoyance in his life. There'd been no word of Thomas Loefler, although his company's online presence had disappeared.

As he relaxed on his balcony, the sun on his closed eyes, he started wondering if he should move on from Berlin. He enjoyed it, but he didn't plan on staying in one place forever. France had been on the edge of his mind for a few months. Maybe Paris, but it might be nice to have a base in the south of France. He looked forward to a more relaxed lifestyle.

As he daydreamed about French food and wine, his phone rang on the table in front of him. It was a local number, but not one he recognized.

"Hello?"

"Hello, Christopher." *It took only a second for the unexpected voice to register in his mind.*

"Ah, Thomas. I assume you're doing well, unlike Mr. Crighton." *Christopher closed his eyes again. Thomas must be angry about Alexis, but no need to bring that up right away.*

"Very well. Have you enjoyed Berlin? I've always wanted to visit." *Thomas's words were full of meaning. He was already there.*

Christopher moved the smallest amount in his chair, peering through the railing of his balcony down to the ground below. He didn't see anything out of the ordinary. He gazed at the buildings around him, but saw no apparent threat. He cast a glance back through his apartment toward the front door, but everything seemed the way it should be.

"Yes, it's an amusing place. I'm sure you will enjoy it," *Christopher responded, leaning back.*

"You didn't understand David's warning?" *Thomas asked.*

"I'm not interested in threats."

"You shouldn't have run from Manhattan, Christopher. New York's leader wasn't pleased by your cowardice." *Thomas's voice morphed as he said these words. When the last two were spoken, Christopher understood who Thomas really was. And everything made sense.*

"Ah, hello, John," *Christopher addressed the former leader of the organization's California chapter—the man whom Christopher worked for as a project manager for many years before being transferred to Manhattan.* "I was wondering why the CEO of a pharmaceutical company cared that much about a random woman in California. It was a ruse."

"I've been invited to lead the New York chapter since your last boss met with—a sudden accident," John said. "California is still crawling with feds. As it won't be available to us again anytime soon, this opportunity was well-timed."

"Of course," Christopher responded.

"I wanted to bring you back with me, even with the bridges you burned when you ran," John continued. "You were still one of my best project managers. But then you showed me how much your talent for project planning has slipped."

Christopher nodded to himself, a smile on his face. The whole scenario was a test. An impossible, ridiculous test. "I never intended to go back to the organization, so I'm afraid you wasted your time. And what was David in this ploy of yours? When it became obvious he was obsessed with Alexis himself, I did wonder if something else was going on. Not to mention you were both imbeciles who couldn't follow the simplest of directions."

"David was a means to an end," John sighed. "An expendable piece of flesh. He was easy to manipulate and bend as I needed, because he wanted that woman so much. I didn't reveal my true identity to him, because I knew at some point, somehow, he would tell you. He knew I wasn't really Thomas Loefler, but that didn't matter to him. I told him I was giving you a test, and he was happy to comply with whatever gave him the resources he needed to become a part of Alexis's life.

"Initially, I was going to work alongside New York's leader. As you know, that state has more projects than it can handle, so more leadership was necessary. I was making plans for additional project managers. He was not willing to consider you, but I wanted to give you another chance. I was having you followed, trying to think of a way to demonstrate that you were still a valuable asset. Then I met David. I gave him your location in Berlin and created the story he would tell you. Thomas Loefler was a character I'd already thought of, so bringing his pharmaceutical company to life, in case you should need convincing, was not difficult. Even though David is an idiot and couldn't be trusted to do as he was told, I knew you would be too distracted by the money and the thrill of the game to catch on completely."

Christopher ignored the comment and said, "I understand that you and David had a deal. But if it was never your aim to get the woman for yourself, why did you get involved with so much of the fieldwork? Why did you need to participate in the test? You let yourself get stabbed—"

"Because I knew David would fail right away," John said in a confident voice. "I needed another character to keep the plot going until you failed. I played my jealous, impatient real estate agent well, wouldn't you say? A good project manager knows how to handle their operatives, Christopher. You lacked in this. It would have been easier if you had come back to California. As for the stabbing, that was an example of a hole in your plan. She shouldn't have had any weapons. Why was that not addressed beforehand? Your work was subpar at best. What happened? You used to enjoy these projects, especially the little intricacies that had to be just right to make them work. You promised David and I the abduction plot would be air-tight, but that wasn't the case. Your time outside the states has ruined you."

It was Christopher's turn to sigh before he said, "A real project would not have included an operative hell-bent on seeing the project manager fail. You were biased when you began this so-called test. I'm assuming you had no real intention of recruiting me to the New York office. You were scared I would reveal some of the organization's deepest secrets after I moved to Berlin. You were angry that I left the organization behind to keep myself alive and out of prison, although you did just the same. You pitched this project to your New York colleagues, knowing it would fail—that you would be told to kill me. At some point, you butted heads with the leader, most likely because you are both men who refuse to share control. So, you killed him. Now you are in charge and do not need anyone's permission to kill me. That is what this is all about.

"Unfortunately, you also made yourself look like a fool," Christopher continued. "Your argument is that I could not control my operatives. Therefore, the project failed. But won't the project reviewers wonder why you didn't try to turn things around—come up with your own plan to get the woman? You didn't want her, but David did. As the New York chapter leader, shouldn't you have found a way to make that happen? He did pay you a substantial amount of money to work with you, did he not? I know you would not have teamed up with him for free. And now, not only does he not have her, but he is heading for federal prison. Don't you think the project will end up looking like just as much of a failure on your part as mine?"

"Getting the woman for David was never the goal of this scenario," John growled back.

"Perhaps that is how you see it, but it may not be how others do." Christopher said. "Do you think this will help you keep your new title, John? Or do you think another man with greater ambition and fewer grudges about the past might challenge you for it?"

"Are you insinuating that you will try to take the position from me?" John laughed.

"Certainly not! I have no interest in being a slave to the organization after experiencing the freedom I have now. And to lead a group of other slaves more pressured than I to succeed? The idea is horrifying."

As he was speaking, he heard the door of his flat open. His back was to it. He did not let himself flinch. He'd memorized the particular noises of his apartment—the subtle squeak of the door, the creaks of the floor and where they were most prevalent, the cracking sounds his windows made when opened for the first time in the morning on warmer days. One of the reasons he'd rented this flat was because of its noise—a built-in alarm system.

Christopher gripped the thirteen-inch throwing knife that sat next to him on the chair. He always kept it by his side on the balcony. He had others hidden in various spots throughout the flat.

He whirled, feigning surprise, as John's voice floated through his front room. The man was holding a gun equipped with a silencer. "Good thing you'll never have the chance at that title," John said, raising the gun.

Christopher let his knife sail. Another thing he liked about his home was the straight line of sight from the balcony to the front door. He'd kept larger pieces of furniture out of its path when he'd planned the layout of the space. He was very good at knife throwing. He'd spent hours a day practicing from the time he was a young teenager. His goal this time was to not immediately kill his target. The knife landed in John's abdomen. The man let out a surprised yell, dropped his gun, and stumbled to the ground.

"This isn't a movie, John," Christopher said, keeping a casual air as he walked the distance between them, sitting down on the couch. There was another knife shoved between the cushion and arm rest. "You shoot right when you have clear sight of your target. It would have been possible for you to kill with just one bullet. You should know this. Maybe you did once. Your time behind a fancy desk ruined you," he continued, spinning John's words against him.

"For years, you allowed everyone in the California chapter to do the difficult work for you. You sat back romancing clients, making money, and murdering people in your office. I respected you when I worked in California, but when you sent me to Manhattan, I witnessed a true leader. The New York leader knew how to control the employees and projects under his command. It is very disappointing that you were able to murder him—to put yourself in a position of such magnitude."

John grunted in pain. At least he was smart enough not to remove the knife, as he would most certainly bleed out. Blood was already pooling around the wound and soaking into his clothes. He reached for his gun, but Christopher had moved to stand in front of him and picked the weapon up from where it lay, two feet from John's fingertips.

"You should not be here. You should have sent someone to do this for you. You should stick to murdering people on your turf. When you enter your target's space, you give that person the advantage," Christopher said.

John attempted to stand, his eyes moving around Christopher's body. Christopher spun to see two men climbing over the railing of his balcony. He fired two quick shots from John's gun, each hitting its target. The men sailed back over the balcony to the street below.

"At least you had the decency to bring some backup," Christopher sighed.

"You know you're not going to make it out of this building," John muttered, *moving to push a button on his watch. Christopher fired a shot at it. John cursed in renewed pain as the bullet went into his arm.*

"Very much the opposite. I know this building, this neighborhood, and this city like I was born and raised here. I know that I will get away and continue my life. With that knife wound, you will have a very difficult time leaving here. Although, I'm sure you have others coming, so maybe someone will save you," Christopher responded, grabbing two bags he kept ready in a far corner of the room. They held everything he would need to start a new life.

"You'll never be free. The organization will find you," John said, but his words ended in a groan of pain as he collapsed back to his knees.

"Perhaps," Christopher answered with a shrug. "Part of me hopes you do manage to survive. Wouldn't it be fun to continue this game in the future? You can hone your field skills, make it more of a challenge. I'm sure by that time you will have another new face for me to enjoy."

As John fell forward, Christopher left the flat he'd called home for more than two years, locking the door behind him. He made his way downstairs, killing two more operatives in the process, and into the city's streets. A crowd had gathered at the front of his building, an ambulance having just arrived for the men who fell over his balcony. He gave them a quick glance, put on his sunglasses, and headed toward the train station. The trip would take more than nine hours, but at least he could enjoy the scenery. France was calling.

CHAPTER 32

Alexis hadn't been under the assumption that coming back to Sacramento would be easy. She'd been right. She had her job at the Arden coffee shop, but missed Valle Coffee. She'd tried to reapply, but there weren't any openings. Her former manager was also pretty unhappy with the way she'd left, which Alexis understood. Her teaching job had also been filled. That was okay, because those classes required her full attention, and she was having trouble concentrating these days. Her creative flow also seemed to have left her after all the paintings she'd cranked out in isolation.

Her relationships had taken their own beating. Eileen said she was fine and happy to have her daughter back, but Alexis could tell her isolation had taken an even bigger toll on her mother this time. She'd turned thirty while she was gone. Her mother had always talked about throwing her a big party when she "survived the last year of her twenties." This theme seemed appropriate for Alexis's life, but of course, the party hadn't happened. Alexis told Eileen they could just pretend she was turning thirty again on her thirty-first birthday. Eileen laughed, waving away the idea, insisting they didn't need a big party. Alexis didn't let on that she was disappointed.

Her interactions with Kassie and Brett were more uncomfortable. Brett acted awkward most of the time they were all together, as if holding his breath to see if Kassie might snap. Kassie was trying, but Alexis knew her friend was hurt. The resulting complicated emotions were not so easy to smooth over. She knew Kassie understood why she did what she did, but that she also didn't agree with it. Alexis assumed it also brought back painful memories from when Kurt had threatened Kassie into her own isolation from Brett. For now, she tried to keep their conversations light. Maybe when their relationship felt stronger again, they would get into the tough stuff. Alexis was doing that enough with her therapist anyway.

A relationship Alexis hadn't expected to develop was with Nora, her former shift lead at Valle Coffee. Nora came by Alexis's new shop to drop off her final paycheck. They chatted briefly, Nora telling Alexis her husband left her for a woman he worked with. Now that they didn't work together, Nora was kinder and willing to listen, even though she was going through her own stuff. Alexis needed that. After the coffee shop, they met for lunch a couple times, once with Nora's son Owen in tow. He was a shy three-year-old, but Alexis managed to get a few smiles from him. It was nice to have more friends.

Then there was Luke. Alexis thought about him every day, but hadn't seen or talked to him since their last unpleasant conversation. Kassie and Brett never brought him up. She still had the key to his apartment. She knew she should give it to Brett to give back to Luke, but she couldn't bring herself to. It was the last connection she had to the short time they'd had to love each other. She tried not to look for him everywhere she went. Somehow, she had to let him go.

There was one piece of her old life that remained—she still had her job with The Painting Palate. Although her name and picture had been splashed through the local news again, no one attending those events seemed to know anything about her. Or maybe they just didn't care. Every time she instructed a wine-and-paint event, she had a couple hours where she felt like she could relax and breathe.

On a Friday morning in late August, several news agencies reported the testimony in Langley's case was complete and both sides were beginning their closing arguments. Her hand twitched as she forced herself not to pick up her phone to call Luke. She was sure his emotions weren't treating him well.

She wanted more than anything to know he was okay. She could ask him that much, right? But as she went to select his number from her contacts, she chickened out. How would she start that conversation? *Leave him alone, Alexis.*

The next night she walked into The Painting Palate, glad to lose herself in guiding a group of people through painting the Tower Bridge.

"Hi, everyone! As you come in, pick your seats. It's best to keep your personal items on the floor or on one of the extra tables in the back of the room so they don't get paint on them. You should have everything you need at your seat, but we'll go over that when we get started in a few minutes," Alexis said with a smile as people filtered into the room.

She could tell those who had participated in this kind of event before from those who hadn't through their excited chatter or nervous looks. Wine bottles were opened. One bigger group of twenty-somethings had a cheese tray to go with their zinfandel. She turned to make sure she had all her supplies set. She'd already checked the tables twice to make sure her customers had their initial paints, brushes, and water ready to go.

"Any seat?" asked a deep voice with a hint of the South.

Alexis couldn't make herself turn around, because the world seemed to have stopped. It couldn't be him. He would never be caught dead here.

When she did turn, her heart did a flip. It *was* Luke, and he was standing very close to her. His hair was still on the longer side, which she had to admit she liked. She looked up into his dark eyes like she had countless times before, his presence wrapping around her. How had he managed to come in without her noticing?

"Um, yes," was all she could think to say at first. Then, "You're here."

"Yes. Kassie told me you'd be here tonight." There was a hint of a smile on his lips, but the way he shifted his body weight from one foot to the other told her he was nervous.

"You—You realize what this is?" She gestured around the room at the customers already sitting by their canvases. Easy conversations floated around them. Everyone was with at least one other person, except for Luke, it seemed.

"I do. Although, I didn't bring any wine," he answered with a smirk. Her heart skipped.

"You don't have to—" she cut herself off with a sigh. *Why is he here? Is he going to stay? Will he really participate?* "So, the world must be ending, then?" she asked in a reference to their old joke. She'd been sure the question would make him laugh, but his smirk disappeared. His face became serious.

"Yeah," he said. "It's a pretty desperate situation."

He looked for a moment like he wanted to kiss her. He couldn't want that. Not after their last conversation. Not after how unforgiving they were to each other.

Then she realized some of the customers were looking at them. She glanced at her watch. It was a few minutes past the hour.

"Sorry, I need to let you get to work. Can we talk after?" he asked.

She nodded. He took a seat at one of the tables farthest from her. She watched as he took in the canvas in front of him, the paints, brushes, and cup of water to his right. She thought he looked a little queasy.

He's staying? He's actually going to stay and paint the Tower Bridge?

She gave him one more glance and took a deep breath. *I can do this. I can do this. I can do this.*

As she led the group through the steps of bringing the landmark Sacramento lift bridge to life, she tried to look everywhere in the class but at Luke. The couple times her eyes strayed to his face, it looked focused. He seemed to be staring only at her easel and his own.

Horizontal, vertical, diagonal, she thought to herself, focusing on all those lines to keep herself on task.

By the time the class was moving on to the scenery around the bridge, the flowing Sacramento River below, a bit of Old Town Sacramento to the left, and the river bank to the right that was the very edge of West Sacramento, many of her customers were tipsy from the wine. Teasing laughs and loud conversations filled the room, almost covering Alexis's amplified voice. This was normal for this far into the class. She laughed and chatted along with them, pointing out tips for their paintings if they asked.

When her eyes flitted to Luke, he was watching her. His eyes looked sad, even though his expression and body language hadn't changed. It made her heart ache, but she couldn't think too deeply about it. She had to get to the end of the night.

As things wrapped up and she gave her thank you spiel, there was a kind round of applause. Alexis took pictures of different groups holding their art in front of them. Some of the groups blended a little more now, a sign of new friendships sparked over the evening. Alexis loved when art was a catalyst for bringing people together. She made sure to ask them all to get home safely. In reassuring tones, many of them mentioned using rideshare companies.

"We'll text you when we get there," one of three sisters grinned with a wave as she and her siblings headed out the door.

"Sounds good!" Alexis laughed back.

As everyone else filtered out into the night, Luke hung back. She watched him in her peripheral vision as he cleaned up his supplies. She walked the studio, gathering items as she went. She'd turned Fleetwood Mac on for the task. *Gypsy* drifted through the speakers.

"I can see why you like this job. It's a painting party," he said, his deep voice cutting through her racing thoughts. "And you were amazing. It's nice to see you in your element."

She was rinsing brushes, but passed him a small smile, ordering herself not to blush. "Thank you. With all the insanity in this world, it's nice just to be somewhere where people are creating—where they're happy."

Luke nodded, holding her gaze for a few moments, then went back to helping with cleanup. When she was finished and had taken one last look around, grabbing her own supplies and digging the keys out of her purse to lock up behind her, he made his way over to her again. He looked relaxed, but his eyes told a different story. Her heart slammed in her chest.

"Still driving your dad's truck?" he asked.

"Yes," she breathed in response, studying those eyes.

"Can I walk you to it?" His voice grew quieter.

"Sure." After they let themselves out, she jiggled the door handle to make sure she wasn't so distracted she forgot to lock it.

It was dark outside. The August air swirled around them on a warm summer breeze. Strange that a year ago, they'd been discovering their love for each other. Alexis had lost so much time and trust with her mom and friends when she left. She hoped she could get back the trust with hard work. But her relationship with Luke had already been damaged—their separate lives seemed too overwhelming for them to share a life together. Could they come back from that?

When they got to her truck, an awkward tension enveloped them. He looked over her head into the distance. She studied his painting, which he gripped in one hand.

She let out a small laugh, but immediately covered her mouth to try to stop the sound. He looked down at her in confusion, following her eyes to his painting.

A smirk developed on his lips, giving her the confidence to joke, "Well, I can tell it's supposed to be a bridge."

"I didn't want to brag in front of everyone, but it's pretty obvious I'm a natural at this," he responded, the smirk growing into a grin.

"Oh, yes, I see definite Picasso inspiration there." Her laughter continued. His face took on an exaggerated expression of disappointment.

She gave his arm a light push, then felt she shouldn't have. Her cheeks grew hot as she lowered her gaze to fiddle with her bag.

"Alexis," Luke said, but she didn't look up. "Miller." His voice grew soft.

The use of her last name had her finding his eyes. "Luke, how can you be standing here about to say what I think you're about to say with everything that happened?"

"Because I love you, Miller."

She shook her head in disbelief. "You were so angry with me. So much has happened. How can that feeling be so easy for you?"

"The feeling is the same as it always was. I was angry because I love you and knew I came close to losing you. I know a big part of the reason we broke up is because I shut you out. I put my needs before ours. I'm sorry about that." He kept his eyes on hers, but put his hands in his pockets. His look of vulnerability reminded her of their day at the Crocker Art Museum.

"Thank you. I'm sorry too. The Zeke sightings were getting to me. I knew something terrible was coming. I was angry and scared for you, yes, but I was also trying to make my life easier in any possible way," she responded. After a moment of quiet, she continued, "I heard they're starting closing arguments in Langley's case. How are you doing?"

"Yeah," he responded with a heavy sigh. "I'm okay. I'm working on it with my therapist. There's a lot of anger still, but some relief and a small amount of peace mixed in. I had a conversation with Susan this morning. It was the best we've had since Emma died. She and I probably won't be talking much anymore. She's going through a lot of very difficult healing of her own. But there's an agreement that we can reach out to each other if we need to. The prosecutors have no doubt the jury will find Langley guilty. I feel like the right thing was finally done for Emma. It stretches beyond solving her murder. She wanted Langley brought to justice for aiding in the serial killings. I feel like we honored her with that."

Alexis nodded. "You did. I'm glad you were able to solve the case."

He gazed down at her for a few seconds, his eyes dark. "Even with what it did to our relationship?"

She sighed, looking past him at other people walking to and from their vehicles. "I think you're forgetting the way I treated you during and after I was in hiding."

The smallest smile touched his lips, and a gleam grew in his eyes. She knew he was about to say something he just couldn't help. "I was the one who asked you to sleep with me. That night's not something I could forget."

She rolled her eyes, forcing herself not to give him another push. "I *meant* leaving town without telling you, not having any form of communication with you, sleeping with you and then leaving before you woke up, ghosting you when I got back to Sacramento—"

"I understand." He paused. "*Now,* I understand." He put his hand up to stop her response, moving closer to her in the process. "I'm sure I'm not going to word this right, so bear with me. I know I was obsessed with Emma's case and you wanted to take care of things on your own. But I want you to know now that you can lean on me for whatever you need or want to. I will do anything I can to support you. I don't want to argue anymore about how I thought you should have handled things with David. It's done now and you're safe. But there will still be difficult things in the future."

"David's trial," she nodded, knowing exactly what he meant. Her former coworker had already pled not guilty to all charges, but a date for the trial hadn't been set.

He nodded. "Having gone through Langley's, I can imagine testifying is going to be—unpleasant—for you. I'm sure there will also be more media attention."

"I'm sure you're right," she responded, thinking of how she wanted to continue. "I hated isolation, Luke, even more than the first time. It was harder this time, because I didn't have as much money and didn't give myself as much time to prepare. I also knew how much I was hurting everyone who loved me. Especially my mom, who had been through it once already. I finally have my life back. It's not the same as it was before I left, but I love it. I'm never giving it up. I won't be running again. I'm staying right here." As her words ended, she was proud of the confidence behind them.

He nodded, his face reflecting the pride she felt.

She sighed, studying him again. "Luke, how would we manage this? All of these words and feelings are wonderful now, but do we have a viable foundation of trust? I don't want to lose you again. Maybe it's too much of a risk. We can work on our friendship." The last sentence felt flat and weak.

He searched her eyes, bringing his hand to her cheek. Leaning down, he whispered in her ear, "I want to be your friend, your best friend. But I also want so much more."

She shivered at his breath on her face. He lowered his mouth to hers and kissed her slowly. She moved her body closer to his, a light hold on his arm. When he pulled away from her, she had trouble remembering what she'd been saying.

"Well, damn it," she murmured in a breathless voice.

"I know you mean what you say, Miller. I can see the conviction in your eyes. I want to focus on this relationship. I want to do whatever work we need to do to be in the best place for us."

"Couples therapy? So sexy for a dating couple," she laughed.

He shrugged. "Fine with me. We're both already seeing therapists. Why not see one together? It'll make us stronger. And there will be plenty of other sexy times," he ended with a grin.

She laughed again, excitement coursing through her. "You're too persuasive."

"Need to be," he answered, his face becoming serious. "Do you still love me, Miller?" His lips were near hers again.

"Yes, Kruger. You drive me crazy, but yes, I love you very much."

His smile lit up his face. Her heart swelled, grateful to be the one to make him look like that. He pulled her into another kiss, lifting her feet off the ground as he held her close. Yes, being back in Sacramento was different. Time and all its tests had changed things, including her. But this moment, full of joy and soaring love, felt as familiar as a field of wildflowers flowing to life through the strokes of a brush.

EPILOGUE

Luke knocked on the wooden door, feeling like he'd been transported back in time. The church dated back to the 1400s. It was difficult to comprehend the history its walls had seen. He still couldn't believe they'd pulled this off—a wedding in County Galway, Ireland. The home of Alexis's ancestors. Only their immediate families and a few close friends, including Kassie and Brett, were in attendance. They'd have a bigger celebration back in California in a few months.

Alexis had been in a constant state of awe ever since they'd stepped off the plane in Dublin, wanting to soak in as much of the country as she could. They'd be there another two weeks, so she had plenty of time. Luke had never felt the level of joy he did as he watched her study everything around her, finding countless things she wanted to paint.

"Come in," Alexis responded to the knock, her voice quiet.

"Should I close my eyes?" he chuckled as he opened the door to her bridal room. "Isn't this bad luck for our marriage?"

"No, you don't need to close your eyes," she said with a small laugh, but he could hear her nerves through the happy sound.

He caught his breath at the first sight of her. Her hair, which was once again long and red, was gathered in a fancy knot at the nape of her neck, a bejeweled comb holding it in place. Her beloved diamond earrings adorned her ears. Her silken skirt flowed from a beaded top. Her neckline was low and what he would call square-cut, like something out of the Jane Austen books she loved. Small, lacey sleeves covered just her shoulders. His heart picked up speed as he took her in. For a moment he wished he could lock the door behind him and forget about the wedding. He forced himself to take a breath. There would be plenty of time for that later.

"You're gorgeous, Miller."

She blushed, but grinned back. "You look pretty nice yourself, Kruger."

He wore a classic black three-piece suit with a white shirt and black-and-white-striped tie underneath. His wavy hair was still on the long side, because Alexis liked it that way. He'd been happy with the way he looked in the mirror, but now he shrugged it off.

"No one's going to give a crap what I look like when they see you looking like that," he responded. He still stood back, unable to take his eyes off her.

It'd been two years since they'd gotten back together, nine months since he'd proposed to her. Along the way, they'd fought to keep their relationship strong: going to therapy and communicating without fear.

Alan Langley and David Crighton were both in prison. Alexis had hyped herself up as much as possible, but David's trial had been exhausting. It made her past fresh and raw again, and it dragged on longer than prosecutors expected. Luke felt powerless, frustrated, and angry as her testimony and the media attention took everything from her. But he was there for her every step of the way. When David was convicted and sentenced, she cried for hours and slept for a day. Then things got brighter for her; like she was finally able to breathe in a place that used to be filled with smoke. He knew she'd never be able to completely move on from everything that had happened to her, but at least now she could move forward.

The FBI was still searching for Thomas Loefler. The pharmaceutical company that served as a front for whatever his business really was, had disappeared from Sacramento, and then seemed to shut down all together. Its online presence was destroyed. Agents were tracking anyone they could find who seemed connected to the company, but a number of false identities were involved, leading to dead ends. As Loefler had disappeared and left David to take the fall, Luke tried not to worry about the missing man. Alexis told him she would live her life as if Loefler didn't exist, because she had to put the fear behind her. Luke was sure the FBI would find him someday.

As Alexis moved into her future, her relationship with her mother had grown strong again, just as Luke knew it would. Things with Kassie and Brett seemed back to the way they used to be. Time and lots of talking had done wonders. Nothing had been easy, but having Alexis back with them made it all worth it.

Luke had supported her in the decision to focus on her painting. So, a new teaching position at Sacramento City College, The Painting Palate, and selling her art became her life. Her work was displayed in several Sacramento and Bay Area art galleries, and her sales exploded. He'd attended several gallery events with her and felt like he would break apart with pride, especially in seeing the confidence that grew in her every day.

The passing of the days also made his pain and anger toward Langley easier to handle. But when the roller coaster of grief put him through another loop, he opened up to Alexis, telling her everything. She was always ready to listen, holding his hand as he talked. He appreciated the physical connection along with the emotional one. He found himself more able to focus on his job, his friends, and her, because pushing everything down for so long had taken much more energy than he'd realized.

In one of their many conversations, she'd revealed that Laoise was her birth name. She'd been born Laoise Elizabeth Kelly. Memories of meeting her for the first time in a tiny interview room flooded back. He could remember seeing the name on paper and not knowing how to pronounce it, but she'd said it aloud just once. He felt guilty for forgetting it in just a year's time, especially with how well his memory usually worked. But that didn't upset her. She said she loved the name. It would always be special to her, but it wasn't her anymore.

"David called me that name in the park," she'd told him in that same conversation. "That's how he'd first known me. But I think he was using it to scare me—to point out that he knew more about me than most people in my life. I initially changed my name to protect my identity, but it's more than that now. I've become a new person since I left San Francisco after the rape. As Alexis, I've been through my own darkness. I want to strengthen this version of myself, so I can truly thrive." Tears had filled her eyes as she continued, "I told my mom to call me Laoise again if she wants to, but she said she's going to start calling me Alexis. She said she wants to fully support who I am now."

They were both growing stronger, independently and together, which is how he knew it should be. And now here they were on their wedding day, the gateway to the rest of their lives. He felt truly at peace. But as he studied her standing there in her dress, he could see that she didn't.

"Cold feet, Miller?" he asked with a smirk.

She rolled her eyes. "No, I plan to experience the lifetime of your charm and wit that I signed up for."

A laugh escaped him, and she smiled. "No, I just have a bit of a plot twist," she said, her voice shaking.

"Okay. I can handle most plot twists," he answered, but felt his own nerves kicking in.

"The conversations we've had about having kids? You know, where you joked about being afraid of being an old dad, but I think you *are* actually afraid of being an old dad?"

He nodded. He felt a little numb, in disbelief of what she seemed to be telling him. He was forty now. He wasn't sure if he had really pictured himself having kids, but he was sure he would have imagined starting before now.

"It looks like the decision's been made for us. I'm pregnant, Luke," she said in a near whisper, her eyes never leaving his face.

"Uhhhh," he responded, running his hand through his hair and taking the nearest seat. As a police detective, he'd seen and experienced some pretty surprising things, but they all seemed to pale in comparison to this moment. His mind raced as he tried to comprehend that he was going to be a father.

The words of Susan and Eileen came back to him. They'd been very different in the way they spoke about it, but both reflected on the powerful feelings that came with being a parent. Apparently the universe liked foreshadowing. His thoughts began to clear as he reminded himself that he was marrying an incredible woman he loved more than he'd thought would be possible again in his lifetime. He was more grounded than he'd been in many years. He was actually feeling pretty good about this particular twist.

"Looks like it happened when I changed my birth control. It was such a small amount of time in between, but just enough, I guess," she explained. As Alexis continued to watch him, tears welled up in her eyes. "I'm scared, Luke. I've decided I want this baby. I want to be his or her mother. I hope you want to be a father. But we didn't get to choose the timing, and raising our own little human with everything we've been working through sounds—"

He jumped up from the chair and was pulling her into his arms before she could say anything else.

"Kassie forbade me to cry before the ceremony because of my makeup," she said, her whole body shaking.

"Kassie always means well, but I have to call bullshit. Cry if you want to," he responded, rubbing her back, then pulling her away from him to look into her eyes. "It sounds overwhelming and scary, but we're in a better place in our lives and relationship than we've ever been, so I think the timing makes sense. And yes, I'll be a respected elder when this child turns twenty," he continued with a laugh, a grin spreading across his face as she laughed too, "but I want to be a father. And with the passion you put into everything you do, and the care I see you have for everyone you know, I can't see you being anything other than an amazing mother."

Tears were flowing down her face, but happiness shone in her eyes as she pulled him into a kiss. He was going to be a father. The idea still seemed unreal, but excitement for their future bolted through him.

"So, maybe we should go get married, Miller?" he teased when he pulled away from her, wiping away tears. Just then there was a quiet knock behind him. He heard Kassie asking if they were ready.

Alexis grinned up at him, pulling him toward the door. "Yeah, Kruger, I'd say it's about damn time."

THE END

ACKNOWLEDGEMENTS

I continue to receive so much love on this writing journey. I couldn't travel down the path of being an author without the support and guidance of so many people. To my husband Greg and our boys, thank you for your endless love and for giving me the time I need to immerse myself in writing. You mean everything to me, and I'm lucky to have all of you! To my parents, Rick and Stephanie, and my in-laws, Ron and Fran, thank you for all the help and love you give us every day.

Alli, thank you for being the best beta reader there ever was (as well as a wonderful friend)! Your ideas always make my books better, and your love for my stories means everything. And, of course, thanks for all the bagels (hee hee)! Taylor, thank you for your unending support and for the motivation I need to get out there and promote my writing. You are an amazing friend and person! I hope the importance of your namesake in this story makes you proud! To Jack, Sally, and Ashley Valle, thank you for letting me use your name to bring Valle Coffee Co. to life. The three of you have had such a big, wonderful impact on my life, and I love you all so much! Stefanie and Mano, you inspire me on the daily with the hard work, love, and sacrifice you've put into Flour Dust. You make me want to keep working to pursue my dream. Love you both! Cori, thank you so much for your encouragement, friendship, and ideas for social media content! To my Mom Squad, Katie, Christy, and Stephanie, I love you ladies! To all my other friends and family, thank you for your continued love and support!

To MP Smith, thank you so much for being an amazing editor! You've taught me so much, and I have such fun talking writing with you! I'm grateful for our new friendship. To Lisa Montanaro, thank you for teaching me so much about the business of writing, introducing me to the bookstagram world, and encouraging me to join WFWA and Every Damn Day Writers. Being an author can feel so isolating at times; it's so nice to be part of a writing community. Thank you to Lindsay Heider Diamond for the beautiful cover. You knocked it out of the park again! Thank you to Colleen Sheehan for formatting the interior. I'm glad we got to work together!

Finally, thank you to my readers. It means so much that you take the time to read my books, spread the word, leave reviews, all of it! You're helping me make my dream a reality. I hope to give you many, many more stories as the years go by.

ABOUT THE AUTHOR

Bridget Sheppard has been deeply in love with writing stories for as long as she can remember. Born and raised in Northern California, she enjoys reading, music, the beach, TV shows from the 1970s and 80s, and anything having to do with Ireland! She published her debut novel, *Light in the Chaos*, in 2020. *The Chaos of Time* is her second novel, and she hopes to be sharing stories for many more years to come. Bridget lives in the Sacramento area with her husband, three sons, and two dogs.

Made in the USA
Monee, IL
12 January 2023

23471105R00173